IT'S UP TO
CHARLIE HARDIN

BAEN BOOKS
by Dean Ing

Anasazi

Firefight 2000

Firefight Y2K

The Chernobyl Syndrome

In Larry Niven's
Man-Kzin Wars Series

Cathouse

For a complete list of Dean Ing books and to purchase all of these titles in
e-book format, please go to www.baen.com.

IT'S UP TO CHARLIE HARDIN

An Adventure by

DEAN ING

BAEN

IT'S UP TO CHARLIE HARDIN

Copyright © 2015 by Dean Ing

A Baen Book

Baen Publishing Enterprises
P.O. Box 1403
Riverdale, NY 10471
www.baen.com

ISBN: 978-1-4767-8030-6

Cover art by Dan Dos Santos

First Baen printing, February 2015

Distributed by Simon & Schuster
1230 Avenue of the Americas
New York, NY 10020

Library of Congress Cataloging-in-Publication Data

Ing, Dean.
It's up to Charlie Hardin / Dean Ing.
     pages cm
Summary: In the summer of 1942, young teen Charlie Hardin is set loose in Austin, Texas, with one command, to stay out of trouble, but there are some situations he cannot ignore and he comes to understand that, no matter the cost, when danger arrives he must be brave, resolute, clever, and just a little bit crazy.
ISBN 978-1-4767-8030-6 (hardback)
[1. Adventure and adventurers--Fiction. 2. Friendship--Fiction. 3. Family life--Texas--Fiction. 4. Austin (Tex.)--History--20th century--Fiction.] I. Title. II. Title: It is up to Charlie Hardin.
PZ7.1.I54It 2015
[Fic]--dc23

                                    2014042703

Printed in the United States of America

10 9 8 7 6 5 4 3 2 1

TABLE OF CONTENTS

For our irrepressible Lena

IT'S UP TO CHARLIE HARDIN

PREFACE

This is the sort of confession a man may indulge in if he is too lazy to commit the autobiography his grandkids asked for, and too self-absorbed to scribble the books his publishers wanted more of. It is also naked homage to Mark Twain, who in 1875 half-fictionalized the lively times he had enjoyed in his Missouri village thirty years earlier.

So Charlie Hardin is my Tom Sawyer, infesting my small Southwestern city during World War II. Charlie's settings and tribe were chiefly as described, and many of our adventures too. Many locations still exist, though I have furnished everyone with camouflage. One, with his brilliant deceptions and a hair-raising addiction to risk, failed to survive his teens. Some of those risks were real.

Sixty-five years later, Austin's capitol grounds have been robbed of that lily pond, and Shoal Creek has been choked into submission, but recently the castle and the dogapult park were still in place.

Nothing should go without saying, so let me say I lack the vanity to imagine that the following pages could stand comparison to *Tom Sawyer*. The book inspired many a writer, yet no one else has written its equal.

—Dean Ing

CHAPTER 1:
✈ ATTACK AND RETREAT ✈

April 1944: "Blam, blam-blam!" Captain Charlie Hardin froze at the voice of the Nazi gun. *That must be the command post,* he decided. With infinite care, his blond thatch an inch below the enemy's view, Hardin turned his head toward Sergeant Aaron Fischer, his second-in-command. Hardin twitched a gesture that drew a nod from Fischer, who hurried crabwise up the ravine in a flanking move.

Risking a careful glance through tufts of grass, young Hardin resumed his study of the terrain, the kind of broken country that floods could transform. Brush and saplings might change in a season while a few big hardwoods remained. Sergeant Fischer would need those trees for cover, or this commando raid would end in retreat with heavy casualties.

When he heard shouts from the command post, Hardin knew that Fischer had been spotted. A high-pitched hammering staccato erupted from a second Nazi, and Fischer, caught in the open, spun clutching at his breast. Moving at breakneck speed, he sprawled in a rolling dive, sliding to a stop in high grass. He lay unmoving, face up.

3

With a thrill of gooseflesh the thought came: *now it was up to Charlie Hardin.*

To his right, the ravine deepened to thirty feet with vertical sides, but near its top a gnarled root the thickness of his wrist looped from the turf. He decided it would hold him. If it didn't, the fall could break his neck. Muscles straining, Hardin picked his way along the face of the embankment; footholds few, handholds fewer. A trickle of sweat moved down the bridge of his nose. It seemed that he could feel Fischer's open eyes staring into his back, and this spurred him. Stamina and planning were the strengths of Captain Hardin, and now he used them both, grasping that python of root just as his footing crumbled.

Moments later the young commando pulled himself over the top and wormed between small boulders above the ravine, mouth open wide to quiet his breathing, and exulted. Nothing moved in the glade nearby, but the place held only one tangle of old brush against a slanting tree that might hide Nazis.

A blind rush across that exposed slope would be foolhardy. He was near enough to hear excited enemy voices and knew they must be expecting his attack, but by the rules of engagement he must not let his weapon speak until he could see the enemy. He discarded two plans before asking himself the trigger question, the one that so often pushed him beyond himself: *what would Uncle Wes have done?*

It worked. Grinning despite desperate odds and the memory of Fischer's sacrifice, Hardin slid behind the vee of boulders and lay between them among a scatter of smaller stones. The stone he hefted was flat as slate, the size of his fist and, again watching the stillness, he wondered if it would make enough noise. He brought his arm up quickly and released the stone without revealing himself, watched it arc over the concealing brush, and saw it scythe into grass near his fallen comrade.

Tufts of grass moved and, instantly, the command post spoke again, then fell ominously silent. Hardin smiled, knowing the enemy had now realized the ruse—but too late. He had seen an arm lance out from beneath a fallen hackberry limb to point toward that quaking grass. He could not move nearer without exposing himself, unless . . . He reached into a hip pocket and withdrew the weapon he had kept in reserve, had not even shared with Fischer. He flicked a thumb expertly under a projection on the oval mass, counted silently to four, and hurled the thing with all his might.

Fascinated, Hardin watched the eruption that followed. His little weapon dropped perfectly behind the slanting tree trunk, better aimed than he could have hoped, and the explosion he heard was one of anguish. A thin, sad-faced boy squirted into view on hands and knees and Hardin fired with telling effect: "Powpowpowpow!"

An instant later he saw Aaron Fischer, wonderfully renewed, leap to his feet in a suicide charge on the command post, firing nonstop: "Dowdowdowdowdow," until cut down by a single oddly muffled "Blam!" from the hollow tree.

Charlie saw Aaron get it again, this time in the belly. The charging commando flipped heels over head with one mortal scream and then rolled, writhing magnificently, to lie still again. *That Aaron,* thought Charlie, *he's the best durn dier in the business.* Aloud he cried, "Powpow, Jackie, you guys are both dead! I got you with my pine grenade, and I saw you real clear, Roy!"

Grown-up curses and a voice emerging from boyhood told him Jackie Rhett did not take defeat gracefully, for grace was not Jackie's specialty. But as Charlie Hardin trotted downslope toward the other boys, he worried. Something very unNazilike quavered from behind the tree. It was a wail, and it was real.

Aaron hopped to his feet and moved toward their dead

enemies, one now struggling from the hollow of that big tree trunk trailing a chain of curses potent enough to be worth keeping for future reference. This special language skill was a major reason why, among neighborhood mothers, Jackie Rhett was roughly as popular as measles. Charlie shook his head and marveled that Jackie could force his plumpness into such an opening. Jackie's T-shirt hiked up to reveal welts down the length of his oversized stomach. Devil take the pain, if Jackie wanted into something he *would* get into it. That was one reason why Jackie was one fat kid in the sixth grade who didn't get picked on. Another reason was that at thirteen, though no taller than Charlie or Aaron, Jackie was thirty pounds heavier and a year older.

And two years older than Roy Kinney, a fifth-grader they allowed to take part in games like Commando because, no matter how aggravating Roy managed to make himself, four was one more than three. Jackie wouldn't compete if the odds were against him.

Charlie and Aaron knew without thinking about it that the wails weren't Jackie's; the very idea was foolish. Besides, half the time, Roy's singsong "OW, ow, owowowowow" in a descending musical whine was the reliable siren that announced the end of many games.

Charlie sighed. Squatting, the three older boys watched Roy's spindly calves thrash like a swimmer's. The rest of him, all but the noise, had evidently taken root in the underbrush. "C'mon out," Charlie begged, but was answered only by renewed drumming of Roy's Cub Scout shoes.

Aaron pleaded with the same result, while arguing with Jackie that he'd stayed dead fair and square until an enemy had been killed to renew him, and finally Jackie, fists against his sides, growled, "Awright, longWord it, Roy, you're makin' me tired and it's almost suppertime." He kicked the sufferer's shoe soles.

Roy lay still then, but the siren persisted. "Here, you

chickenWords, help me," said Jackie, and sneered when the others declined. Jackie's persuasion was indirect. First he pulled Roy's knickers off, no small task wrestling elastic cuffs over scout shoes. Next Jackie made a few opening remarks on the subject of nakedness in general, then got specific over Roy's vile nudity even though Roy still wore his knit shorts. All without result. Once Roy got himself wound up this way you had to let him run all the way down.

Without pausing in expert cussing that held the others spellbound, Jackie took a small stick and, with each curse, began to switch a metronome beat on Roy's legs, which soon caused the boy to scramble from the brush with his tears renewed. It was not the stick that exhumed Roy so much as the regularity of it. Jackie could have brought Roy out just by tapping on his rump with a fingertip, over and over again. The rhythm was the pain; almost any kind of regularity, kept up long enough, is agony to a boy of eleven. It is, at least, unless that same boy is creator of the rhythm, which can be heavenly music to him.

Believing himself safe behind his shelter of hackberry debris, Roy claimed, he had been struck painfully in the left cheek by some object both blunt and sharp—which Charlie knew was a small gray pine cone. He quickly explained it as his grenade. Charlie spied it in a clump of johnsongrass and displayed it to them. "It's even the right size and everything," he said proudly.

"Well, jayWord-ceeWord, no wonder," Jackie burst out, noting tiny pinpricks of crimson on Roy's face that matched a pattern on the pine cone.

"No fair throwing rocks or pinecones and no rubberguns, right? Nobody else had any Word grenades anyhow; you're plain nuts about grenades. Where'd you get a longWord pinecone anyhow?"

It was a good question. None of the boys knew of any nearby trees that bore such warlike fruit. Austin, Texas, had

its share of towering pecan trees, groves of elm, steel-barked
hackberry and vast live oaks with limbs that seemed to
spread half a county wide, but pines were rare.

Charlie explained that he'd found it rummaging through
his mother's Christmas decorations. It was hardly worth
pointing out that any December debris packed away until
April was treasure, and treasure was fair game. "And it's not
a rubber band or a rock," he said, knowing he had tossed a
hunk of slate too, but only as a diversion, so it shouldn't
count really.

Instead of meeting Jackie's hard gaze, Charlie licked his
thumb and rubbed it across Roy's cheek, and the glance he
shared with the older boy was full of silent understanding.
Roy's companions all saw that he carried tiny new war
wounds on his cheek, yet it was best for all concerned if Roy
did not know it. The other boys took a few scratches as the
fortunes of war, but any time Roy discovered he was leaking
in color the siren would begin anew. Roy was, at best,
inferior war material, but of all the neighborhood boys he
alone could be wheedled into such roles as quisling, Japanese
spy, or Italian soldier. Every second-grader knew that
nobody, not even real Italian soldiers, wanted to be an Italian
soldier.

Leaning against the hackberry trunk, Aaron picked
judiciously at his nose, inspected the result, and sided with
Charlie. "You can rule it out next time 'til we find more
pinecones. But this time it was Charlie's secret weapon
without a rule against it, so it was legal."

Argument was in Jackie's glare, but he shrugged because
Aaron, by neighborhood consent, was the legal authority in
these things. All the boys took it for granted that, if your dad
specialized in something, you just naturally inherited that
knowledge. Coleman Hardin was a city officer with the
juvenile authorities whose badge gave him the status of a
detective, so Charlie claimed imaginary knowledge of police

matters. Raised by his grandmother, Jackie was the boys' expert on wheeled vehicles, though he might never drive his gram's school bus. Roy's dad sold insurance, which made Roy a specialist in risk assessment. And Aaron's dad was a lawyer. It was an article of faith that any boy who denied the logic of all this would throw their whole social system into chaos.

"Tell you what, Roy," said Charlie, "you keep my grenade for next time and we'll trade it back and forth."

Roy's face brightened, then fell. "So I get bunged only every other time?"

As Roy considered this risk, Jackie suddenly snatched the offending vegetable and ground it underfoot. "That settles that. No more throwin' *nuthin'*, and that's my rule." Jackie stood with fists on hips, waiting.

No one moved. It was not exactly Charlie's cone; it was a family Christmas cone. To an Austin boy, personal injury was scarcely visible compared to the slightest insult to his family. Asked what he must do if a maniac took a step toward the boy's sister, that boy was expected to leap at the fiend. Charlie's problem was even worse because his distant uncle Wes Hardin had been a true paragon of violence half a century before, a historic real-life killer at age fifteen. And Charlie, at twelve, was still searching vainly for his killer instinct. He swallowed and wondered when he was going to develop the heart for it. His heart was thumping hard at the moment.

Charlie, alert to his dad's conventional wisdom, had memorized several myths given with good intention. One of them was, "All bullies are cowards, son."

Jackie Rhett was the exact image of a bully, so in the fourth grade Charlie had challenged Jackie to a prizefight, using pillowy boxing gloves some well-meaning ass had given him. Jackie had not needed to foul the smaller boy, and every kid in school learned the outcome—because

Jackie told them, complete with sound effects and pantomime. Charlie wondered if Jackie's gram had taught him how to punch. It was a neighborhood scandal that the old woman must be his diction coach.

Charlie knew Aaron was too honorable to help against the older boy. Pal or no pal, you didn't fight two on one. Aaron might feel every blow to Charlie as a blow to himself, but Aaron knew the code. And Jackie knew that Aaron knew.

Now, after a long moment, Charlie shrugged as carelessly as his trembling shoulders would allow. "That ole pinecone was thrown away anyhow," he lied and added with fuddled bravado, "I bet you couldn't use a grenade, Jackie, you couldn't hit the Word side of, uh . . ."

"The broad side of a Wordhouse," Jackie smirked. "If you're gonna say it, get it right."

Charlie wheeled away, face burning. To dare one of the awful incantations and stumble on it was almost as bad as a whipping. Over his shoulder he said, "You coming, Aaron?"

Aaron came. The two boys trotted off along the creekside trail without conversation, goaded by the mocking laughter of Jackie Rhett, as Jackie intended. For a distance equal to a city block they quickened their pace, Charlie from shame, Aaron in camaraderie.

Their path snaked across thickets in soil that was replenished perhaps once a decade, each time Shoal Creek flooded. At one point, the boys were obliged to hop through a break in what they called the storm pipe, a concrete drain pipe four feet high that carried flood waters from suburban streets to this untamed creek, which led to the nearby river. The resulting jungle seemed a wilderness to the boys, though it meandered near the center of a city of low hills and a hundred thousand people—currently more in wartime, with its crowds of uniformed young men. Along the meadows near the creek a boy could organize a war or a pretend cattle

drive without a glance at fine homes barely visible through
trees that skirted the useless bottomland. One needed only
to shinny up an elm to see the spire of the state capitol, a
fifteen-minute walk away.

The boys scrambled up an embankment near the Tenth
Street bridge, still in silence until they reached macadam,
and shook hands as comrades-in-arms. The Hardin
bungalow lay two blocks ahead, the Fischer place three
blocks south.

Charlie was arranged on stouter bones than his friend
and, for over a year, had stayed wary of Aaron not so much
from the playground label of "jewboy" as for suspicion of
any kid who acted so much like a teacher, which is to say
Aaron was studious and scrupulously fair. When the
Fischers first moved to Austin from North Texas when both
boys were eight, Charlie had taken his own physical
superiority for granted. Aaron revised Charlie's opinion the
day they got into a punching, dirt-wallowing fight that
Aaron finally pronounced a draw, though they both knew
Aaron had got the best of it. Aaron looked skinny, with tight
dark curls roofing classic Aramaic features on a head a few
sizes too large to match his frame. But Aaron had a secret
weapon, too, one he would share with Charlie; it was called
Dynamic Tension, and he had taken it from the back cover
of a comic book. Aaron had read the tale of Mr. Atlas, the
one-time ninety-seven-pound weakling, knew he failed to
qualify by at least ten pounds, and financed his mail-order
muscles by clerking for a week at a fireworks stand. After
that it was only a matter of following instructions and
faithful calisthenics.

Aaron's wrists and ankles were still girl-slender, but his
agility was superhuman. Watching Charlie try to pin his
friend in a good-natured wrestling match was, as Coleman
Hardin put it, ". . . like shoveling fleas with a pitchfork."

For a moment after their handshake, neither boy spoke.

Then Charlie began, "That guy is really lucky. If I ever get mad at him, boy . . ." and trailed off.

Aaron gave a quick nod of agreement followed by a slow negative headshake, which Charlie understood perfectly: agreement, then irritation. All he said was, "What a momzer," and then loped off down the tree-shaded avenue. Charlie accepted that while Aaron's dad was lenient on some points, for some reason he wanted Aaron at home by sundown on Fridays.

Charlie trotted home constructing great towers of retribution for Jackie Rhett that always crumbled when Charlie struck them with blunt reality. Jackie was a fact of nature that defied all Sunday-school logic; he was social Darwinism in the raw. Mean-spirited, pudgy, quick-tempered, badly raised, by all rights Jackie should have been a pushover. Yet Jackie pushed everything else over with regularity. Jackie could hit harder, bear more pain, add a column of figures quicker, and catch more sun perch than any of his classmates.

Charlie never thought about the likelihood that in a taller, tapered form and without the touch of acne, Jackie might have been the class hero. What Charlie did consider was that most likely he would fall asleep that night replaying his inglorious retreat from the older boy.

But Charlie was wrong. His last thoughts that night were that he'd give a nickel to know what a "momzer" was.

CHAPTER 2:
✈ FUNDS FOR A SATURDAY ✈

Charlie waked to the distant music of plates clattering in the kitchen, and seconds later he was underfoot there. Five days a week during the school year he emerged from his room as if drugged and might not struggle fully awake until midmorning recess. On the sixth day he was atingle at the first flutter of his eyelids. His mother had only to murmur, "Charlie," for him to materialize at the breakfast table. Since the age of ten he had graduated to shoes and something that might pass for a T-shirt. When younger, often barefoot and shirtless, Charlie had been formally dressed for Saturday.

Coleman Hardin, already in the alcove called a "breakfast nook," crinkled a smile over his coffee cup toward his son. Then as Charlie slid into the bench opposite, his father placed the cup in its saucer with surgical precision.

Charlie knew the signs. So far he had heard only one word: his name. Yet a huge amount of communication had passed through the little family. His mother had nodded her welcome and smiled toward the alcove table as she forked strips of bacon onto a paper napkin. A good sign, and her

13

pretty, fine-boned features were defined by lipstick and an obvious touch of rouge, which meant she was ready to confront whatever the world might hold.

And Charlie's dad had smiled, usually another good sign—but he wore his old khaki work clothes, a bad sign. He hadn't fixed Charlie with that flinty arctic eye feared by all sons, but his smile was not entirely convincing and he had taken special care with his cup, as though it was half-full of nitroglycerine. His fair hair had been combed but was now mussed, a clear sign that he had already engaged in some undisclosed work. Before breakfast. And Charlie's dad would stroll over hot coals sooner than do manual labor before breakfast.

Now the elder Hardin lowered his head, eyeing Charlie in the manner of a man peering over invisible bifocals. Even before his father spoke, Charlie was fidgeting. "Very good job on that mesquite, Charlie."

Understanding and shame crossed the boy's face. He bit his lip and said nothing, but risked a glance at his mother. He knew she was listening though she appeared to give all her attention to frying eggs in bacon grease, a wartime economy that would be complete only when a jarful of that grease was donated to the war effort.

His mouth still set in that fraudulent smile, Coleman Hardin lifted his cup again; swirled its contents. "Yep, a good job, even a fine job. You left it in my way because you knew good and well I didn't really want to paint that side of the porch this morning," he said, his drawl-and-twang peaking on "good and well," then diminishing in a friendly way. He sipped and watched the boy without malice.

Charlie worried because his father showed no sign of distress, a sure hint that he had devised some punishment to fit Charlie's crime of forgetting to haul away several armloads of mesquite trimmings stacked near the house. Charlie kept his eyes averted, hoping his dad would develop some steam behind the rebuke, to vent in words and not in deeds. Charlie's dad could be a booger with deeds.

Warming to his topic: "I took one look at those clippings and I said to myself, why, that boy knows I wanted to do the whole job later, I said. I said yep, and he's willing to make sure that I do it, too, running off to the creek after school yesterday instead, most likely. He won't mind doing it this morning, says I; he won't even mind if I dock his allowance."

Charlie jerked at the key word, "allowance." "Aw, Dad . . ."

"That's what I told myself, Charlie. I realized you wanted to work this morning, and save me a quarter too."

"Couldn't I just save you thirteen cents?" Though no math scholar, Charlie could subtract in an instant, from a quarter, the price of a twelve-cent ticket to a Saturday matinee at the Queen Theater.

"A *quarter*," was his father's reply, a few decibels added to offset a twitch at the corners of his mouth and a flickered glance toward his wife. "I reckon it won't destroy you to miss a chapter of *The Lone Ranger*." It was well known that Charlie cared little for the main feature every Saturday. It was the serial that drew throngs of boys to the Queen Theater once a week, as a magnet draws iron filings.

"It ain't *The Lone Ranger*, it's *Flash Gordon*," Charlie replied, "and it's on with *After Midnight with Boston Blackie*! Aw, please Dad, *pleeease*," he pleaded.

Proving she had missed nothing in the exchange as she delivered two plates of bacon and eggs: "Don't say 'ain't,'" said Charlie's mother.

"I know where he gets it all," his father said, his fork held aloft as a preacher might hold a Bible. "It's that fool Rhett kid I've told him a million times not to associate with."

"Jackie's not a fool," Charlie blurted before he remembered that negotiations were underway. "Your tongue will burn in heck, Miz Taylor said so," he added, invoking the mighty name of his Sunday school teacher.

Charlie's mother sat down quickly. "Your father didn't actually call anybody a fool, Charlie," she said, though the darted glance at her husband was cool. "It was just a figure of speech. He meant to say," and again the glance, "he meant to say, that fool*ish* Rhett kid."

Charlie's dad had not intended to ground the boy completely until this moment; had meant to motivate him into a furious assault on prickly mesquite clippings and then to part with seventeen cents, enough for the movie and a nickel sack of popcorn. But somehow Charlie had managed to enlist a man's own wife against him. This was the trickiest sort of treachery, thought Coleman, and it needed strong measures. "That fool Rhett kid and that fool Hardin kid," he exclaimed. "Maybe it's our son who's the bad influence!" In the silence he had produced, Coleman Hardin addressed his breakfast with furious speed, drained his cup with a gulp, and swung up from the table. "I'll tell you one thing, sonny boy," he said, tipping Charlie off by use of the diminutive that he was really angry at someone else, "if those clippings aren't gone by lunchtime, I promise to run you through 'em at the end of my belt. Now if you will excuse me, Willa, I have to buy some brushes and thinner." And Charlie's dad stalked out of the house, having threatened a punishment he would not dream of fulfilling.

Now Charlie knew where most of his father's irritation lay. Both parents normally called each other "honey." When they didn't, they were prissily formal; and when formal, they were either angry or at a church picnic.

Willa Hardin knew that correcting her husband in the boy's presence had "tipped Coleman's madbox over." If Coleman was the best of husbands and fathers, like many others he had emerged from the recent national depression so thin-skinned in a few places that an unwary wife could poke a hole clear through him. Many a breadwinner still waked in the night shivering with sweat from a remembered nightmare in which he slumped at a breadline or swung a pickax eighty-four hours a week for a twelve-dollar paycheck. When a man has so recently escaped an era when his pride was all he owned, he is likely to keep that pride oiled and polished and automatically functioning far too long for his own good.

So it was that the Great Depression made Charlie spend much of that Saturday forenoon armored by shoes and shirt hauling mesquite to the neighborhood dump, which was only a sinkhole in a vacant lot near the creek, where locals disposed of such things. From time to time Charlie greeted other boys, all of them gloriously unemployed. A few times, he tried to make it appear such fun that any sensible person would rush to help, but apparently every boy in Austin had read the same books as he. As one said in parting, "Don't hand me that Tom Sawyer crud, Charlie."

It was only a block or so to the sinkhole, and the total weight of those clippings would not have outweighed the boy. Yet any opinion that Charlie's job was an easy one can be held only by one who lacks intimate experience with mesquite. When God made the world and found it good, He rested. It was while He was resting that someone noticed that He had left the Southwest without any truly spiteful trees. God chose not to bother further with such things. And that is how the devil inherited the job of inventing mesquite.

In crusted caliche desert, mesquite keeps its head down and seldom rises higher than a shrub. But when it can steal enough water to wet its whistle, a mesquite tree will tower over a four-story building. Its leaves divide into slender leaflets the size and usefulness of a broken shoestring, and if they promise shade, they lie. Its beanpods can be fodder for a determined cow of an experimental turn of mind, but since the Texas longhorn was the result of this research, it merits no applause.

More: the unwary dude who sits under a mesquite for long will go away gummier and wiser; the demon tree drips a useless sap. And all of this evil intent grows pale beside the main feature of the mesquite, for it is the grand champion porcupine of the vegetable kingdom, a living snarl of barbed wire. A mesquite branch as long as a boy's arm grows thorns as long as his finger. None of your spindly undernourished thorns, either; at its base, the thorn is as thick as a pencil, honed to a point that can penetrate a truck tire. Tell an Austin boy that an army tank sustained thirty-six flats driving over a mesquite and he will believe it.

No wonder, then, that Charlie piled branches on his old Radio Flyer wagon with such respect, and why his black and white fox terrier, Lint, could not be coaxed into pulling the contraption. Lint liked a good joke as well as the next dog but a stray mesquite thorn was outside the joke category. It took Charlie two hours to deliver the last of those clippings to the sinkhole.

And ten seconds to realize that he had created a shield for a boy on the run.

Charlie stood gazing down at his work for a long time. The sinkhole was five yards across and, with its new contents, almost up to ground level. He saw that if a fugitive could keep that sinkhole between himself and a pursuer, he could gain temporary refuge. No one would dare try to jump across; failure to clear the gap would be like falling into a den of pit vipers. And after a boy regained his breath he might find, or make, a special path through other nearby shrubs to stave off pursuit.

As it was, every turn of every path in the neighborhood was known to every boy. But why should this state of affairs last forever? Charlie filed this idea away and trundled his wagon home. It was nearly eleven o'clock, and he decided against trying to wheedle money from his dad. There were, after all, other sources of income.

As Charlie neared his best pal's house, he slowed his gait and dropped the tongue of his wagon so that it was hidden by the sidewalk hedge. He could not have said why he did this, but the wagon implied work of some sort and Charlie understood vaguely that one boy's Saturday was another boy's Shabbes. On the Jewish Sabbath the Fischers, while not overly strict, could be depended on for mysterious habits. There would be bread pudding to fill the inner boy, but there would not be "anything happening," including chores or loud play, and the Fischer pace in walking or talking would be, for Charlie, artificially slow. Yet Martin Fischer knew his son too well to expect total immersion in the traditional ways. His son Aaron could be depended on to avoid work on this day—on most days, in fact—but Fischer knew that few things are more holy than a boy's love of life. Aaron was permitted a bit of Saturday in his Shabbes.

Standing on the sidewalk before the Fischer bungalow, Charlie cupped his hands as if holding some rare insect, then blew between his thumbs. A soft mournful note hung in the air. He repeated this quickly, adding a higher note and returning to the original tone. It was the song of a flute with laryngitis, and several of Charlie's tribe had mastered it for such tasks as calling a pal outside without voicing anything.

Presently a similar *tootle-EE-oot* rewarded him from inside the house. Moments later Aaron followed his toot outdoors, wearing shoes and shirt as always. "Eat yet?" he asked, falling in step as Charlie pulled the wagon.

A shrug. "You?"

Identical shrug, but Aaron flipped a quarter and caught it to show that at popcorn time he would be financially equipped. "Got your money?"

Headshake from Charlie. "Thinkin' about a bottle run," he said. "I figure we've got an hour."

Aaron no longer wondered about the wagon. "Can't work today, but I s'pose I could play Find the Bottle with you," he said. A few blocks uphill, finer homes with bigger yards sat farther back, marking families that did not save empty bottles for the deposit. Their empties were left for trash collection behind back fences in alleys used for little else. With a nod toward noble impulse, some of the well-to-do might leave those empties beside their trash cans. A Hires root beer or Dr Pepper bottle could be sold to any grocery for two cents, and a milk bottle was worth a full nickel. It never occurred to the boys that trashmen might value those pennies too, but because trash was never collected on weekends and the boys gathered bottles only in extremes, bottle runs went unnoticed.

Lint heard the wagon's particular squeal from a block away and joined the troop, wary of other dogs behind fences, alert for cats to chase. It was a moment of pride for Lint when he was allowed on such tours but a galling rebuke if Charlie said, "No. Home, Lint. Go home." And Lint would obey. This was not a trick anyone had taught the terrier. Early in puppyhood, Lint had somehow learned what "home" meant and reacted to the word as if he had just noticed a signpost: SMALL DOGS WILL BE EATEN. Charlie soon learned to avoid using the word for any other purpose when Lint was in earshot. If Aaron, in a forgetful moment, happened to remark, "I should be home by dark," Lint might pause, or even stop undecided. If Charlie said it, Lint would instantly head for home as if his master had hurled a clod in his direction.

Several blocks up the hill they turned down an alley, gaining two cents from a Nehi bottle. The next block was without profit. The third block produced two milk bottles and four bulbous little Coke empties that inflamed both boys with expectation, but now all those bottles rattled in the wagon so that every dog in the neighborhood began to make pointed remarks. And some wealthy folks kept big dogs.

"Maybe we should pack trash around the bottles," Aaron said, and mentioned a comic radio program's most infamous sound effect. "We sound like Fibber McGee's closet."

"Fill my Flyer with actual garbage? I reckon not," Charlie scoffed.

Instead, he took off the shirt he no longer needed and stuffed bottles in its sleeves, muffling their progress. Presently they walked to another alley and headed back downhill, finding a trove of RC Cola empties that virtually filled the wagon. Charlie added his shoes to the mix, which helped silence the racket somewhat until they discovered a litter of half-pint milk bottles. Now, even granting Aaron a share, they had more than enough to fund Charlie's movie. By now they needed to hurry their clattering treasure down to the tiny store which, before home refrigeration, had sold only blocks of ice. Since the Ice House owner now sold a bit of everything at all hours and knew the value of goodwill, he was obliged to redeem bottles.

"We might not make it in time," Charlie said, guiding the wagon with difficulty because, downhill, it kept darting left or right without warning. "You go on, save me a seat."

"Nuh-uh," said Aaron staunchly. "We can make it if we run." He meant only that they should run the half-mile from the Ice House to Congress Avenue and the theater.

But Charlie was not one to leave a good idea alone, and thought to improve Aaron's. "I'll steer," he said, flipped the wagon tongue back, and mounted his clattering load as if it were a saddle. Now, if all went as planned, he could keep the front wheels properly aimed. "You better keep up," he warned, taking it for granted that Aaron would maintain his grip on the wagon. It has been mentioned that Charlie was an optimist.

For a few moments their strategy worked, Charlie sticking his bare feet forward beyond the wagon like bumpers, Aaron bent double with both hands gripping the wagon's tail, Lint trotting at Aaron's heels barking encouragement.

And then those few moments passed, and the strategy began to fail when Lint, goaded by Aaron's trouser cuffs flapping so temptingly near, began to growl and nip at them in a friendly way. By now gravity was exerting its influence, Aaron moving as fast as he could with his head down, rump high in the air, trying to kick the dog—in a friendly way. Small grooves across the sidewalk were not much help to Charlie, who still managed to control what had now become a squealing, jouncing juggernaut. The time for braking was at hand, and Charlie lowered his heels to the sidewalk as he did when wearing shoes.

But Charlie was sitting on his shoes. His bare heels were thick as boot leather but, thanks to friction, grew hot as a skillet within seconds. "Brakes," he called, lifting his feet again. "Braaakes!"

And Aaron tried, the only way he could. Still gripping the wagon, he stretched out full length, facing the cement, dragged cruelly downhill by a wagonful of bottles plus eighty pounds of nitwit. Aaron could feel his belt buckle scraping over grooves, shirt buttons grinding against cement, until his chin hit the sidewalk and he lost his grip on the wagon.

Aaron shouted the only counsel he knew, which was, "Slow down;" good advice though fruitless, and Lint galloped happily alongside Charlie barking expert advice as his master looked ahead with a desperate calculation in mind.

A driveway loomed ahead, the only place where cement led smoothly to the street, and Charlie leaned far to the side as he steered into a steep right-angle turn. He might have succeeded if not for Lint, who was not expecting this maneuver and crashed headlong into the wagon as it teetered on two wheels.

Wagon, boy, bottles and dog went tumbling, clangs and yelps competing as the load cascaded along the curb for the next twenty feet toward a nearby storm grating. Lint was first to recover, rushing to Charlie as the boy came to a sitting position, helping inspect heels and elbows with medicinal licks.

Aaron brushed himself off as he approached the crash site and retrieved one of Charlie's shoes from the gutter. Shards of glass were strewn below the curb, though half the bottles remained unbroken and, as Charlie tied his shoes, Aaron placed their surviving loot in the wagon after one darting glance toward a gray stucco bungalow nearest them. "I think we better clean this stuff up." He began to shove the larger chunks of glass toward the grating of the storm drain.

"No time," said Charlie, getting to his feet, wiping spit into one elbow.

"Yes there is, if you don't want us both in trouble," Aaron insisted. "Don't look now but I think I saw a face watching us from the spook house. I said don't look," he protested, and sighed because Charlie had immediately looked toward the gray bungalow. Another time, they might have given further thought to Aaron's claim, but by now no face could be seen and the boys were busier than two ants on a junebug.

Grumbling, they spent precious minutes using their shoes to guide splinters of bottle into the iron grating next to the street. Charlie's injuries proved slight, an angry scrape on one elbow and a trickle of blood from a finger. He worried more about Lint, who kept growling into the storm drain and limped until Charlie removed a needle of glass from a paw.

Aaron watched, plainly impatient, as Charlie performed the surgery and Lint thanked his master with saliva. "They're not gonna hold the movie while that pooch drowns you,

Charlie," he said. The little troupe left the scene in a run, and ransomed their surviving bottles minutes later for all of thirty-seven cents.

Charlie left his Radio Flyer behind the Ice House. Disposing of the dog was even simpler with the magic incantation, "Home, Lint." Then the boys loped off toward the Queen Theater, with enough spare pennies to share a tiny bag of candy corn from Woolworth's department store. They gave no more thought that day to the storm drain or to the face Aaron might have seen framed by gray stucco.

CHAPTER 3:
✈ THE REMAINS OF EASTER ✈

On the Friday before Easter in Charlie's world, most people might claim without reflection that they took the holiday seriously. In practice, if you were Charlie's age, Good Friday was merely the first of two Saturdays in one week, with an added neighborhood tradition the boys never mentioned though it could linger for ten days.

Charlie's mother did her part, donating a dozen fresh eggs to what she thought was merely an Easter egg hunt and supplying a ten-cent packet of aspirin-sized dye tablets. Roy Kinney's parents allowed his friends to use a dirt-floored storage space under their house and grandly called the place a playroom. They also supplied another dozen eggs. Sue Ann Kinney, a long-haired blonde colt of fourteen, was old enough to oversee the boiling of eggs in their kitchen, yet young enough to accept the dangers implied by several boys meddling with liquid dye. It was Mrs. Kinney's belief that no harm could arise from this.

Sue Ann supervised the boiling process and carried the steaming, vinegar-scented potful of eggs outside before entering the storage room where four boys waited on wooden crates, having set up a plank as a table between storage boxes. A half-dozen old cups, each with a dye tablet, awaited hot vinegar water from the pot.

"You busted one of Charlie's and one of Roy's," said Jackie Rhett as he watched eggs being dipped out with a wooden spoon.

"How can you tell?" Sue Ann said, unmoved. "They might both be yours."

"Yeah, eggs is eggs," Roy added.

"Alla my eggs better be perfect," Jackie grumbled.

Aaron said, stressing the first word, "*Whose* eggs?"

Jackie glared a reply but said nothing because Sue Ann represented adult supervision. Aaron knew, because Jackie bragged about such things, that all six of the eggs Jackie supplied had been obtained by stealth in Jackie's pockets from the big Checker Front Grocery.

Aaron had brought no eggs, claiming that Easter was a topic his mother preferred not to explore, so the boys were soon pushing thirty hardboiled eggs around on the plank while Sue Ann slowly half-filled the cups with water still hot from the pot. "Not yet," she said, as Roy isolated an egg. "Wait for the fizz to stop." And with this she began to stir the brilliantly colored, briskly foaming stuff in the cups with her spoon handle. "Charlie, can you roll the cracked eggs onto that old cup towel? I can make egg salad for lunch and there'll be seven eggs for each of you. Okay, Jackie?"

A quick nod from Jackie and three sighs from the others; Sue Ann was a born diplomat. Charlie pushed the two damaged items aside and knelt beside the girl, their heads nearly touching, and while the other boys foraged in corners for small sticks they had brought in during earlier projects, Charlie was content to kneel there, inhaling a scent more mysterious than vinegar. It disturbed and intrigued and ensnared him, and reminded him of another encounter with Sue Ann the previous October.

✳ ✳ ✳

It had been the day Roy broke a favorite Kinney vase and promptly disappeared, and Sue Ann had enlisted Charlie in a search. Because the girl seldom seemed to give much attention to Roy's friends, and Charlie was teasing a tiny horned lizard with a twig at the time, he had said, "Why me?"

And she had tossed that yellow mop of hair from her face, and batted her eyes, and smiled. He later decided her power was the smile, or maybe the faint hint of lilac he had never noticed before. "Because you're nice. And smart. I bet you know everywhere Roy would hide. I bet you know just about everything, Charlie." And because Charlie did not know that half of diplomacy is allure, something in him had glowed like a lightning bug.

Horned lizards were common enough and Charlie abandoned his task, especially with the stirring of something new in his breast. Soon, at his suggestion, they arrived at a historic local mansion, a stone pile set on a steep slope and known to all as "the castle." Charlie peered into bushes that surrounded the high ancient stone wall, knowing those bushes were favorite hideouts for Roy. Sue Ann had stopped at the wrought iron bars of a gate that had once admitted horse-drawn carriages to the grassy courtyard inside, a space dominated by an enormous live oak. "I don't know if he could squeeze between these bars," she said.

"He can, but he'd better not," said Charlie. "Sometimes they yell at you from the castle." He had paused to gaze at the vast stone structure that squatted uphill from above the courtyard. "I don't think he's here."

"Just us." For a moment they had stood at the massive gate in silence that, for Charlie, seemed perfect. Then: "Charlie, there's something I need to know. I think it's bad but I can't ask my mom; I think she'd have a hissy fit."

"Moms will do that."

"And Daddy? Worse."

"Uh-huh. What's it about?"

"A word. Just a word a boy asked me about after class. He acted like I was supposed to know. Charlie, I didn't know what to do. If a person asked you—I mean, would you ever tell they had asked?" Charlie had shaken his head. "Ever, ever? Cross your heart?"

This time his headshake had been more firm, with a forefinger tracing an X on his breastbone. After a timeless moment he said, "Am I supposed to guess?"

"If you were me, what would you do if a boy said—" and then she pronounced the whole Word right out loud, and stunned him with all the force of a lightning bolt between his ears.

Charlie had heard it enough, but never from a girl. It was a Word so potent, so full of adult mystery, that Charlie had only a vague notion of its exact meaning because it wasn't in the dictionary, and he would not even refer to it by its letter. He was more comfortable thinking of it as the Word after an E Word but before a G Word.

His tongue had clung to the roof of his mouth as if glued there. He sensed that Sue Ann, though taller and older, was asking something heroic of him; not heroic in deeds but in wisdom.

"Charlie, what should I have done?"

At least he knew what always worked for him when faced by life's great unknowables—such as that very moment. "Run," he blurted, and took to his heels.

Sue Ann was as fleet-footed as Charlie, but caught by surprise, she was left two paces behind all the way home. On the way her mood changed from uncertainty to suspicion and by the time Charlie swerved toward home he could tell by Sue Ann's tone that he had failed to cover himself with glory.

"Better not tell, you little scutter," she had called,

reluctant to cross the Hardin property line. "You just better not, is all." There had been tears in her voice, and since that day they had treated each other with the reserve of near-strangers.

Today, Charlie sensed that he was finally forgiven for the crime of being a boy unequal to the needs of a girl—that is to say, any boy. Sue Ann produced a pencil stub and let him print a "C" on one end of each of his seven eggs, then guided Roy through initialing his eggs with the understanding that any mix-up in those identical eggs would be a disaster equal to a Biblical flood. While the others followed suit, Roy became first to baptize his property by the simple tactic of whining to his sister about being the youngest and therefore always the most carelessly mistreated. When Roy saw Charlie preparing to dunk an egg, he insisted on having first turn at all six colors, with the result that Roy had one egg of each color with one left over while the other boys were forced to wait.

Aaron had more exotic tastes. He had brought a tiny birthday-cake candle and used it like a pencil to draw invisible designs, marks that became visible when the dye failed to tint the egg through that tracery of candlewax. If Sue Ann wondered why Aaron's designs featured block letters and words like "never miss" and "bam," she chose not to ask questions.

Charlie suspended eggs so that bands of different colors would decorate an egg. With the eventual fate of his eggs in mind, Jackie tinted every one of his a bright orange; he had noticed the previous year that a flying object of that color is easiest to track.

It took the whole group some time to discover why Roy was now sobbing. With one egg still white, he had resolved to dye it in a manner as multicolored and spectacular as any of the others. But some choices ruled out others, and Roy did not realize this until he had dyed all his fingers and smeared the colors and achieved Jackie's ridicule in the bargain.

"Bee oh emm's not a word," Jackie said.

"Sure it is," Roy replied. "A bomb, like you drop from a plane."

"Nope, you needed another 'b' on the end," Aaron said, and spelled it out. This was by now an impossibility on an egg that looked as if it had been decorated with ugliness in mind.

"That's crazy. It'd be 'bombuh,'" Roy insisted, tuning up his eyewash equipment.

"I'm sorry, bubba; Aaron's right," said Sue Ann, forgetting that taking sides against her little brother absolutely guaranteed tears. Roy flung the hated egg away into distant shadows and folded his arms over his face with a barrage of boohoos while Sue Ann sought ways to comfort him. Meanwhile: "Somebody find that egg," she said to no one in particular. "If it starts to stink my mom will skin us alive."

Jackie took no notice of this mission, content to enjoy Roy's troubles, but Charlie and Aaron began searching hidden crannies of the place. Charlie wasn't surprised to see that his pal had managed to carry a cup into the shadows with him.

"You said yellow," Aaron muttered, and set the cup down.

"Yeah, but—" Charlie began, but stopped when he saw Aaron carefully draw a pair of undyed eggs from a jacket pocket. "Oh boy," he finished with a grin, and turned away to resume hunting Roy's errant egg. It seemed that Aaron had, by prior agreement, brought a couple of eggs with him after all.

Presently Charlie discovered the lost egg, now severely cracked and flattened, and by now Sue Ann had persuaded Roy to glorify one of the cracked eggs she had set aside. Charlie showed his trophy to Aaron, who was blowing two bright yellow eggs dry. He pocketed one and gave the other to Charlie. "And guess what I found," Charlie said, holding up his other hand. Dangling from his forefinger was a fat one-gallon glass jug, roughly a third full of some dark pulpy mass. "Our jam. We forgot all about it last summer."

Aaron frowned, remembering. Several boys had spent an entire afternoon collecting dewberries along the creek, mixing them with stolen sugar and tap water, shaking them into an awful mush in that jug, then finding it was easier to get a berry into that narrow neck than to get it out again. Aaron made an upchuck face. "Wow, don't drop it. Talk about stink," he said, and made a worse face. In Aaron's experience, anything forgotten in a cellar for six months was not going to smell of incense.

"Let's see if it does," said Charlie, and began to unscrew the metal cap. The first hiss that emerged was so loud Charlie nearly dropped the jug, but when he inhaled, Aaron's fearful grimace quickly turned inside out. The two boys gazed at each other in delight, then looked into the jug again. A mass of foam now nearly filled the container, and an odd sweet tang filled the air.

"What're you guys doing?" called the girl.

"Nothing," Charlie called, tightening the cap again, pushing the jug behind a box. "But I found that ol' egg." And he made his way back to surrender his find.

Sue Ann promised to refrigerate the eggs until Easter and, before leaving them, told the boys to put everything back as they found it. This did not fit any plans of Jackie, who claimed his gram expected him at home. Moments later, with Jackie and Sue Ann gone, the other three boys sat listening to a screen door slam upstairs.

Roy began to smile because he saw the others doing it, then reconsidered. "Why are we smiling?"

"'Cause Jackie didn't wanta help," said Aaron.

"So he scooted," Charlie added, "so he won't get any jam."

Roy's eyebrows shot up. His lips formed a silent "jam." His smile was instantly reborn. "You brung some?"

"We all did," said Aaron, climbing back over storage boxes, grunting as he snagged something from the shadows. "Last summer, remember?" Aaron could not know how near he—all of them, in fact—had been to an explosion, thanks to the six-month buildup of pressure inside the glass jug. Charlie's accidental release of some pressure had spared the boys some serious grief.

"Gol-leee, dog," said Roy. He studied the foamy half-liquid gunk through the glass. "I got dibs," he announced.

"Oh, I just bet you do," said Charlie, dripping scorn. "I found it, and Aaron's next." And he unscrewed the cap again. The hiss was not so fierce this time, but it produced a glance between the older boys that said, "This may not taste like it smells." Now bubbles of foam filled the jug and popped at its mouth.

But the smell had them all salivating; sweet and wild and tangy and—something undefinable. "It's my house," said Roy.

"And my sugar," Charlie countered.

"And if I don't get first dibs, I tell."

Aaron took a turn at the scorn business. "That you hid it away? So what?"

"So I tell Jackie," said Roy.

"Aw, let him go first," said Charlie, who had intended this from the moment he first wondered about the taste of the stuff.

One glance at each of the older boys was enough to make Roy wonder if he had won this privilege too easily, but when Aaron growled, "Here, gimme that thing," Roy snatched up the jug and licked at its mouth. Then he licked again. Next he tipped the jug up and took one small sip. Followed by a very large one.

The others grabbed at the jug together when Roy was

seized with a spasm of coughs, and while Charlie took an experimental sip, Aaron watched purple stuff spray from Roy's nose. Coughing, sneezing, Roy groveled in the dirt while the older boys ignored him and sampled their lumpy fluid.

"Wow, I wish my mom's jam was this good," said Charlie, blinking away tears.

"Don't hog it," said Aaron, who knew Charlie's capacity for sweets. He swirled the jug and drank more of the runny pulp while Charlie waited his next turn.

Charlie slapped lightly on the smaller boy's back until, blinking while his eyes streamed, Roy sat up again. The others expected his usual snivel but, after one look at the way Aaron gulped at the jug, Roy made a brave decision. "Gimme it," said Roy, and claimed the jug.

While Roy swilled a half-cupful, Charlie wiped his eyes. "Tastes kinda hot," he said. "Pepper hot, not stove hot. But maaan . . ."

Aaron, blinking his own tears away, watched Roy with a pensive air. "Yeah, like Passover wine," he said. "Smells like it too, a little." The two shared another glance. Then, "You know what I think? I think a little jam like this will go a long way. Hey, Roy! Now you're the hog." Roy managed to shake his head without taking his lips from the jug.

"Leave some for Jackie. Or we'll tell," Charlie chimed in.

Roy lowered the jug, grinned, and produced a belch that really needed a larger boy. "Bites your tongue," he said happily.

Charlie screwed the cap back on the jug and hid it away where he had found it. "We gotta remember this."

"Next time, a whole pound of sugar. And two jugs," said Roy. He looked around, blinking. "I'm full," he decided. "You guys got any marbles on you?"

At any given time, a boy's pockets might contain a penny

or two, a pink blob of bubblegum (chewed only a little) wrapped in waxed paper imprinted with a tiny comic strip, a rubber band, and half a dozen cheap glass marbles. So, though Roy needed no answer, the older boys dug into their pockets and found enough colorful little spheres to have a game.

"Hot in here," Roy said, wiping sweat from his brow. "Let's go out." And as he led the way into the tree-shaded backyard, he paid no attention to the murmurs of the older boys.

No Austin yard was very useful to a boy without a room-sized plot of barren dirt with the flatness of a table. A twig might serve to scribe a two-foot circle roughly in the middle of the plot, with a straight line drawn three paces distant for "lagging"—a competition to see who could toss a marble nearest the line, which established the order of business. A favorite marble for shooting was a "taw," and a boy who insisted on using a taw larger or heavier than the norm was likely to find himself playing alone. This, because a boy captured a marble by shooting it out of the circle with his taw, and a heavy taw had an unfair advantage.

Moments later they had forgotten all about eggs and liquid jam while they knelt in the dirt and exercised their thumbs, shooting from outside the circle, with urgent calls of "knucks down, you're ooching," and "missed by a mile." They were not playing "keepsies," in accord with a common belief that playing for keeps was as sinful as any other form of gambling.

The first time Roy hiccuped, no one paid much attention. The second time, he was taking careful aim and grunted in irritation as his shoulders jerked. Aaron, patiently waiting his turn, sighed and leaned his head against Charlie's back. Charlie did not notice. Then Aaron giggled. Roy, hunkered down with his knuckles properly touching dirt, turned his head sideways to see what Aaron thought so funny. And then, very, very slowly, remaining bent in a kneeling position, Roy fell over, his hair in the dust inside the circle, and still holding the marble.

Now Charlie began to laugh too. So did Roy, in total silence with eyes closed as if in unspeakable joy or agony, and after an endless pause he flicked his marble, which soared away nowhere near the field of play. It was then that Aaron saw the wet patch spreading from the crotch of Roy's pants, and pulled himself fully upright. "Charlie?"

"I see it. And smell it too." He toed at Roy's arm, none too steadily. "Hey, Roy. You peed. You know what? You are one dumb kid."

Aaron snickered again. "Shikker," he muttered.

From Charlie: "What?"

"Drunk. Charlie, he is!"

Charlie bent down to shake the smaller boy's shoulder, lost his balance, and found himself sitting. "I think he's snoring," said Charlie, and blinked. "And you're fuzzy."

"Charlie, we're all drunk," Aaron said suddenly. "That jurn dam—durn jam did it, and we're in big trouble."

They both risked a look toward the house, expecting a frown from every window, but no one was watching. "Not yet we aren't. We better carry him back under the house," Charlie said.

"I don't think so. Maybe we can sit him up," Aaron said.

The deed was done with more haste than skill, but moments later Roy slumped with bowed head in the sleep of the innocent, more or less sitting, hands in his lap, legs splayed before the scribed circle while two larger figures melted away over the Kinney back fence.

Charlie had no hope of avoiding church services on Easter morning, and because his hard-boiled eggs were still in the Kinney refrigerator, he took care to craft a special, unusually earnest and detailed prayer. Mostly it involved homemade jam, good intentions, and avoidance of punishment. Evidently God was in a forgiving mood. When Charlie migrated to the Kinney home after lunch, no one seemed curious about Roy's long nap the previous Friday. After Sue Ann distributed the eggs, each of the four boys took a turn hiding all the eggs in a neutral location, which was the ill-tended grounds of the public library a few blocks away. They might have preferred the small adjacent park but had learned in previous years that younger egg-hunters with watchful parents would be numerous as insects there on this day. Since the library was closed on Easter Sunday, no one would shoo them away. They managed to lose two eggs and crack a few more that afternoon, but took these setbacks in good humor and each took his eggs home for future use. No bright yellow eggs figured in any of this.

For the next few school days, Easter and its products were forgotten, but on Thursday, Jackie Rhett declared war. Charlie learned this when, at the end of morning recess, he saw Aaron in the hallway of Pease School. Aaron rubbed an ear with one hand and displayed a badly flattened egg in the other. "Just thought I'd give you fair warning," he said. "I'll tell Roy at lunch if Jackie doesn't see him first."

Charlie studied the missile. "Jackie's?"

"Gotta be, it's orange. Shoot; I never saw him. Got me good. I hadn't thought about bringing our egg war to school."

Charlie nodded, shrugged, and said, "Almost late for art class," as he turned away. He was almost inside the classroom when he felt a solid thump between his shoulder blades. Aaron was already halfway down the hall, looking back with a grin, and those pieces of egg at Charlie's feet were no longer in a condition to be used again. Thus was the annual egg war declared, each boy against all the others.

Since Aaron had come to school eggless, Charlie waited for him after school as usual. His plans changed the instant he saw his pal burst out of the building between two girls, pursued by Jackie Rhett. Everyone knew how fast those stubby legs could propel the older boy, but Aaron managed to dodge and weave among others as he made his way across the playground. Aaron stayed a healthy fifteen yards ahead as they sped across the street and Charlie guessed the chase would lead along the byways of Shoal Creek.

Charlie trotted home alone to his trove of ammunition, which lay on a shelf in the Hardin garage, and filled his pockets. He left his yellow egg, which might need another few days to develop its full authority, and hurried down the street toward a spot near Aaron's home where one of the trails climbed away from the creek bottomlands. With skill and surprise, he might splatter both opponents.

But he had taken too long. A half-block from the trail Charlie saw that an exchange of pleasantries had already taken place because Jackie emerged first, watching the expanse behind him; watching it so intently that he didn't see Charlie. That meant Aaron must be armed now with what remained of one of Jackie's eggs. It also meant Charlie was in luck.

Running almost silently, Charlie was within a few paces of Jackie before Jackie heard him and dropped to a crouch, so that Charlie's egg sailed inches over his head. Facing this new enemy, Jackie hurled a handful of nothing toward Charlie at point-blank range, but this trickery was an old tactic, and Charlie had seen that Jackie's hands were empty.

Aaron's were not. As Charlie veered away to hide among shrubs at the trail, something that might once have been an orange egg found its target of naked skin in the exact center of Jackie's back between his pants and shirt, just as Jackie leaped to his feet. His "Yow!" said all that Aaron wanted to hear, and most of that eggy debris slid from sight down the crevice in the back of Jackie's pants.

Now Charlie had another egg ready, and this time his aim was better. Jackie, in full flight, took the blow on one arm without slowing and found safety behind a pomegranate bush. "No fair, no ganging up," he called.

"Who's a gang?" Aaron cried in protest, bobbing up from cover.

Charlie, realizing his friend hadn't seen him, yelled, "I am!" With that, he air-mailed another perfect strike, catching Aaron on the shoulder.

Aaron lost his balance and fell from sight downslope, giving Charlie time to pull another missile from a pocket. Jackie, seeing that he had not been unfairly singled out, but now eggless while Charlie was armed, took this opportunity to set off for home. Every few steps, small bright orange shreds of his own ammunition dribbled from the legs of Jackie's pants, which Charlie watched with great satisfaction.

From nearby, but well hidden: "Where'd you come from, guy?" cried Aaron.

"Shangri-La," Charlie called.

"Durn you, Charlie," said Aaron, laughing.

"Durn yourself," said Charlie, advancing.

Aaron heard those footsteps. "I got my yellow bomb," he warned, his voice more distant.

"Oh, sure you do, and so do I," said Charlie, knowing both claims were false. He skulked among the shrubs until he saw, beyond his range, a curly head hurrying toward the bottomlands. "I guess that'll teach guys to mess with Charlie Hardin," he called, with a quick look to be certain Jackie wasn't in earshot.

Charlie walked home whistling, inhaling the sweet air of the victor, replaying the past few minutes and revising and polishing each detail until it suited him to perfection. Finally in sight of home, he had convinced himself that superior Hardin skill, and not luck, was the secret of his triumph.

He did not alter his opinion until he felt the thump of Ray Kinney's mottled mouse-brown egg, hurled from behind the Kinney hedge, against the back of his head.

CHAPTER 4:
CHARLIE'S HIGHWAY

In the next few days, the egg-warriors learned that it had been a mistake to bring war to school. Roy had no classes with the bigger boys and merely kept a wary eye peeled at lunchtime. The others soon developed headaches from frequent dartings of the head, and a whole-body flinch at every sudden move by some other student. Even then, Charlie was grazed between classes by something that might once have been most of an egg—though after being molded into a missile between Aaron's hands it looked more like a blob of paint-flecked cement—and the same day, Aaron's locker door took a direct hit as he was about to close it.

Aaron didn't see the marksman, but an hour later, when called with Charlie to the principal's office by school loudspeakers, he soon got a broad hint. From fifty feet away they saw through the office doorway that someone sat almost hidden across from Principal Frost, but they recognized a familiar pair of rundown cowboy boots.

"Whad you do," Charlie asked softly, "tell on him?"

Aaron, his lips barely moving: "Nah. He'd just tell back. And then get me later."

41

Charlie was nodding agreement as they stopped in the doorway. "We were s'posed to come, Mr. Frost," said Aaron as he locked eyes with a Jackie Rhett who looked as if all the meanness had dribbled out of him.

"But we can come back later," Charlie put in.

"Ah, Fischer and Hardin. Right on time, boys," said the principal, and swung around in his chair without rising. Mr. Frost was a small man of economical movements and eyes that shone with sly intelligence. It was rumored that his bow ties numbered in the millions. "An eyewitness tells me you young thugs have been terrorizing this poor lad with Easter eggs," he said calmly. A flicker of his glance made it clear who that eyewitness probably was.

"Not me," said Aaron. "Ask anybody, Mr. Frost; it has to be somebody else."

Frost's gaze flicked to Charlie who only said, "Nossir," with a shrug that practically hid his head in his shirt.

"But what am I to think when this innocent boy is so terrified of you that he throws eggs at your friends?" said Frost, still at his mildest.

Charlie and Aaron lifted eyebrows at one another. "I dunno," said Charlie, thinking of Roy. "What friend?"

"Felice Gutierrez," Frost replied, with a friendly nod toward Jackie.

The other boys stared at Jackie as if he had begun singing opera in some dead language. Aaron managed to squeak, "Sir?"

"Sixth grade, never talks, scared of everything," said Charlie, and Aaron nodded. "What about her?"

"She's with the school nurse, getting boiled egg combed out of her hair," said Frost. "It was her distinct impression that young Rhett hit her deliberately."

In an effort to make sense of it all, Charlie turned to Jackie. "What did she do to you?"

"I was aiming to egg you back," Jackie said abruptly,

then added to the principal, "I don't even know that greaser kid."

"But now she knows you," Frost replied, resigned to such disrespect for Tex-Mex children from the likes of Jackie. "And I expect her brothers will, soon. They're both in Austin High, you know."

The boys digested this in silence. Austin High School stood just across Twelfth Street, facing this very school. It did not take an honor student to figure out how quickly a pair of offended Latino teens could launch a search-and-destroy mission after school to find one short-legged Anglo egg-thrower. "She didn't mention me or him?" asked Aaron, indicating Charlie.

Frost shook his head. "I didn't tell her you two caused young Rhett to do what he did." And after the tiniest of pauses: "Yet." Rich in experience, Frost could build a threat the way an insect builds a sandhill, grain by grain. When none of the boys replied, he said, "Have you two been bullying poor Rhett?" Seeing rapid headshakes, he went on, "I'll put it another way. Would you happen to be carrying any food in your pockets? Eggs, for example."

Charlie thought furiously, wondering whether his answer could refer to "eggs," plural, or to the one he suddenly remembered that lay, at this exact moment, in his pocket.

But Aaron had Frost's attention, quickly reaching into both pants pockets. He turned them out without a word, producing two marbles and a pink eraser. No eggs.

But Mr. Frost's eye was good. He saw the five small flecks of eggshell, one orange, one blue, and three crimson, that clung to Aaron's pocket. When Aaron noticed the evidence and drew a long breath, the principal stared him down. "You're going to say you sometimes bring hard-boiled eggs to school for lunch. Aren't you?"

"Yes, sir," said Aaron.

"Don't say it," the man said.

"No, sir," said Aaron.

"You didn't answer me, Hardin," said Frost, not unkindly. "Is it possible you could have colorful reminders of ancient food with you as well?"

"I might have forgot something," Charlie admitted, and placed a hand over the pocket that bulged with his one partly flattened egg. "Uh-huh, I did. In fact, here it is." And Charlie carefully detached his lime green, much-abused egg from the fabric.

Frost knelt, sniffed elaborately, nodded. "And you boys both eat hard-boiled eggs at lunch?"

"Sometimes." Charlie looked to Aaron for agreement and got it.

"Very well. Hardin, divide that disgusting thing in your hand into halves. No no, over the wastebasket, for heaven's sake. Fischer, you choose which half of it looks less repulsive. Then you will both prove to me that you eat antique eggs at school." And seeing their pleading looks, he added, "Yes, right now, unless you want your parents here in my office to discuss all this. Wait," he said suddenly. "Rhett, you seem to find this entertaining. I can have the nurse bring what she recovered from the Gutierrez girl for you to eat—I imagine it will include some of her hair—or I can put you in study hall for an hour after school every day next week. Just to keep you safe from thugs like these two after class, mind you. Your choice," he finished. While the principal's words continued to paint Jackie as a victim, his tone lacked sincerity.

Jackie swallowed by reflex as he watched Charlie begin to nibble. "I'll take study hall," he said, his face in an awful grimace.

"A wise decision. So it's back to class for you. Right now," said Frost, and waited as Jackie hurried out of the office.

Charlie struggled to swallow a bite. "You got any salt, Mr. Frost?"

The principal sighed. "Just eat it, Hardin. Children are starving in Europe."

Aaron and Charlie walked home together that afternoon, swollen with pride at being called thugs by Principal Frost, though they suspected the label had been applied in gentle sarcasm. "But that went over like a German zeppelin with Jackie," Aaron said. "I think we better cancel the war while we're still ahead."

Charlie nodded. "Goes without saying."

"This is Jackie Rhett we're talking about, Charlie. For that guy, *nuthin'* goes without saying. And we say it to him together so Jackie knows we agree."

Charlie was more than willing, but in his mind the pair of yellow eggs lingered like the last two plump kernels of popcorn in a sack, tempting and unconsumed. "One thing I'm durn sure not gonna do is tell anybody we fixed those eggs special," he said. "I'll flush mine down if you'll flush yours."

Aaron did not reply for so long that Charlie knew he was thinking ahead, as he did when playing checkers. At last: "More fun if we just put 'em somewhere so they'll get found someday, like they'd been lost ever since Easter Sunday."

"Found by who?"

Aaron grinned and shrugged. "Anybody but us," he said. So the boys disposed of their yellow bombs together, nestled out of sight at the base of a shrub in the hedge of a childless neighbor. The disposal was noticed by no one; well, almost no one.

Ever since he stood over that tangle of mesquite at the sinkhole and grasped the notion of a secret path in plain sight, the idea had festered in Charlie's mind. After supper on Friday, he rummaged among garden tools in search of something powerful enough to help him cut small branches but soon realized that the task was beyond him. He might have enlisted Aaron, but Friday evenings in the Fischer home were devoted to other things. Besides, something in the solitary nature of his project appealed to him, something he knew might fill his pal with awe. So when Charlie spotted his mother's new rose clippers, a new use for them sprang into being in an instant.

The tool wasn't too big, and its scissoring blades were sharp as knives. And while his original escape highway had begun to seem too much like work, he did not need much time to settle on an alternative that was closer than the creek.

When Charlie slipped away up the street at sundown with the clippers in a hip pocket, he knew exactly where he was going and thought that he might get a good start on his project before the April twilight faded.

His goal was a solitary midsized oak that leaned in toward the old stone wall surrounding the castle courtyard. From open windows in homes along the street he could hear bits of dialogue and laughter from radios, though television had not yet infected Texas airwaves. No nosy adults lurked in porch swings to wonder why some neighborhood kid was fooling around in a tree during twilight at the castle wall.

Once, he had been small enough to hide in bushes as Roy still did. But Charlie had grown enough to shinny up the oak which hung over the wall, its branches drooping far down inside toward the sunken courtyard. Another oak, huge and spreading, stood in the courtyard's very center, and Charlie had vague plans for it.

Neighborhood myth claimed that, long ago, a boy had once tried to climb the outer wall itself. No one Charlie knew had ever been so foolish because a century before, such walls were erected with broken bottles cemented into their tops. Standing at the smaller oak Charlie could see the last rays of sunlight glinting from cruel shards that might injure generations to come.

But Charlie had once seen Jackie Rhett use the oak as a path, merely to show off, daring anyone to follow. Jackie had picked his way up ignoring welts from tough little branches, well above the top of the wall, then across and finally, hand over hand and aided by gravity, down inside through foliage to the sunken meadow of the courtyard. At last Jackie had hung there for a full minute, his feet still more than a man's height above the ground, before trying—and failing—to climb back up. Eventually he had dropped to roll in the weedy meadow, then limped proudly to the carriage gate before squeezing his belly out between rust-scabbed iron bars. That was when Charlie knew Jackie had found no special path, had formed no highway of his own. An idea of that sort was not like Jackie Rhett.

Ideas of that sort were up to Charlie Hardin.

The first few feet of oak trunk were nearly vertical but, pressing his back against the wall, Charlie found that he could thrust his feet against rough bark and walk up the trunk far enough to grasp low branches. After that it was easier to pull himself up to where the trunk sloped inward toward the wall.

Here Jackie had fought his way across dense foliage a few inches above broken glass, through branches too thick to trim with mere clippers. But after snipping off one finger-thick branch, Charlie moved higher until he could stand on a big branch while gripping still higher ones with both hands. It was a simple matter then to walk safely across above the wall.

It looked like a slower route, but it wasn't. Soon Charlie was several feet past the wall, high enough to grasp leafy handholds Jackie had never reached. As he moved farther out on the branches they all became thinner, more springy, and several more times Charlie sliced away bits that interfered. He rejoiced to see that the farther out he moved, the more the branches drooped, and presently he found himself much nearer the ground than Jackie had managed, little more than an arm's length above courtyard weeds. Almost as soon as he dropped to the courtyard he was on his feet again.

The job had taken only minutes! Charlie was so elated he ran to the massive iron-barred carriage gate and slipped through, snorting with self-congratulation. It took him half a minute to run around the corner and up the hill to test his new highway through the oak again. He went up the tree with the ease of a squirrel, climbed to the pathway he had cleared, and in his overconfidence would have fallen onto the terrible glass except that both hands gripped the handholds he had memorized. Then across the bigger branches, then farther still until they grew small and began to sag with him, and this time when he plunged to earth Charlie ran directly to the middle of the courtyard. He had mastered the smaller oak, and fairly dared the big one to defeat him.

Standing before him was a tree six feet thick whose branches spanned half the entire courtyard, fifty feet high. There was no way a boy could scale an oak trunk thicker than he was tall, if its first fork began more than ten feet up. But centuries-old specimens like this tended to spread so far that the tips of larger branches spread downward again almost to the ground, far away from that mighty trunk. This boy-friendly arrangement meant that Charlie could simply reach up, find any branch thicker than a broom handle, and climb into the tree hand over hand.

This tactic, climbing toward the trunk, was new to Charlie and in gathering dusk he did not find the smaller, mean-spirited twigs so much as they found him. Cheeks, ears, and chin all felt the insults of this monster vegetable. As soon as he could grip its foliage safely, he began to counterattack with the clippers.

In this way he moved up into the tree until the branch

supporting him was as thick as his waist and the ground below was littered with neatly severed twigs. The supporting branch sloped upward enough that he could walk on it as easily as climb it, so Charlie took the clippers in his teeth and grasped handholds with both hands.

But the bitter-sour tang of metal in his mouth made him grimace, and in an instant the clippers were gone to fall silently, invisibly, far beneath his feet. Charlie felt an instant of desperation. But how far away could the precious clippers be? He retraced his path in the dimness, swung his legs to one side, and felt leaves scrape his cheeks as he dropped to the courtyard.

The clippers seemed to have scuttled off somewhere in the gloom, yet he knew perfectly well they lurked near, teasing him. He told himself they didn't really have legs, and since they couldn't hide in daylight he could find them in the morning. Still, he kept up his search until he heard a rhythmic series of faint reports that sounded like firecrackers far down the street. He ran to the carriage gate. Those reports were his father's handclaps calling him home, and two minutes later Lint met Charlie as he shuffled into the driveway with, "I'm ho-ome."

As long as he was near enough to obey those claps, Charlie rarely had to give a detailed account for his comings and goings. To avoid any questions he immediately set about mixing canned dog food with table scraps set aside earlier by his mother, and when the last twilight faded, Charlie was sitting at the back porch steps beside Lint listening to the dog's bowl scrape across cement.

Charlie stayed outside talking to Lint much longer than usual that night. He knew that his parents had a supernatural ability to read his face for any guilt he might be carrying, and once they faced him squarely with probing questions, any sin on his conscience would soon be known. Boys like Jackie or Roy might escape by lying, but Charlie operated with a stricter code: he simply did not know how to lie convincingly and had learned long ago not to try. Aaron suffered the same weakness but had worked out strategies to deal with it, and bit by bit Charlie was learning them. The creek was forbidden territory, so if you played there, you also played for a few minutes at the schoolground or the park, and later you volunteered the safe location. If you had done something spectacularly dumb—like losing your mother's rose clippers—you stayed out of sight or threw yourself into some task that demanded your full attention.

Lint's supper had provided that escape, and as he scratched between the dog's shoulders Charlie resolved to try his new highway again the following morning on his way to recover those clippers. If he failed to find them, he would have to buy a new pair, at a price he could not hope to meet by selling a few measly bottles.

CHAPTER 5:
✈ MINING THE DEPTHS ✈

With the nation at war, most families recycled their paper and metals, and tended vegetables in tiny plots they called "victory gardens." The garden behind Charlie's home grew tomatoes, radishes, beets and cucumbers in a space the size of his bedroom. If no other work was needed on a given Saturday, Charlie weeded the plot in return for his weekly quarter. On this day he hurried through his task and received his quarter fully expecting to have the missing clippers safely back in place by midmorning.

So much for Charlie's plans. At the castle wall, with a quick scratch to soothe doggy feelings, he sent Lint home. Then, just for practice, he scrambled up through the small oak improving his memory for handholds, across the dreaded wall, and down into the courtyard, running quickly to where he knew the clippers lay. Then he dropped to his knees and began to grapple in the weeds, slowly coming to realize that what he "knew" did not fit an awful fact: the clippers were not to be found.

At this point Charlie's internal map of his day's business fell apart like a rain-soaked newspaper. He climbed into the huge central oak as he had done the previous evening, then sat balanced above the scene of this disaster and carefully scanned the area. Still no clippers.

He swiftly reviewed a supply of remedies. He would run off and join a circus—but the circus, as everyone knew, lived in Florida, and Charlie did not have the price of a Trailways bus ticket. Moreover, he was strictly forbidden to hitchhike. Well then, he would buy another pair of clippers—after collecting a mountain of bottles, enough bottles to produce a sum so princely it made his head swim. Or he could do without the Lone Ranger for as many Saturdays as it took to accumulate the price of those confounded clippers. Or he might even sell the secrets of his highway to Jackie Rhett.

None of these fancy schemes seemed quite real even to Charlie. He knew the answer to his problem could be summed up in one word: money. Charlie knew boys who claimed to have earned scores of dollars with newspaper routes. But by some secluded rule that parents left unexplained, none of Charlie's friends were allowed to have a paper route or any other job beyond the home. Charlie reasoned that a regular salary could make him much more independent. He had not figured out that, to his parents, a more independent Charlie would be as welcome as a Japanese air raid.

Presently, Charlie noticed a figure moving along the street a block away, coming nearer. A host of oak leaves prevented him from making certain, but by blowing familiar sad little hoots so hard that spots appeared before his eyes, he was rewarded. The walker paused; continued; paused again to listen; cupped his hands near his mouth. And the answering hoot told Charlie that the walker was Aaron.

Invisible on his perch, Charlie enjoyed his pal's puzzlement as he hooted Aaron through the old gate, under the limbs of the mighty oak, and finally almost beneath the hidden hootist before Aaron knelt and fumbled in the tuft grass. When Aaron stood up, it was Charlie's turn to be mystified.

"You found 'em," Charlie exclaimed.

"Who chased you up there?" asked Aaron in surprise, holding the clippers as he stared aloft.

"Never mind," said Charlie, hoping to keep his highway secret as he struggled lower to a safe height. He dropped to the ground, lost his balance, and found himself sitting at Aaron's feet. "Gimme," he said, and held his hand up. "Those are my mom's."

Aaron studied the tool. "What would your mom do with an old busted pair of snips?"

"Clippers," said Charlie, rising. "And they're not old; not busted either. You better gimme."

"Take 'em," Aaron said with disdain, and dropped the clippers on the ground. "No good for anything anyhow."

A faint moan escaped Charlie as he examined the clippers. "Ohh, boy. You've done it now," he said, hoping to share the blame. "You busted the little doodad on the end."

"Me? I just got here. Tell me how I broke 'em before I ever found 'em."

Something in Charlie seethed for release, anything to vent his misery. And here stood his best friend, squinting with hands on hips, ready for anything up to a yelling argument. In a flash of mixed memories Charlie realized this was a drama they had enacted a hundred times, and not once had it ever ended pleasantly for either of them.

"Well, they weren't busted when I dropped 'em," Charlie said.

Aaron's gaze measured the distance to Charlie's lofty perch. "When you dropped 'em," he echoed. "Gee, what does that tell us?"

What it told Charlie, he admitted, was that he expected serious trouble unless he could buy new clippers. Charlie's punishments tended to fit his crimes, and this combined the crime of breaking a prized tool with the crime of borrowing it without asking.

"Get your money yet?" Aaron asked suddenly.

"Boy, don't I wish," said Charlie. "We oughta talk about that. All I got is my quarter."

"That's what I meant. I was on my way to your house. Got an extra dime, so we could go buy a zoom plane before the movie." Small balsa gliders with "zoom" lettered across the wing were more fun between two boys than a baseball because the flights were unpredictable. "You ready?"

Moments later the boys were trotting toward Congress Avenue, once a main trail for cattle drives, still a hundred yards wide and now Austin's central traffic artery. Theaters such as the State and Paramount shared Congress Avenue frontage with the less ritzy Queen and "dime" stores like Woolworth's and Kress's, where a boy might shop for model airplane kits, candy and marbles. At Scarborough Hardware they priced a pair of clippers and walked more slowly afterward, agreeing that $2.49 was an outrageous price for anything so easily broken.

At Kress's, Aaron bought his zoom plane and assembled it on the spot. To cheer Charlie he pointed out that the Lone Ranger would not be *Hi-Yo*ing on the screen for more than an hour. The blockwide park between the governor's mansion and the state capitol building was four blocks up Congress, usually an ample space for a zoom plane. Aaron mimed tossing the glider. "Wanta?"

Because a public hug for a pal was unthinkable, Charlie responded with a grin and a gentle fist against Aaron's upper arm. In another five minutes, free from any trees big enough to steal a boy's toy, they were adjusting the little balsa craft for longer flights. After another ten minutes one of Aaron's tosses ran afoul of an unexpected breeze, and in moments the model had soared to a height they had thought impossible.

"Whoa, you're gonna lose it," Charlie called, marveling.

"Your turn! You're supposed to get it," cried Aaron, who was no more a slouch than Charlie at dodging blame. Both boys set off together, the glider a tantalizing wisp that flew at a sprinter's pace. As the model began to settle far beyond them, it crossed the street and bounced merrily at the curb, vulnerable to anything on wheels.

Charlie and Aaron might have waited for traffic to clear but Aaron, thinking more about tactics than about Charlie's safety, remembered a phrase that was only an inch from magic. "It's up to you, Charlie," he said, and saw the fire of the fanatic kindle in Charlie's eyes.

Charlie darted across one lane ahead of a sedan, adjusted his path to avoid being collected by a coupe in the second lane, then realized a car in the third lane was moving in the opposing direction. Charlie stopped dead on the center stripe but the driver of the approaching car, suddenly alerted, swerved into the adjoining lane as he skidded to a halt. Since that lane was occupied by another car, a brief symphony of squalling rubber, car horns and Word-laden yells serenaded Charlie as he sped to the far curb and snatched his balsa prize up, then continued on at top speed to the lawn of the state capitol grounds.

Nor did he stop then, seeing two drivers exit cars that stood crosswise and immobile while other traffic began to clog the street behind them. The capitol grounds provided Charlie with several screens of shrubbery, and he used them to abandon the scene, finally taking refuge behind a young couple, both sightseeing in uniform, who took no notice of the boy.

By the time Charlie took advantage of bushes to squat and look for pursuers, the street traffic was moving again though Aaron was nowhere to be seen. Charlie moved to the broad central walkway leading to the capitol building, a massive pile of rosy granite that dominated the skyline. He waited for strollers to clear the area near him, then gave Aaron's balsa bird an easy toss knowing that it would be a beacon for Aaron the way a pigeon draws a hawk. A few more modest flights proved that he was right, when Aaron appeared from distant bushes and raced to compete with Charlie in chasing down his toy.

Charlie won. Mindful of the outcome of Aaron's last flight, he prepared to resume the game with a modest toss until Aaron, ready to be the retriever, teased, "Remember if it goes in the street, I'm not as big an idiot as you are."

Charlie paused, his expression darkening. Was it fair for a guy to endanger his own property, urge a buddy to risk his neck for a heroic recovery, and then call the hero an idiot? The perfect accuracy of Aaron's wisecrack only made it worse. "Not in the street," he said, "but this one's up to *you*, smart guy." And with this, he sprinted across the lawn toward the nearby lily pond.

Aaron guessed his friend's intention and gave chase two paces behind, panting, "No, nuh-uh, it's a dime, a dime, a dime," to no effect. He knew that if the glider became water-soaked it would be too heavy to fly again until it dried out. Charlie hurled the zoom plane straight across the broad, tree-shaded pond, narrowly avoided splashing into it over the low curb, and stopped to watch the result. The toy looped, seemed destined to settle on cement, but suddenly plopped down on one of the platter-sized lily pads that decorated the scummy pond like green doilies on a greener tablecloth. Weighing only an ounce, it might still be flown again and lay temptingly near, no more than ten feet from dry cement. "Your turn," said Charlie, hiding his relief.

A whiskery old idler on a nearby bench laughed. "Look out for sharks, sprat."

Aaron hugged himself, toes touching the curb, and sent a gloomy look toward his wayward property. With a headshake: "Might as well be in the river," he said.

"Aw, it's okay," Charlie said. "I dare you to roll up your pants and wade over there."

"Could be water moccasins," Aaron rejoined, and folded his arms. "You did that on purpose. Dares go first."

This was a common challenge; a boy who issued a dare must be willing to take the same risk. Charlie hesitated, searching the pond surface for any sign of poisonous water snakes, wondering how deep the pond might be, because the stagnant water, smelling of green scum, was not appealing. Then he saw the penny on the lily pad with the zoom plane.

Rarely has one cent brought more sweeping change. Twenty feet distant on a second pad lay another coin, one of the gray steel wartime pennies. And unless Charlie's eye lied, a coin that might have been a buffalo nickel sat impudently on a pad, a silent dare more potent than anything Aaron could say. Visiting young servicemen were known to use such ponds as wishing wells, foolishly tossing small coins at lily pads to impress girls foolish enough to be impressed.

Charlie's feet were already bare and as he rolled his pants as high as they would go, he said nothing about coins. Instead, he muttered about the danger, the genuinely icky smell of the pond, the unknown depths—and then sat on the low cement curb and eased his feet down in search of firm bottom.

The bottom was only knee-deep, and it was cement, and slimy. And as Charlie moved out toward his goal, gliding along slowly as if on skates to avoid sloshing or, worse, a headlong fall, he had a moment of skin-prickling, wonderful clarity. He realized that the pond had been visited not by a few coin-tossers but by hundreds of them, maybe thousands, maybe bazillions. And for every tosser whose coin had found a lily pad there had been countless others whose coins had dropped through murk to the bottom. And suddenly Charlie knew that he would have no trouble replacing his mother's clippers. Because in the scummy slime under his toes lay more round metal discs than he could count, and each one was worth at least One Cent. He stopped, sweeping a foot experimentally to broom the coins together. But even if he managed to shove them to the edge of the pond, the man on the bench was chuckling his enjoyment. Who knew how the old codger might complicate this operation?

Aaron, because Charlie had stopped: "Getting deeper?"

Charlie: "Stinks. Real bad. I think I'm gonna throw up." A pantomime of a dry heave thrust Charlie's head forward. He turned, shuffling with both feet, and moved back to the low curb, seeming to ignore old Mr. Benchman while giving every sign that, at any moment, he might deposit his breakfast across the cement near the man's feet.

"I don't need this," said Benchman to nobody in particular, rising with a grunt, limping out of Charlie's life exactly as Charlie had hoped.

"It's okay, Charlie, you tried," said Aaron, reaching over to help his pal from the pond; and with this proof of his devotion he assured himself of riches.

Until that moment Charlie had thought he might retrieve the glider and only the few visible coins, leaving all the rest in their drowned condition until much later, perhaps at dusk, but certainly alone. Now, still looking after the departing old fellow who was well out of earshot, Charlie grinned. "I'm okay. Aaron, have I ever lied to you?"

"Lotsa times. But if you say you're—"

"Not just fibs. Big old lies, guy." Charlie's gaze was intense, with the imaginary heat of uncounted wealth underfoot.

Aaron blinked and thought it over. "Well, there was that time in—"

Exasperated, Charlie burst out, "D-Word it, Aaron, just trust me, okay?"

Aaron allowed full force to Charlie's use of this forbidden

Word and grimaced as if pained. "Okay, okay! What did I do, Charlie?"

"Nothin'. It's what you're gonna do. If you trust me, lie down here and reach past the curb as far down as you can. It's yucky and kinda cold on the bottom. But Aaron, Aaron, ohhh man, honest—*you won't care.*"

It was not his pal's words that drew Aaron down on his belly so much as it was the earnest eye-roll that accompanied, "you won't care." For a few heartbeats, a tiny part of Aaron was afraid; not of Charlie, but of the unexplained, indeed, maybe the unexplainable. Then, reaching into the water so near Charlie's shins that he could smell the scum on them, Aaron found the bottom. And not just the bottom, but what Charlie's bare feet had shoved along ON the bottom, which explained everything.

Aaron giggled, thunderstruck. "Oboy," he murmured, scrabbling about in the muck. "Oboyo*boyo*boyoboy, Charlie, this is it! This is where all the pennies in the world go to die. It's like the elephant's graveyard." As he began to scud a handful of coins up the cement wall he risked a glance around, wary of prying eyes.

Meanwhile Charlie, seeing that no one else had noticed two boys playing at the pond, slowly waded across to the pad with the nickel, then recovered the glider and its penny. There were fewer coins farther out, though the pond was no deeper there. Charlie knew he was losing some through sloppy footwork, but finally could feel that he was herding so many pennies, the sneaky little things were escaping around his toes. He became a more careful prospector now, leaving his new trove near the first one and leaving Aaron to deal with the spoils.

After ten minutes of this Charlie began to tire. Besides, he itched to slide his fingers into riches as Aaron was doing. "Now you," he said, plopping his rump on the curb, setting the glider aside.

But wealth brings its own problems, and Aaron could not sit up without a struggle. He had filled his pockets lying full length, weighing himself down so much that his pants sagged dangerously below his waist as he scooted to a sitting position. "I can't go out there. If I fall, I expect I'll drown," he said.

"Then get away. There's more, isn't there?"

"Lots," said Aaron, taking a death grip on his pants. Soon, Charlie had taken Aaron's place while Aaron waddled to the park bench and repositioned the contents of his pockets. Less tidy than his pal, Charlie spent less time rinsing bits of green guck from each palmful of coins with the result that what went into his pockets went in as colorful as a Disney cartoon.

Presently, in part because a few passersby seemed almost ready to ask questions, Charlie took careful note of cracks in the cement and managed to sit up, intending to return for further strip-mining. With a glance toward Aaron: "How you doing?"

"How do I look?" Aaron stood up, holding fast to his belt, and Charlie snickered. Aaron glared back. "Hey, you expect me to bury it someplace?"

"You look like a squirrel," said Charlie.

"Try standing up and see how you like it," Aaron countered, sitting down again.

This was easier said than done but, with lumps the size of oranges weighting pockets fore and aft, Charlie joined his pal on the bench. They waited until no spectators were in sight and then, walking like brittle-boned little old men, they made their way to shrubbery far from walkways.

It was Aaron who announced that one of them must empty his pockets and mount an expedition to find suitable containers. While Charlie thought about that, Aaron sighed, piled his coins on the ground between them, stood up to rearrange trousers showing patches of dampness, and said wistfully, "Could I have some of it?"

Charlie, in a gruff off-handed way: "Not much. Only half."

"You're keen," Aaron replied, and set off in a loping shuffle.

Soon Charlie had added his coins to the pile, and discovered a surprising number of nickels, a few dimes, and from some blessed madman, a single authentic, unimpeachable half-dollar coin the size of a milk bottle stopper. Many of the coins had lain in state long enough that they were hard to identify. Still, Indian heads were big, and Lincoln's was small. Charlie would spit on a penny and rub it until its disguise wore thin, then start with another.

He had hardly begun when Aaron returned with a discarded Dallas *Morning News* and a question. "We still going to the movie?"

"I guess," Charlie shrugged, though he had forgotten such trivia in the excitement of sudden wealth.

"Then we can count this later." As he spoke, Aaron was lining up sheets of newsprint, transferring the heavy coins to the center of the papers with cupped hands. Charlie watched, fascinated at this show of ingenuity, then noticed that Aaron was wrapping only half of the treasure as a wrinkled metal-filled tube. Without a word he chose several sheets of the remaining paper and copied Aaron's work, twisting the ends like the wrapper of a colossal hard candy nugget.

With a fresh goal and mindful of the fact that *The Lone Ranger* waits for no boy, they sprinted from the capitol grounds, trotted the next few blocks down Congress Avenue carrying their assets like footballs, and finally trudged exhausted into the last-minute line of boys at the Queen Theater. Not until they were at the ticket booth did they realize that every cent, including their original coins, was now wrapped in Dallas newsprint. Aaron loosened one twisted end and paid for both tickets. The ticket lady, experienced in the ways boys carried cash, touched the damp coins only with a fingertip sheathed in red rubber and nodded them past without comment.

Inside, when Aaron turned toward the men's room and Charlie asked him why, Aaron shamed him with a look, displaying palms that were a portrait of grime. "I'm gonna get popcorn and a Three Musketeers. Maybe go back again. But I'm not gonna touch any of it with these hands," he promised.

So Charlie, too, washed his hands, and later wolfed down two bags of popcorn and three Baby Ruth bars, and that night at supper, wondered why he had no appetite.

CHAPTER 6:
✈ SECRETS OF THE STORM DRAIN ✈

On Sunday, the boys held a council of three—though Lint was not a voting member—in a favored refuge under the workbench in the Hardin garage. Counting the loot disabled their brains in different ways. "Half of forty-four dollars and sixty-three cents," Aaron enthused, his eyes like brown moons as he gloated over coin stacks, "makes, uh—"

"Plus the movie and the stuff we ate and the zoom plane," Charlie itemized. "You remember what that came to?"

"Nope. Don't ask me, Charlie, it makes my head hurt. Besides, you found it. If I kept more than twenty bucks of this it'd be like cheating you. I don't even know how to explain this to my folks."

"Me neither," said Charlie. "So I'm not gonna. I found it fair and square."

"Stole it, you mean."

Charlie recoiled as if bitten. "I never! Who from?" Alerted by his master's tone, Lint ceased sniffing at the coins. He knew that barking in such close quarters was rude so he contributed the faint growl this occasion seemed to call for.

"I don't know who from," said Aaron, mostly to the growler. "Whoever owns the pond."

"For Pete's sake, nobody owns it! No, wait a minute; everybody owns it, and some of it was right in plain sight for anybody, only nobody but us went and got it. So we earned it. I mean, it's our durn state capitol, Aaron."

Nervous with doubt, Aaron said, "Wonder what the governor would say."

"You can find out. His house is right next to where we were flying the zoom plane." This was true; the governor's mansion faced the capitol building near Twelfth Street.

"Aw, he'd say it was his."

"Then you go ask him, and we'll do what he says." The boys swapped stares. Charlie could see that his pal was giving the idea serious consideration, so, "We'd have to pay him back for all that stuff we ate," he added quickly.

This complication was too much, and Aaron's position crumbled.

"Then I guess it's finders keepers," he said, "but you told me there was lots more in the pond. Whose is that?"

"We'll leave it for the governor," Charlie offered, charitable in his new wealth.

So it was agreed that, while they had done nothing wrong, they'd better not do it again. This wisdom extended to avoiding any mention about their little expedition to an adult. Or to Sue Ann or Jackie or, in fact, anybody else on Planet Earth. "What we need is a bank," Aaron said.

Banks were another full-blown mystery, with Charlie suspicious that a bank would ask exactly the kind of questions they hoped to avoid, and Aaron just as worried that a bank would demand payment for keeping track of such a huge sum as theirs. The simplest solution, Aaron said, was for Charlie to use up nickels and dimes in buying new clippers, and for Aaron to beg a few paper coin tubes each week from different grocers.

They had liberated a small flour sack to hold the coins, and neither boy wanted to risk hiding such riches where they might be discovered. Aaron was especially firm on the point since his mother had the habit of searching every corner of her house on washday looking for stray socks and such. "My mom's a boogerbear on finding stuff. I can't even hide a piece of taffy," he complained.

"If we can't hide it at home, we've gotta do it like pirates," Charlie said after a dozen ideas had been argued to pieces. "They kept stuff forever."

"Buried it," Aaron nodded. "Yeah, but—nah, this stupid dog would just dig it up. Probably eat half of it. Remember those two cherry bombs we buried? Lint wasn't even there when we hid 'em but he smelled 'em through the dirt. Chewed 'em to gumbo, too."

Drawn into the conversation by hearing his name, Lint awarded a tongue-lolling smile to the boys until he recognized his owner's sad headshake for what it was. "I was afraid to pet him for a week," said Charlie, who had great respect for gunpowder. "But you know what? I bet we could hide it under a rock too big for him."

"Or a hunk of concrete. There's lots of it down at the storm pipe." Years before, a ferocious downpour, channeled partly by several storm drains, had sent an epic flood down Shoal Creek, carrying entire trees to the river while the concrete drainpipe lay almost submerged. One of those leafy battering rams had struck the pipe sidelong, scant yards beyond the usual creekbed. After the creek returned to normal, occasional storms still poured from the drain's broken mouth, but now hunks of concrete large and small lay scattered for half a block beside the creekbed.

Instantly persuaded by such an easy solution, Charlie pocketed more than enough coins for the clippers and forbade Lint to follow. Presently the boys made their way to the creek carrying the sack, judging this curve of concrete too large, or that fragment too small, finally choosing one the size of a sofa cushion half-hidden under runners of ivy. Lifting it was full employment for them both, and beneath it scuttled a civilization of bugs they should have expected. They kicked the insects aside, Charlie holding the curved slab on edge with wary glances around them while Aaron dug a football-shaped hole in the dark, pungent earth.

Some distance away, disappearing into a shallow embankment, the sinister dark throat of the big pipe drew Charlie's attention as it never had before. He knew its mouth held a cool musty stink and once he had seen Lint, hackles raised, reject it as a thing to be avoided. This in itself was enough to give a boy ideas sooner or later. After Aaron bedded their sack in the cavity he had dug, together they lowered the slab and stood back to view the job. Aaron rearranged bits of ivy, then gave an expert's nod of approval.

"As safe a treasure as Captain Guy's," he said.

"You mean Captain Kidd's," Charlie corrected, glancing again at the drainpipe. "Ours is okay, but when we put those pennies in rolls we can find a better bank. I might have found one already." He walked a few paces, then faced the pipe where it emerged from the embankment.

"But all the big pieces are down here along—" Aaron began, not seeing Charlie's focus. But when he did, "Naw, drop it, forget it," he said swiftly. "Nuthin's in there that I want, Charlie Hardin, or you either."

Charlie's eyebrows asked the question without words.

"It's haunted, is what, and you know it," said Aaron. He saw Charlie's pitying look, as he had expected, but he was ready for it. Alone on the creek, in moments of utter quiet, the boys had heard sounds from the old drain that would begin with a hiss, rise quickly to a faint moan, then fade into silence again, like the breathing of some unearthly thing asleep deep in the earth. Or—though neither boy had ever considered the possibility—like the sound of automobile tires several blocks away, passing very near one of the storm drain inlets installed along the streets.

"I don't believe in ghosts anymore," said Charlie, rubbing away the subtle prickling of hair on his forearms.

"Not much you don't." Aaron's tone said, *Durn right you do*.

"Well, there's bad ghosts and good ghosts. You don't know, maybe it's the ghost of some poor old cat that crawled up there a hundred years ago and wouldn't hurt a fly."

"Maybe. Go keep him company, why don't you?"

It wasn't quite a dare, but Uncle Wes would not have backed down. "Maybe I will," Charlie muttered. "But cats don't need flashlights."

"You're rich. Buy one," Aaron said, and this came closer to an outright dare.

On such a bright Sunday afternoon, the whole notion of weird hisses and cat spooks carried less weight in Charlie's mind than the chance for him to make a show of bravery.

"You're rich too. You buy one, and I'll take it in there clean to the end of your kite line."

With that, Charlie pointed dramatically into the drain. Three blocks away, a bald-tired taxi passed within inches of a gutter grating. The big concrete pipe heard it. A second later the boys heard it. Charlie, wishing his finger didn't shake, locked eyes with Aaron and held his stance.

"My kite line reaches to the moon," Aaron said. "First thing after school tomorrow, we can go to the store together."

Charlie found an exact match for the clippers immediately on Monday, a day of damp breezes that brought towering masses of cloud by late afternoon. The boys visited several stores to find the least expensive flashlight. Aaron found a bargain at Kress's, where they managed to resist the candy counter (candy corn 19 cents a pound) but not the new shipment of glass marbles, featuring the 100 Giant Pak,

100 for only 29 cents, that matched the gleams in their eyes with its own glimmers through a cheap net bag. Neither boy had ever owned so many marbles but neither had ever been wealthy until now. "We can split fifty-fifty. Jackie's got most of mine," Aaron said.

"Never play keepsies with that guy," Charlie replied, having made the same mistake with the same result. "We can keep most of them with you know what."

They dug into their pockets, feverish with desire. As the saleslady watched her hand fill with pennies and the occasional nickel, Aaron fed Charlie a warning squint. "If you can't get everything back from your hifalutin' old hideyhole, remember this was your idea," he said.

"Scaredy-cat," Charlie said, hefting the marbles.

"If it *is* just a cat," Aaron retorted, which made Charlie shudder. For the joy of it as they left the store, Aaron followed his remark with, "'Course, it could be a real cat. A reeeal big one," he added ominously, making claws of his fingers.

Charlie refused to rise to this bait, but his silence prodded Aaron to continue his teasing expedition. Aaron had wrung most the juice out of it when they neared the turn that would bring them to the Hardin place. That was when Charlie whistled a shrill variation on the *tootle-ee-oot* that he and Aaron shared. Aaron turned but saw that his pal did not, and he quickly fell into stride again toward the creek. Neither boy was surprised a minute later when Lint, whose ears had doggy-sensory perception, loped up the sidewalk with a happy little bark and kissed his master on the hand.

"Charlie, don't be mad," Aaron said sadly.

"He thinks I'm mad," Charlie said to the dog, and without stopping, planted a lavish headscratch on his tail-wagging worshipper. Then he fixed Aaron with a firm look. "You wanta make me happy, hand me that flashlight and go get your kite line. You know where to meet us."

Aaron surrendered the flashlight but stopped. "This is crazy. Nobody knows what's up in there."

"Then I guess that's up to Charlie Hardin," said Charlie, not looking behind him.

When Aaron raced back to the creek ten minutes later he had already felt a few stray raindrops of the three-to-the-dozen variety, drops so plump that each one made an audible splat as it struck the sidewalk. Protected by the big-leafed canopy of their favorite fig tree as he sat waiting, Charlie had felt no raindrops but he could hear them stutter among the leaves overhead. Moreover, he had heard low rumbles of distant thunder and identified bass notes from the nearby drainpipe as merely faithful echoes of those thunder peals. Meanwhile he had poured a dozen marbles through a hole he tore in the net bag, and now as Aaron handed him the kite line, Charlie traded him half of those marbles.

No one needed to remind Aaron that those little glass orbs were as good as coins. To most boys, depending on how many marbles they had lost and how desperately they wanted back into a game, a marble might be worth more than a penny.

Charlie pocketed the kite line. "I need help to lift the chunk," he said, and waited for Aaron to grasp the concrete lid of their temporary bank. With the coin sack recovered, they lowered the lid again and took a few more coins for pocket change as befitted young men of great wealth. Turning toward the pipe, Charlie said, "You can come along and carry some of this stuff if you want to."

Aaron needed a few seconds to compose the right reply. "Somebody should stay out here with the end of the string, Charlie. We'll wait for you."

"We? Just you." It had not occurred to Charlie that Lint might have doubts about the adventure. "We'll yell if we see your old cat."

"Bet your life you will," said Aaron, still hoping Charlie would relent. When offered the loose end of the kite line near the mouth of the pipe, he tried one more time. "Any last words?"

Every boy knew that American paratroopers leaped from airplanes shouting the name of a fearless Apache warrior. Feeling every inch a hero, Charlie said, "How about 'Geronimo'?" With that, he hunched over enough to clear the pipe and stepped inside, bags on one arm, kite line in the other hand.

Before he could take another step into that forbidding darkness, Charlie heard the penetrating whine of a friend in great distress. Lint knew that smelly hole as well as he wanted to from the outside, where all sensible dogs belonged, and had once given his opinion of the inside as clearly as he knew how. His suspicions had not involved the slightest possibility that his master was a lunatic, but now it seemed to be a fact. His protest was a plea for sanity.

Aaron held a similar opinion. "I guess he's not so stupid after all, Charlie. He's smarter than you are."

Charlie looked back. "Lint." Another whine. More sternly: "Here, Lint. Good dog. Come on, boy," he urged, his voice holding the beginnings of an echo, and if ever a terrier sighed, Lint did. But he saw Charlie take another step into the unknown, and he was not a dog to abandon his master. Lint hopped into the pipe, nails scrabbling like tiny pickaxes on the cement, until he stood between Charlie's feet and growled into blackness as they began to advance. The constant growl was not a challenge; Lint calculated that if he sounded fierce enough, whatever was waiting in that smelly hole would not gobble him up quite as quickly. And Lint had heard the boys say, "cat," and understood it, and knew what size hole an ordinary cat needed. He was not filled with encouragement; this hole could house a pride of African lions.

As Charlie's eyes grew accustomed to the gloom, he noticed more details of the pipe: gritty debris on the bottom, a circular joint in the pipe just ahead, discolorations of mold along the sides. The smell was no better but perhaps no worse as he moved farther up the pipe's slight incline. Charlie placed the bags inside his shirt, the heavy coin bag against his left side so that he could use the flashlight, the bag of marbles giving his skin a shuddery chill on his right. When he patted Lint's flank he could feel his small companion trembling.

At first, whenever he looked back, Charlie could see Aaron and his surroundings plainly, but even with the flashbeam, the path ahead quickly became a blank nothingness. A rumbling echo raised hackles on boy and dog alike, but Charlie quickly realized it was only thunder somewhere ahead and spoke gently to Lint. Soon the mouth of the pipe was only an indistinct glow behind them, and presently he found a smaller pipe that entered from the left, one so small he would have to investigate on his knees or not at all. He could not have turned around in it, imagined trying to scoot out backward, and immediately chose the not-at-all option. He noticed that where the smaller pipe fed into the larger one, it ended with a thick circular ledge, and he deposited both the coin sack and the marbles atop the ledge.

He had taken a few more steps up the main pipe when he heard a familiar voice, made spooky by the pipe, call, "Charrrr-leee."

It made him flinch, and in irritation he shouted, "WHAT?" completely unprepared for how loud a roar a boy can produce by accident when he has advanced the distance of a city block into a storm sewer. It made him jump, which made Lint bark, which sounded like a hound too monstrous to fit in a storm drain. Lint did not repeat his experiment again and neither did Charlie, who felt something wet and warm trickle onto his sock. The flashbeam told him that Lint, with no fireplugs handy, had done what fearful dogs do, directly onto Charlie's ankle. Charlie's underpants told him that Lint was not the only one reacting to the uproar, even one they had made themselves.

"You don't tell, I won't tell," he whispered, patting his dog as he made the pact.

But now he could hear Aaron who was speaking slowly to make himself understood despite the confusion of echoes. "Look—out—for—the—rain."

Charlie made no reply, fearing another ear-splitting bark. Instead he tried to decode some strange new sounds between increasing rolls of thunder that boomed down the pipe. Some of the noise seemed to come from nearby, and when he turned the flashbeam behind him he discovered that a tiny waterfall was beginning to trickle from the small pipe into his larger one. The sensible fragment of Charlie that he had thrust into a far corner of his mind began waving wildly for attention but now, too, his eyes detected a faint hint of light coming from ahead. He flicked off the flashbeam, heedless of the dear-lord-what-now whimper that erupted from Lint.

Now he was sure he could see reflected light ahead, and hear almost continuous thunder from that direction, as well as a noise like muffled radio static. As much as he wanted to turn back, he yearned to see where the drainpipe led, so he promised that fragmentary inner Charlie that he would continue for only ten more steps.

By this time Lint was whining a fair imitation of a dog with three broken legs. Charlie turned the flashlight on again, took one last step toward the light, and saw the dazzle of his beam on broken bottle glass. He knew that glass: bits of small milk bottles and a green chunk with "7-UP" on it. He had pushed it through a cast iron grating the day he dumped a wagonload of bottles in the street, which meant the daylight glow and a growing trickle of water came from that same street grating. And half-invisible in gray concrete, a few steps further beyond, lay rubble from a major break in the side of the drainpipe.

Returning creekward as he tried to picture a map of the pipe and its path under the street, Charlie found that the faint light from the creek was enough without Aaron's flashlight. He paused to place it with the bag of marbles, thinking about the staticky noise.

But the radio static was no longer a riddle. It lay explained as the transformed echo of a light rain shower on a city street, little more than a sprinkle but continuing as water began to flow in the drainpipe. The inner Charlie supplied one brief moving picture of that water becoming a flood, and sent the rest of Charlie careening back toward the creek with Lint a split-second ahead of him.

Aaron could hear the onrushing commotion and welcomed it because he was not encouraged by the trickle he had seen growing from the drainpipe. Still, he was not prepared for the refugees that shot out of darkness to sprawl into wet ivy.

Aaron resisted an impulse to shout for relief, and remained seated under the fig trees. Instead he said, "Where's my kite line?"

"I dunno," Charlie admitted sheepishly. "You can wind it up from this end, or I can do it. Your flashlight's with our money," he added, brushing himself off and crowding under their fig umbrella as Lint wedged himself between Charlie's feet.

"Where's the money?"

"With the marbles," Charlie replied.

"And where's the marbles? Or have you decided you're not gonna tell me?"

For a moment Charlie sat and listened as the empty threat of rain began to pass beyond the neighborhood. Then he said, "I left the stuff on a ledge I found. High as your shin; you can't miss it."

"Yes I can," Aaron retorted. "'Cause I know a guy so dumb he'll holler Geronimo and go get it for me." Another pause. "What if this had been a sure 'nough knockdown-and-dragout gully-washer? You're lucky it was just barely a shower, you know."

"Uh-huh. I know something else, too."

"Charlie, sometimes I wonder if you know anything at all," Aaron burst out, aggravated past all patience. "But tell me anyhow."

Charlie gave his pal the kind of knowing squint that was intended to convey secret knowledge. "I know if you could wiggle down the hole in the gutter where we shoved those bottles we broke, you could end up right here."

Aaron tried to connect his memory of the bottle calamity to the notion of an underground path to the creek. Finally he said, "If you think I'm gonna wiggle down in broken bottles to get my money back, you can just have yourself another think."

"Tell you what else. There's a big hole busted in the pipe, a few feet from the grating. It's too high on the pipe for a little drizzle like this to leak into," Charlie said, nodding toward the outflow that trickled from the pipe, "but somebody better fix it someday."

Aaron stood and began to wind up his kite line. "I guess you didn't find any ol' cat in there," he said. At Charlie's grin, he added, "But just 'cause something didn't find *you* doesn't mean it's not there."

CHAPTER 7:
✈ BRIDGER AND PINERO ✈

Cade Bridger was a short slender man partial to overalls and snuff and the kind of whiskey that could melt the fillings in his teeth, and he could not have named Charlie or any of his pals. Yet in the past weeks Bridger had spied them all at one time or another from windows of the tree-shaded gray bungalow that the boys dubbed "spooky." To a boy not yet in his teens, any house was haunted if its lawn was unkempt, no lights ever shone from its windows, and no one seemed to occupy the property. For men of a certain sort this was perfect camouflage.

Bridger had leaned on shovels for a city paycheck, without making many permanent friends, since 1930. His social world widened the night he met lean, swarthy Dom Pinero at the illegal dogfights in East Austin. Both men won betting on the same dog and then made the same complaint, which was that the ink on ten-dollar bills should not appear even the tiniest bit smudged. Their arguments were not well received, and in a fistfight against the same enemies they became friends.

Later, comparing bruises as they sat in Pinero's old car

and shared a bottle of tequila, Bridger would admit he might not have noticed that the money failed to reach the usual standards if he hadn't heard Pinero complain. And Pinero, made talkative by booze, would say it was an outrage that anyone would try passing such shoddy materials to a man who had printed better stuff while drunk.

Even with a pint of rotgut tequila in him, Bridger realized what that meant: Pinero himself could produce what gangsters called funny money. Pinero's counterfeit bills had been Mexican money, but he said the principle was the same: you made good clear copies, you tumbled them for a while in a tub of dirt to give them a touch of realism, and you spent them where people were too dumb to take a close look. That's how Bridger learned that his new pal was a printer with a powerful thirst and friends across the border. And when Pinero found that Bridger's cousin worked for an agency in Austin's roaring real estate market, it seemed to them that their partnership was bound for glory.

Bridger knew things about his cousin that would have interested police, so that cousin could be made to do small favors. Working alone, Pinero had not found a nice quiet place to set up a small printing press; in fact, when he met Bridger he had not yet found a press he could steal. It did not take many days for them to go into business together. Because Bridger had no more patience than an average five-year-old, it was Pinero who explained that it takes time to develop a business.

Their first step was to find a proper place to operate a printing press for illegal purposes, which meant they would have to wrestle a stolen machine weighing as much as two men into a dry place away from prying eyes. Electricity and lights would be ideal but even Bridger, with gallons of greed and half a pint of brains, knew that the city hooked up the lines and must be paid for services. In Mexico, said Pinero, people learned how to deal with such matters. They would not even need electricity because small hand-operated printing presses had been developed centuries before electric motors. Pinero patiently explained all this to Bridger. During wartime, Austin had more people than housing, so small houses were in great demand and the list of vacancies supplied by Bridger's cousin was not long.

They finally chose the gray stucco place near Shoal Creek, which had stayed unrented because it stank terribly of mildew, thanks to water damage. The water leak had been caused by a break in a storm drain adjoining the property, and one of the men who had gone through the basement and repaired the leak was Cade Bridger.

When Pinero heard this, a less careful man might have said, "Cade, you idiot, you might have told me this earlier!" But Pinero needed his partner in crime, at least temporarily, so he was patient. He said, "So you figured a smart gent like you could dig us a secret tunnel out to that old drainpipe?"

Bridger's cousin lent them a key to be copied, and then falsified the records so that the house could still not be rented until "serious health hazards" were repaired. In this way, the scoundrels obtained a house without renting it. By the time Pinero had furnished the basement with necessary equipment, Bridger imagined that the tunnel was his own idea, to be used only as an escape route in case they were ever trapped while at work in that rancid basement.

Soon after a suitable hole had been smashed in the concrete drainpipe, Pinero located a press that two men might haul away from its rightful owner in the trunk of a small panel van. Brave with booze late one Friday night, they cussed three hundred pounds of printing press from the van to its new basement home, and after such heroic labor a man needs his sleep.

When Bridger awoke on his pallet with the usual pounding headache his hangovers brought, it was roughly noon on Saturday. In one corner of an unlighted basement and without a wristwatch, he had no idea of the time, so he staggered up rickety steps to the ground floor and, hearing what sounded like a miniature auto accident somewhere outside, he peered from a dining-room window. That was the moment when he saw Charlie Hardin in the gutter among a jumble of broken bottles, and was spotted for an instant by Aaron Fischer.

Bridger was not in the habit of taking blame for things and saw no reason to tell Pinero he might have been seen by some neighborhood kid. The boys went off down the street, so Bridger went back to sleep off his hangover. In the weeks since then, everyone concerned had made great progress toward the calamity that would follow.

CHAPTER 8:
✈ THE DOGAPULT ✈

One of the few German words that wartime brought to Austin was "ersatz," meaning imitation. Materials needed to fight a war were suddenly hard to find at home, and familiar things were replaced by new ones, often of poor quality. With good natural rubber going into tires of fighter planes, the new synthetic rubber for civilians was like that: ersatz.

A small box of prewar natural rubber bands, found after years of storage in a cool dark place, could still be used to spin a model propeller. Aaron had linked a dozen bands together to power his model until the rubber looked dangerously weathered and likely to break during the windup. This would be certain death for the model. At that point Mr. Fischer had discovered Aaron's discovery and claimed the entire box, and bought his son a box of synthetic rubber bands in a spasm of fairness.

Aaron's first attempt to use his ersatz rubber ended in the worst possible way. While Charlie held the model Aaron had built from balsa strips and lovingly covered with tissue, Aaron began to wind its propeller expecting the rubber to twist the usual three hundred times. He had counted to a hundred and forty when, with a report no louder than the clapping of a toddler's hands, the rubber snapped.

When a twisted loop of rubber snaps, it does not simply fall limp; nothing that genteel. Both halves instantly become demon knots, destructive furies that leap away from each other becoming shorter, thicker knots, coiling like snakes as they retreat. Faster than an eyeblink they become little rotating flails tearing furiously at the balsa and tissue from the inside. In a split-second the model's fuselage becomes an unrecognizable, utterly unrepairable mess crushed as if by some tiny invisible fiend. After the necessary yelling argument with each boy blaming the other, Aaron experimented and found the rubber to blame. For a time afterward, they set aside hopes of using rubber for their projects.

It was Jackie Rhett who put them back in business. Jackie had a special knack for "finding" things—often before other people lost them. Democratic about the property of others, Jackie did not discriminate against adults or, for that matter, any creature that might be said to own property. A dog with the slimiest tennis ball for a chew-toy soon learned that if that ball landed in the hands of the pudgy kid, it might not be seen again.

Jackie never said where he found his excellent prewar inner tube of natural rubber, but it was the genuine good old stretchy stuff. Some of that rubber soon became strips for his slingshot; some he used as ammunition for an evil device called a rubbergun that was forbidden to other boys and shot a big rubber loop faster than the eye could follow. More important, it would sting like the devil from many yards away.

Such was Jackie's view of the world that he would then demand the loop back because it was clearly his; he had inked his name on it. Some of the remaining tube he sold to

Aaron, who now carefully scissored it into thin strips for models.

"You're making a slingshot," Jackie accused, squinting as Aaron wielded scissors borrowed from home.

"Not either," said Charlie, sitting on the workbench of the Hardin garage as he watched Aaron's progress. Because Aaron's tongue was caught between his teeth as he worked, Charlie unconsciously did the same until he unlimbered his tongue to add, "Couldn't even shoot an acorn with strips this thin."

"He could bunch 'em up," Jackie growled, fearful that Aaron might develop such a weapon after promising not to, because it was exactly what Jackie himself would have done. "And he promised not to, or I wouldn'ta gave him the stuff."

"Sold it to me, you mean." Aaron did not pause in his task but now proved he was listening. His glance caught Charlie's, then flickered away.

Jackie did not miss the look. "Yeah, and I got more," he teased. "I bet I got nearly as much money tied up in rubber as you guys got in quarters."

No reply from either boy.

"How about it, Charlie? You can buy some, maybe a little more, for only two bits. Same as Aaron bought. Maybe more."

It would have been a simple thing for Charlie and Aaron to utter flat denials but somewhere in their unwritten personal contracts was a casual policy against outright lies, so long as a question could be deflected. Charlie said, "So who's got two bits?"

"He does. Did. And he's got a lot more," said Jackie, nodding toward the scissors-user. Nor did Jackie miss the faint headshake Aaron sent to Charlie, but that might have meant several things. A year before, these two had been as transparent as window glass to Jackie's cleverness. Eventually though, they had learned that what you told Jackie was likely to be used against you. For Jackie, discoveries like this by the boys were like the problem of slaves learning to read and Jackie, as a member of a noble class, felt this was No Fair. Jackie knew in his bones that Aaron Fischer had paid a whole quarter for that rubber with much too brief a trade debate for a kid who earned only a quarter a week, when a movie cost twelve cents. A burning desire to know more about this was Jackie's only reason to be on Hardin property, a place where he knew he was not welcome.

"You got a lot more money, Aaron? Maybe you could loan me a buncha quarters," said Charlie, making it sound highly unlikely.

"Soon as Jackie leaves," was the reply, with equal sarcasm. "Too bad you don't have rich friends like mine."

"I know you got money too," Jackie said to Charlie, and followed this with a knowing wink. "I seen you after school."

"Well, that settles it," said Aaron. "Anybody you see after school must be made of solid gold." He crossed his eyes and let his tongue loll from the side of his mouth: Aaron Fischer, village idiot.

"He was eatin' a Baby Ruth," Jackie persisted. For a moment no one responded. This was different; serious evidence of wealth that, in the past, Charlie had lacked.

This time, the silent look between Charlie and Aaron was longer, and not entirely friendly. Both boys had fiercely sworn to avoid any evidence of their mining venture on the Capitol grounds. Of course each had wasted no time cashing small bits of it, sinning a penny or a nickel at a time, in the hope that no one would notice.

Aaron, who had committed the same sin a day earlier but having the good sense to eat his Butterfinger in secret, realized he could get two revenges for the price of one, on different boys and for different reasons. "Well, he got it the same way you do," said Aaron, just to stir the others up.

Jackie had boasted about his light-fingered ways at candy counters too freely to bother denying it. But Charlie, whose own dad was a juvenile officer? "I bet he didn't," Jackie said darkly.

"You weren't gonna tell, Aaron," said Charlie, unbothered by such a whopper and able to modify his policy about lies where Jackie was concerned. He was fully engaged in this swindle on a moment's notice. "Besides, the owners said it was okay because I always tell them when I know"—and here he deliberately glanced in Jackie's direction—"who else is doin' it."

"You better not, you B-Word," Jackie snarled, but suddenly pale with the fear of the amateur shoplifter.

"How do you know he means you?" said Aaron.

Before Jackie could reply, Charlie made his head snap around with, "Did the police come to your house yet?"

Fearing his voice might crack, Jackie could only shake his head.

"Then I didn't mean you, did I?" Charlie said. "Not yet, anyhow."

Jackie trembled with relief. "B-Word," he said again.

Charlie did not take the insult with helpless anger. "Maybe you'll just flat give me the rest of that rubber, Jackie," he said. "If I can't buy it, maybe you'll purely have to give it to me. Or else."

"Else what?" Even though Jackie knew exactly what.

But Charlie told him anyway. "I tell."

A three-way silence enveloped the shed. Then Jackie said, in a voice tinged with awe, "Blackmail."

Charlie cocked his head as if to consider this charge until, "Yeah, Charlie, it is," Aaron said softly. "If he gives you the rubber and you don't tell, you're a blackmailer. If he doesn't and you do tell, you're a snitch. If he gives it to you and you tell anyhow, he can tell the police on you, so you go to jail with him."

Fascinated by all the possibilities, Charlie said, "But what if he doesn't give me the rubber and I stay mum anyhow?"

After a dramatic moment, Aaron shrugged and began to use the scissors again. "Then I think you're a dummy."

Charlie nodded. But, "Blackmailer is worse," Jackie muttered.

"Dummy's worse," said Charlie.

"Blackmail."

"Dummy."

Louder now: "Blackmail. You calling me a liar?" This was a fighting word, and against a younger boy Jackie was always ready.

Aaron managed to cloud the issue nicely with, "Nobody knows which one he is yet, Jackie. We'll have to wait and see. You can make him either one you want to; depends on what you do."

This kind of debate put Jackie into a state of confusion that he dealt with by stalking stiff-legged to the door. "I don't have to put up with this," he said with wounded dignity.

"Put up with what?" Aaron said, pretending innocence. But Jackie had already sped away. After a moment's silence, Aaron smiled. "Get him mixed up enough and I bet he'd bust himself square in the mouth."

"Why'd you let that scutter know you had so much money?"

"'Cause I need the rubber. Why'd you let him see you with a candy bar?"

Charlie shrugged. "Aw, I just didn't think. This isn't over, guy, he knows we're rich. We'll have to be extra careful."

They hooked pinkie fingers together for a moment in the gesture that sealed agreements, and presently Aaron finished his task. As Charlie stopped in the yard to snap the lock on the garage side door, Aaron began to laugh.

Charlie looked around. "What?"

"Maybe I better not come over here anymore, Charlie.

My dad won't let me play with blackmailers," said Aaron, and pointed to the walkway near their feet.

Coiled in a tight cylinder and bound with wire, with no explanation needed, lay a roll of gray rubber the size of a coffee cup. Charlie claimed it immediately. "At least now we know what Jackie wants me to be," he said, with a headshake. "I wasn't gonna snitch on him."

"You think I don't know that?"

Both boys snickered. Charlie said, "I didn't hear him sneak back here. You?"

"Nope. Loud as he is, that's how quiet he can be," Aaron replied, stretching experimentally at the rubber. "This is the real stuff all right, five times as much as he sold me. I reckon you're about the biggest, worst blackmailer on the planet. Sell me a quarter's worth?"

"Naw. I'll keep it 'til you need it bad and charge you double," Charlie replied with a grin.

In Charlie the urge to compete was plain enough that it might have been painted on his forehead. Days later in the Fischer home, as his ally was cementing tiny sticks to the fuselage of a new model, Charlie rummaged into Aaron's plans from older models. "If I can buy whole sheets of balsa I bet I could build this pretty quick," he said, holding up a plan that showed a graceful sketch. "If you'd help."

"Don't you know there's a war on?" Aaron spoke America's commonest phrase, and applied a razor blade to a tiny stick. "Balsa makes life rafts. So bust up an apple box; the wood's free."

"Way too heavy though, right?"

Aaron paused to consider. "Not much, if you sanded the heck out of it. You have enough rubber to catapult it to Mars, but the only way it'd fly is fast."

"Fast is good," Charlie ruled. "And you'll help?"

"For some of that rubber, sure. Hey, where're you going?"

"There's always old wood crates in the Ice House trash," said Charlie, and promptly disappeared. Since Aaron lived near the Ice House, the seeker was back within minutes with pieces of three thin pine slats, only one of them badly splintered. Soon the boys had used a pencil to draw outlines of wings, a single graceful long oval for tail surfaces, and a fuselage whose rear end swooped up in a rudder like a shark's tailfin. Now, the only way Aaron could resume his own task was to send Charlie home to work. Aaron filled him to the brim with instructions, some of which Charlie might even follow.

By dinnertime, Charlie had used his dad's coping saw to cut all the pieces out following those pencil lines. He might have advanced to the whittling stage by then but for his habit of testing the pieces of pine after he cut them from the slats. His test method with each piece was the same: squint hard, imagine that this piece was finished and connected to all the others, then throw it across the shed, startling Lint with his special "*Neeerrrowr*" sound effect that in his mind represented a powerful engine. It was always necessary to pretend that the piece did not flutter to the dirt floor like a dying sparrow.

"Looks like your durn dog chewed it out," was Aaron's judgment when he saw Charlie's handiwork the next day. So saying, he found enough tools in the Hardin shed to neaten Charlie's work, and used sandpaper to begin forming the wing surfaces. Presently he put the piece down. "I did one side," he said, shaking sawdust from his hair. "Gotta go; I've got homework and so do you. I showed you how to sand a wing, and you can do the rest."

Plainly hoping his pal would relent and do the whole thing for him, Charlie said, "But it won't be as good."

"It would if you'd watched what I've been doing

instead of playing with that pooch," was the retort, with an apologetic glance downward and, "Sorry, Lint," to soften the criticism. A moment later Aaron hurried off.

Anger lent force to Charlie's hands as he copied his friend's work, or thought he did. Any fly on the wall might have noticed in Aaron a careful eye for detail, but a gift for action in Charlie. It followed that if Charlie sanded a pine slat twice as briskly as Aaron, his finished product would be somewhat thinner. He put his experimental sound effects to work, adding the *kakakakakak* of a machine gun for good measure, before smearing furniture glue on all surfaces that seemed to need it. The result would not have satisfied a pessimist, but Charlie's eye was the eye of an optimist. He left his pine missile to dry and went to his room to do homework for an endless ten minutes.

When Aaron next saw Charlie's model, he kept disappointment from his face. "Keen job," he said, noting several ways the left side of the model differed from the right side. What's done was done, he felt, and careful adjustments sometimes resulted in a glide that might satisfy a first-time builder.

"Time to test it. There's probably room in the park," Charlie said, collecting necessary odds and ends.

Privately, Aaron thought there would be plenty of room inside the garage, but did not share his opinion. The little neighborhood park was a block nearer the center of town than the Hardin place, with a steep slope on one side and enough open meadow between live oaks to test-glide a small model. They stopped at the top of the slope and the builder exercised his right to be first to test his creation.

At Charlie's toss, the glider darted downslope instantly, rolling over and over as if spinning around an imaginary tree trunk, then stuck like a dart in the grass but, being stout pine, without damage. "Wait, I can fix that," Charlie cried, and raced to recover the thing. He had seen Aaron adjust models a dozen times.

Aaron watched until he saw that Charlie, with scant knowledge of flight adjustments, was bending a wing's edge exactly the wrong way. "You'll make it worse, guy," he said, and received a disgusted *who's the expert here* glance. "Okay, then," he shrugged, "but you will."

"I reckon I know how to fly my own airplane," said Charlie hotly, and prepared to make another toss.

And in that moment, Aaron Fischer made a grand discovery. It is this: To Avoid Ever Repeating A Cheap Mistake, Make That Mistake More Expensive. "A nickel says it's gonna do a worse barrel roll than before. A nickel, Charlie. Five cents cash. Or . . ." And Aaron sounded the cluck of a hen.

Charlie's eyes narrowed at the hint that he might be, in the slang of that era, "chicken." Without forethought, his teeth gritted, he said, "Make it a dime."

"A quarter," Aaron said calmly.

"A dollar," Charlie said in a hoarse whisper, and followed that with what was, for Charlie, a mighty oath. "A D-Word dollar, and we'll see who's chicken!"

Aaron spat in his open palm and stuck his hand out to be shaken, and Charlie shook it, and only when Aaron stood away and folded his arms did Charlie pause to consider the size of the bet his mouth had made for his pocket to risk. But he had enlarged the bet himself—twice, in fact. He tossed the glider again, and this time saw it flutter down in exactly the kind of tight spiral Aaron had predicted.

No words were exchanged until Charlie returned with the nonflying toy and, on his face, a look of abject disgust. Instead of the "*told you so*" that a lesser failure deserved, Aaron sighed. "Happened to me a few times too," he said. "Maybe we can fix it."

"It's no good," said Charlie.

"It might be. Tell you what: I'll buy it from you."

Charlie's sharp glance searched for sarcasm. Finding none, he said, "What for?"

"For one dollar," said Aaron, and saw understanding flood his pal's face. "Then I get to try and fly it myself."

Silently, sheepishly, Charlie handed over the toy and watched as Aaron began to make changes. A wingtip was shortened by grinding it against the cement sidewalk. A wooden edge was smoothed, then bent correctly. The little glider's balance was changed with half a piece of chewing gum that Charlie, on Aaron's instructions, pried from the underside of a park bench and squeezed to regummify it. After two more tests a piece of gravel the size of a pea was added to the gum and this time the model flew an almost straight lazy glide down the hill.

By this time Charlie's mood was greatly improved. "If we catapult it, maybe it'll climb," he said.

"Wings are too short now," was the reply. "It'd need something more powerful than a catapult."

Charlie, with sudden enthusiasm: "A dogapult!"

Hearing this gibberish, Aaron said, "Are you nuts?"

Charlie dug into his pocket for the wad of rubber. "Five feet of rubber tied to a rod stuck in the ground is your catapult. So twenty feet of it would be my dogapult."

Aaron had suggested more power, but this was far beyond his ideas and it engaged his imagination. Minutes later they had driven a stout oak stick into the soil, tied loops at the ends of the rubber, and fixed one end of the loop to the stick above grass level. And every time one of them murmured "dogapult," the other would cackle.

Finally, when the remaining loop had been slipped into a notch under the model's nose, Aaron backed away holding it by the tail until the rubber was stretched several times its ordinary length. He called, "C'mere, Charlie, you do it, it was your idea."

Charlie needed no more encouragement than this. The rubber's tug was like a live thing, and on its release the glider sprang away with the speed of an arrow. Given so much power and cheers from both boys, it flew up and up above the tops of the park's oak trees with one broad, glorious barrel roll, then slowed and turned its nose down halfway across the park, plunging into a treetop thirty feet above the ground. And there it stayed, barely visible among oak leaves in a prison of twigs.

"Well, you told me to," said Charlie.

Aaron had suffered such losses before. "I'm not going up there after it," he announced. "It's lost for sure."

But the amazing flight of the glider had already given Charlie an appreciation of the power of his invention. "Not if it's up to Charlie Hardin," he said. "Let's go back to my lab'ratory. My dogapult put that durn thing up there and my dogapult will get it down again." And before they had walked a city block, Charlie made his plan clear.

CHAPTER 9:
✈ LINT IS AVENGED ✈

Along streetsides and in vacant lots, Austin's weeds included a fast-growing vine with gourds the size of a baseball. The gourds were easy to find because they were of no practical use. Green and striped with a tough shell, the little spheres were heavy with seeds and stringy wet stuff, but they would bitterly disappoint any boy who broke one open expecting it to taste like a tiny watermelon.

Charlie knew this when he collected one of the gourds on his way home. "We need a pouch to hold this in the dogapult," he said, tossing the thing to Aaron.

"And a forked branch," Aaron replied. "As big as a crutch. But if your mom sees you with a slingshot that big she'll scalp you."

Charlie agreed with a nod. "Even if all I'm gonna shoot is some ol' branches instead of climbing to the top of that tree. A guy would have to be crazy to go up there."

"Or real, real dumb."

"Yeah." Then Charlie brightened. "Hey, you think maybe for a nickel I could get Roy to—"

"No, Charlie. Nuh-uh. Roy might be worth something to somebody, someday. Besides, this way will be funner," said

Aaron, tossing the gourd back, continuing straight ahead as Charlie turned toward the Hardin driveway.

Charlie paused. "Where you going?"

"Down to the creek to find me a crutch so I can play wounded soldier. No skin off my nose if somebody I know can use it for his dogapult."

Charlie watched his pal amble down the street and, as Lint trotted out with salivary greetings, held up the gourd. He hurled it toward a neighbor yard with a command to "fetch!" and the terrier bounded away in pursuit. Gourd, stick, ball, or brickbat, they were all the same to Lint; if his master could throw it, Lint would capture it.

Boy brains are wonderful in the different ways they work, and more so in the different ways they play. The focus of thought in some boys, tight as a burning glass, might sizzle on one point for an hour or more, but Charlie's thoughts leaped like a kangaroo. In his case, a few minutes in fruitless search for a leather slingshot pouch produced enough boredom to approach pain, and curlicues in his strips of rubber reminded him of pretzels his mother believed she had hidden well in the pantry. Nibbling pretzels into shapes that formed numbers and letters diverted him toward algebra, which interested him long enough to wade through half of his math homework, but the plight of two trains leaving the same station in different directions at speeds X and $2X$ sent him scrambling to assemble sections of track for his spring-wound model locomotive. When the locomotive left its track and sped away under his bed, Charlie wriggled among debris to retrieve it. He discovered, in addition to enough dust-bunnies to stuff a sofa pillow, a long-lost tennis shoe, which was not only worn out but by now several sizes too small. And emerging from under his bed, Charlie looked at the tennis shoe tongue he gripped and saw that it could form a slingshot pouch big enough to enclose a baseball.

No wonder, then, that while Aaron Fischer was securing a forked stick of pecan that a boy might carry publicly in the role of fictitious wounded soldier, Charlie trimmed the elastic of his slingshot, ruined his appetite, did much of his homework, cleared the dust-balls from beneath his bed, discarded an old shoe, and linked the slingshot's flexible parts together with stout fishing line. It may be enough to note that to get anything done in this world, the Charlies benefit from the Aarons, and Aarons need their Charlies.

Charlie would have denied that every time he walked past the park for the next few days, he breathed a silent *"yes!"* when he spied the short-winged glider twisting lazily in its treetop. Retrieval was his mission, and no wind or squirrel or tree-climbing fool would have earned his thanks for doing the job.

Late on a Sunday afternoon the boys finished their preparations and trudged up the steep slope of the street, Aaron drawing the pity of strangers with his wrist-thick crutch of hardwood that was too long to fit his armpit properly, Charlie pulling a discarded golf cart. When Aaron asked what the wheeled bag was for, Charlie explained that it was supposed to be a caisson. "But it's really to keep the sling stuff and gourds in," he admitted.

"You got me there. What's a caisson?"

"Beats me," said Charlie, "some kinda box I guess, but in that army song they say those caissons go rolling along, and if you can be wounded, I reckon I can roll a caisson."

"What kind of army?" said Aaron.

"Artirrily," said Charlie. "They shoot big cannonballs."

"It's artillery."

"Yep," was Charlie's reply as he freed a gourd from its vine and dropped it into the bag. Aaron opened his mouth, then closed it again and handed Charlie a gourd that had thought it was safely hidden.

With a half-dozen of these vegetable cannonballs they reached the oak that still unfairly held the glider captive, and only after tying the rubber cords in place did they find—as they might have found sooner if they had rehearsed in the "lab'ratory"—that the sturdy forks of pecan wood did not bend in a way to let them aim directly upward. They walked off some distance, then moved again. The best spot for aiming, they saw, was in the lowest depression of the park with a direct view of a small toy of pine caught high in an oak.

It was clearly a two-boy task, and Charlie made the point that the inventor of a thing, the one who gave it its very name, should naturally be first to test it. So it was Aaron who sat cross-legged with the pole of the slingshot propped against one shoulder and anchored between his feet, gripping the pole tightly while Charlie chose the biggest of the gourds and settled it into the shoe-tongue pouch.

Their first attempt was weak because Charlie failed to stretch the rubber strips far enough. The little gourd described a lazy curve into the tree's lower branches and fell back as if to mock them.

"My turn," said Aaron, transferring the pole to Charlie, choosing a smaller gourd and improving his aim by closing one eye and squinting with the other, tongue caught between his teeth, nodding to himself, with all the other preparations a boy needs to show the world that he is an expert not to be trifled with.

As Aaron hauled back mightily, Charlie shifting a bit against the heavy tension, a breeze moving the treetop, the glider moving to and fro, any exact aim of a gourd was sheer luck. But Aaron's luck was wonderful, and awful too. As the tension departed, Charlie tumbled backward. The little striped globe whirred away and bullied a leafy twig aside before striking the glider with an audible report, continuing in an arc that took it into another tree half a block distant and several seconds later.

"Now you went and did it," said Charlie, as pieces of the ex-glider fluttered earthward. And then he heard the faint commotion as their falling ammunition made its way down through the distant tree, and his frown evaporated. "You hear that? It musta gone a mile!"

"It went pretty good," said Aaron, strolling to collect the shards of a toy that, while he had aimed at, he had never expected to hit.

"My dogapult could shoot clear across town, I bet," Charlie said, ignoring the debris. "Whatta you think?"

"I don't think it's fixable, guy, but I didn't mean to."

"Fixable? It doesn't need to—oh, that thing," Charlie scoffed, his head already filled with fresh possibilities. "Never mind, what we need is to find out how far a Hardin dogapult can throw a hand grenade. You know, one of those," he said, indicating the rest of the gourds. "I bet we could get a patent and sell it to the army tomorrow, but we have to test it for distance first."

Charlie's enthusiasms often moved faster than others chose to follow, but Aaron was adaptable. If Charlie could think beyond the ruination of a new toy, Aaron would help him do it. "We shot high, but if you wanta shoot for distance it might go a lot farther," he said, and with that the Hardin dogapult had a new goal.

An invention gains a great deal of importance by being labeled a military device, and the boys argued in great detail over which direction to launch their ammunition, what location to view it from, whether the grenades should be smaller or larger, and which launch angle would shoot the cargo across the greatest distance. They settled on a sloping spot with an iron-hard shrub so gnarled that the dogapult pole, wedged firmly between its branches, could be erected without a boy to anchor it. The "grenade" was to be launched at a shallow angle in the general direction of Charlie's own home.

Though their labor was dull, they spent the time developing a lively argument over the manufacture of the Hardin Dogapult. Aaron was convinced that they could get by for their first army shipments using only a few dozen used inner tubes and a hundred pairs of old tennis shoes, while Charlie insisted that shoes and inner tubes must be new to be worthy of war materiel.

When at last Aaron was argued out of his status as a war profiteer, he trotted to a prominent hackberry tree and climbed it so that it afforded him a view over neighborhood housetops. "Be sure and aim away from the trees," he called, "and I'll tell you when to fire."

Charlie was stung by the notion that someone else expected to be in command. Moreover, he had heard people testing complicated equipment and intended to do this thing right. So when he heard, "Three, two, one, *fire*" from high in the tree, he only drew the elastic cords back as far as he could.

Then he paused dramatically and sang out, "One, two, three, testing," and released his ammunition aiming between two tiny branches. "That's what you say when you test," he called back.

Because Charlie was heavier and more muscular by twenty pounds, he was able to stretch the elastic farther. When the pouch sprang away, it actually whistled. The little gourd flew fast and high, clearing every treetop in the park long before the top of its flight, drawing a falsetto "Woooooo," from Aaron.

Charlie had fired from a sitting position but now leaped to his feet and peered into the sky. "How far?" he called.

"Still up," was the reply. "Coming down. Can't hardly—" and then Aaron ducked as if someone had dropped a heavy book on his head. A half-second later they heard a clattering crash in the distance, not much different from the sound a sledgehammer might make if hurled against a slate blackboard. Aaron continued to watch, but now seemed to be an unmoving sculpture against the hackberry trunk.

Charlie ran to the base of the tree. "What? What?"

Not so loud as before, Aaron called back, "Hit ol' man Turner's roof is what. Knocked a tile plumb off." As he spoke, both boys could hear the slow distant scrape of large pieces of flat tile as they slid down a sloping roof. Aaron hugged tightly to the tree now as if to hide, though the gourd had struck a full block and a half away, and well below them. Then it occurred to Charlie that even at that distance, Mr. Turner's house made a sizeable target.

The Turner residence lay across the street from the Hardins. Charlie had maintained no opinion of the childless Turner couple until after the day Lint distinguished himself by digging among Mrs. Turner's snapdragons and getting caught at it. A few days later Charlie had observed Mr. Turner using a Daisy air rifle, one so new a price tag still hung from its pump lever, and he was using it on Lint even though the dog was not even near the Turner turf. A Daisy was spring-powered and its BB would barely pierce a boy's skin, but it stung like a bee and could be deadly to a bird, or a window. This is why Charlie might never find a Daisy under the Hardin Christmas tree.

Now, Charlie surprised himself with the vastness of the satisfaction he felt, hearing the progress of that tile. "Stay up there and see what this does," he ordered, already in motion. He snatched up one of the remaining gourds and prepared a launch exactly as before. The two small branches centered his aim again; his second test announcement made it official. Even the wind's whistle was the same.

But this time, Charlie was up and running instantly toward Aaron's perch, peering through trees toward his grenade though any glimpse of it by Charlie would have been a miracle.

Before he had run a dozen steps he heard Aaron call, "It's

gonna—" and then the report of a second shattering collision, faint but emphatic "—hit ol' man Turner's back porch," Aaron went on. Charlie had intended to leave matters at this, until Aaron continued his observations. "Uh-oh. Here he comes."

Charlie molded himself to the hackberry trunk. "Where?"

"Not here, dummy; he just stepped off his porch. Hands on his hips. Looking at his roof. Wow, he's mad enough to pee steam." Charlie would have given a lot to be standing where his friend stood with a bird's-eye view downhill, but these bulletins were satisfying enough. "Gone back inside," the announcer continued. "Boy, I hope your fingerprints aren't on those things; the way he was hopping around he was sore as—oh man, here he comes again, and he's got a rifle."

For a count of two, an invisible ice cube meandered down Charlie's back. Then he said, "Maybe like a Daisy air gun?"

"It's kinda little. Yeah, maybe a Daisy."

"Don't go away," Charlie said, and turned back toward his launcher, then stopped. "Hey, Aaron. Keep up your walkie-talk. He can't see you or hear you anyhow, right?"

"He better not," was the heartfelt reply. By this time Aaron's bulletins were barely audible.

"I told you about him and Lint. He started a sure-'nough shooting war, remember."

"He just went back inside," Aaron called. "I'm coming down, it's all over."

"No it isn't," Charlie assured him, taking the next-to-last gourd from its makeshift carrier. In moments the thing was done, the grenade en route, Charlie hurrying to emplace his last gourd while the other one was still in flight.

"I don't see it," Aaron reported seconds later. "Maybe it didn't—" but then the noise told them both that it did, and if anything the crash was louder. "Holy cats, he just jumped out the back door, I think he thinks we're on the roof." They could hear a man's voice faintly from afar, and it was not singing praises. "Wait, now he's looking up. Kind of in this direction. But now he's turning around."

In his mind Charlie saw the Daisy user scanning the sky, turning slowly, perhaps planning some awful revenge, and in that moment he released the last gourd, then leaped up and began to dismantle his weapon.

"He's climbing up his chimney rocks, yelling like a Comanche," Aaron called. "Now he's on his roof." A final blast of gourd-on-tile floated to them. "Wups, not anymore," Aaron said, and started laughing. "When the last grenade hit behind him, he jumped off and fell into those big flowers. Wow, now his wife's outside giving him hail Columbia."

Aaron spent no more time in the upper reaches of the hackberry tree, sliding down heedless of shoes or shirt-buttons, still snickering as he helped Charlie wrestle the pecan-wood pole loose. "Maaaan," he said as they hurried from the park, "if that guy figures out what you did, you are gonna be in *sooo* much trouble."

"You mean what *we* did," Charlie rejoined. "And he won't, if we don't tell him. Uh, I'm headed for the creek. You?"

"Right. You better keep your dogapult a military secret. First time ol' man Turner hears the army's new launcher doodad was invented by his own neighbor, he's gonna blow a gasket."

This put the invention in a new light. Helping America's war effort was a fine thing, but blistering the inventor's backside seemed a poor sort of reward. And it was not as if they needed money; both boys viewed themselves as wealthy. Charlie hit on a satisfying answer to the problem minutes later when Aaron mentioned a family friend, an army corporal home on leave from the Quartermasters. "You tell him about the Hardin Dogapult," Charlie said. "Be sure he spells it right but no first name. There's Hardins everywhere."

By this time the boys were trotting in single file down a creekside path, bound by unspoken agreement for the ruined storm drain. "I don't think he shoots grenades, Charlie," panted Aaron over his shoulder.

"He might not master any quarters either, guy, but he's an actual corporal in the army," Charlie huffed back. "Tell him it works, okay?"

And so it was settled, with the dogapult experiment shelved indefinitely. Charlie, who seldom threw things away if he had an alternative, knew where he could hide all the pieces of his device. He took them far up into the storm drain, placing the elastic parts above the protruding lip, laying the big fork of hardwood flat in the dry silt of the watercourse while Aaron stayed outside, he said, as a "lookout."

"As a scared-out, you mean," was Charlie's retort.

"I wouldn't mind going in there now if we'd brought the flashlight," Aaron said, to ward off further teasing.

Charlie thought it over. "Yeah, we could put it on the ledge and it'd always be ready. Anyway, there's stuff I wanta look at, lots of new dirt. I don't know where it's from."

Aaron shrugged. It didn't seem important.

Yet.

CHAPTER 10:
✈ THE YELLOW PERIL ✈

Final exams at Pease School were not due until the end of
May and never proved to be as fierce as promised by
teachers, but they loomed like doomsday in the minds of
boys. Because Charlie and Aaron shared several classes, they
used this excuse to "cram" together on weekday afternoons
in May. Some actual studying took place now and then,
though a suspicious parent might have wondered what bits
of wisdom could be gained during time spent with Jackie or
Roy.

In some ways, however, living near Jackie Rhett offered
a kind of education for other boys. It had not taken Jackie
long to discover that two of his victims were, unaccountably,
now marble-rich. He was quick to propose a marble
tournament, meanwhile keeping up constant complaints
about a sprained thumb, though for some reason that injury
did not seem to affect his aim much. The older boys
understood Jackie's strategy and by conspiring against him
without a word, managed to enjoy the excitement of games
in the Kinney yard while losing only a few marbles. Roy
was not so shrewd. It was after finally losing his last four

red-and-yellow "glassies" in one expert turn by Jackie that Roy burst into tears and ran off toward the family storeroom.

"Crybaby, cry," Jackie chanted, unmoved. "Everybody watched, it was fair."

"I'm gonna show you fair," Roy wailed.

Jackie pocketed his new plunder while the other boys gathered their marbles in the belief that Roy would soon be back with an adult. But Roy came charging out from under the house yowling another kind of cry, one that rang with fury. Jackie had never feared anything from the smaller boy, and saw no reason to reconsider now.

But Charlie's hair stood on end, and Aaron's too, almost in the same instant. In each hand Roy held an egg as he sped toward them, and both eggs were bright yellow. And raw. And two months old. Aaron yelped, "King's X," and bolted for the fence. Charlie tripped and fell into ivy but made not a sound, staring in horror as he scrambled up to distance himself from Jackie.

Then Roy hurled the first egg, which missed its target by such a wide margin that it splattered against the top of the Kinney fence a foot from Aaron, who was struggling to disentangle a trouser cuff from a fence picket. "Noooo," Aaron announced, reacting to a stench that confirmed his worst fears. Charlie backed against the fence, a silent study in terror though the horrendous aroma had all been sent in Aaron's direction by sheer accident.

Roy faltered, then stopped for a mental adjustment and stared, having seen—but not yet smelled—that one of the eggs he'd saved was not the genuine hardboiled article. In truth, until that moment the Kinney boy had never thought about the glorious potential of any uncooked egg that has been hidden away for months. Only Jackie stayed in place, not knowing that the eggs were raw or pausing to wonder at Charlie's behavior, grinning as he realized only that the smallest of the boys had saved some old ammunition and was angry enough to use it.

Though still unafraid, Jackie did not intend to be egged. Here was an opportunity to show his prowess once more, to dodge the second missile, perhaps recover its remains to use on Roy, then swagger off after showing the audience his mastery of any situation. Still grinning, Jackie ducked as if to move left, ducked back to the right, ducked left again, in a near-squat, then caught sight of the panic on Charlie's face. And then looked back at Roy. And frowned in puzzlement.

Just as Roy, an arm's span away, hurled a perfect strike that caught the older boy squarely on the forehead.

Roy brayed a single triumphant, "Haaaaa," before the scent overcame him from the rich dark slick gooey mass that spread from the older boy's hair, across his face, and down across the front of his T-shirt bearing flecks of yellow eggshell and other fragrant tidbits. Jackie took a breath—a major mistake—then clasped both hands before his face, which was an even greater mistake. A second later he fell on his knees, making noises like a boy trying to gargle in reverse.

Roy, overwhelmed and undone by his own success, grabbed his stomach, stumbled forward onto Jackie, and without warning deposited over the older boy's back the proof that he'd had tuna salad for lunch. If Charlie had been less thunderstruck by this he would have noticed Aaron's eyes peeping between fence pickets.

For a moment the two sufferers wallowed together, ridding themselves of whatever ailed them, before they rolled apart. Jackie swayed to his knees again and, very slowly, began to pull his T-shirt off while Roy sat up and groveled, now fearful of consequences. Jackie said, "You saved those," though it sounded more like, "Choo slay toes," to which Roy said nothing.

But Jackie did manage to direct a shaky finger toward

Charlie, who might have denied any part in this catastrophe if given a moment to reflect.

Yet Charlie had known from the first sight of Roy's headlong charge that somehow, the eggs hidden and later forgotten had been found, and whatever happened next, the blame would fall at his feet. Carrying such a load of guilt, Charlie lacked the good sense to lie about it.

Jackie's eyes narrowed as he chose who was to suffer for such an insult. Even a skunk would not have attacked Roy at this moment, and Jackie's gaze followed the pointing finger.

"I dunno how he found 'em," Charlie blurted, and no more admission was needed. He saw the look of purpose on Jackie's nastified face, cleared the fence with a superhuman effort, and sped down the alley for home.

Aaron trotted behind his pal, hoping to stay out of the fray, and shuddered to notice that Jackie had crossed the street in time to cut Charlie off. He saw Charlie pause an instant, then begin sprinting down the street away from home. He feared that Charlie had chosen sure destruction.

But Charlie knew better. Two blocks distant lay the castle wall and his secret highway over it. And beyond that lay the massive oak where, if he didn't forget a single handhold, Charlie could scamper through the foliage as if he belonged there. Jackie seemed unable to run with his usual furious speed, spitting and coughing as he pursued ten yards behind his prey, and for once Charlie even widened his lead as he neared the wall with its smaller overhanging oak. He swung up its trunk with Jackie so near, Charlie felt an angry hand brush the sole of his sneaker. But Jackie was shirtless now, and an oak's bark can sting like barbed wire. Charlie regained a foot of advantage while enraged pursuit coughed and snorted and plowed through greenery just below.

Aaron drew near without fear for himself now, peering up past Jackie to see his pal who appeared to have become a two-legged squirrel using both hands with hardly a single clumsy move. Aaron watched this with amazement and the beginnings of hope for Charlie. The voices he heard were louder than the scrape and slap of branches.

"Gonna rip yer pants off," Jackie snarled. "Make ya lick this S-Word off me," he panted a moment later. "Kick some teeth out," he promised, with convincing fury.

And Charlie's reply was—a snicker? It was, though he was now only inches beyond the bigger boy. Hearing this, Jackie growled without words and lunged ahead with renewed rage. Now Aaron climbed up into the tree though staying safely out of reach.

Then Charlie eased out and to Aaron's wonder, climbed up through the branches that overhung the courtyard a chimney's height below. The entire main branch, laden with two boys, began to droop. Jackie accepted as a basic fact that if Charlie could navigate such a thicket so fast, Jackie could do it as well.

Not everyone's basic facts are real. Jackie discovered his mistake as he grasped a tiny branch that snapped, snatched at another and missed, then plummeted down through the rest of the foliage headfirst, yowling as he went. He struck grassy turf on his back with a thump like a hollow log, arms outstretched, eyes and mouth open and gasping like a goldfish.

For the duration of a dozen heartbeats not one of them spoke. Charlie, choosing remembered grips, descended six feet or so, then dropped and rolled near the silent Jackie. He recovered and ran a few steps toward the bigger oak, then turned back. Jackie was not following. Instead, as he recovered his breath, he was using it for another purpose: sobbing. Not only that, but oozing crimson from a dozen cuts and punctures, one of them torn deeply into his cheek.

Poised between joy and worry, Charlie stepped near. "You okay?"

Jackie's mouth worked, but only sobs emerged. From above, Aaron began to pick his way down through the branches like a boy who valued his skin. "I bet he needs a doctor," he said, dropping to the ground.

Jackie managed to nod. "What he needs," Charlie said, "is for us to kick his teeth out. Take his pants to the schoolground. All that stuff he said. That's what Mr. Jackie Rhett needs."

At this, Jackie's sobs gradually merged into blubbering as he wiped an arm across his face and saw how much blood resulted. Rolling to his knees seemed to bring more torment, and with forehead resting on the ground he might have collapsed, had Charlie not steadied him with a shoe sole.

Aaron spoke. "Charlie, if that was you down there and he was where you are, what would he be doing?"

Shrug, and pause. "Laughing, I reckon," said Charlie, and nudged the wounded warrior. "You hear, Jackie?"

"You did this," was the pained answer. The others knew Jackie so well they only exchanged glances in disgust. More crying now: "All your fault."

In some small way, this charge had irksome shreds of truth sticking out of it like short hairs from old chewing gum. It was a novelty to hear such a thing from Jackie only because Jackie seldom needed to fall back on excuses for utter, total failure. Charlie smiled when the only correct reply suddenly emerged from among several others, composed itself as if by magic, and waited for him to deliver it.

"I can make you take that back right now, if I want to," Charlie said. "But I don't want to. I can 'pants' you. Or me and Aaron can tell every guy in school how you got egged by a little kid and then outrun and outclumb by another kid, which is how you got all beat up. Or maybe we won't, if we don't feel like it. Depends on you. Now go home, your gramma wants you," he finished.

Sniveling, Jackie let himself be pulled up by his arms and, after a moment of indecision, limped slowly away toward the distant gate that he must squeeze his plumpness through. To help him home and risk bumping against such a fragrant wretch would have taken a hero more than human, and the boys let him go without further exchange.

When he was too far off to hear soft voices: "For a minute I was afraid he was gonna wallop you good for that," Aaron murmured.

"Me too," said Charlie. "But right now I think he figures I'd whup his tail."

"What do you figure?"

"Maybe I could, right now," said Charlie. They swapped grins as he added, "Tomorrow I better be careful."

As the boys strolled toward the gate Jackie had just struggled through, Aaron said, "You shoulda told Jackie that Roy was in on the egg secret clear back to Easter."

"And get Roy pounded to smithereens? I wouldn't do that, even to Roy." After a moment Charlie added, "How d'you suppose he got hold of those eggs?"

"How would I know? No point in asking him, Roy will tell a fib just for practice. But if we let Jackie wonder about whether we all knew, he might treat guys better; not be such a momzer."

"Yeah." Charlie couldn't stand not knowing anymore so he said, "I give up; what's a "momzer"?"

"My dad's worst cussword, so I'm afraid to ask him. But pretty much, it's just a guy like Jackie."

Charlie nodded, entirely satisfied.

CHAPTER 11:
✈ HOW WHEELS BRING CHANGES ✈

As the time for final exams drew near, the boys sometimes put aside *Action* or *Planet* or *Captain Marvel* comics long enough to consult a textbook for a few minutes. Coleman Hardin, an honor student in his time, had once expected outstanding grades from six-year-old Charlie. By now, though, he had been driven to face cruel reality by his son's consistent mixture of Bs, Cs, and a teacher's scrawled "*Could apply himself much better.*" As always, Hardin reminded the boy that while a final grade of B was rewarded with a whole dollar, each A would bring the princely sum of two dollars. In the past, the very mention of such a payoff had quickened Charlie's spirit in the same way that a cat might hope to catch a flashlight beam. But this year, for some reason, Charlie's eyes did not gleam as much upon hearing that familiar announcement.

For Aaron Fischer, the issue was more complicated. The Fischers had come to expect borderline honor-roll grades, and this year they had chosen to stir the boy up with a bargain so tempting that he kept it secret even from his best friend. But to win his prize, he must earn no grade below a

B. And Aaron had quickly agreed, and then spent the next
month wishing he hadn't.

The pact with his parents chewed at Aaron's innards
because whether he got all As and Bs or not, he foresaw hard
consequences. This time, a single C on his report card would
yield huge disappointment for weeks in the Fischer
household. On the other hand, the honor roll would bring
Aaron a

! ! ! ! ! BICYCLE ! ! ! ! !

In Aaron's mind the prospect was wonderful and awful
in equal proportions. Afoot, his travels were limited to a
half-mile or so; on a bike he could wander for perhaps two
miles, or possibly on special Saturdays even as far as the
Texas Longhorn stadium across town.

But he would have to go without Charlie.

Both boys knew that for Charlie, the bike question was
closed and locked and put away on a shelf by parental order
until the day he graduated to Allan Junior High, more than
a mile across town. Charlie was not left to wonder why; the
reason was all too clear. On new roller skates a week after
Christmas, he had streaked down the steep West Avenue
sidewalk and, out of control, veered into a neighbor's
flowerbed to the ruination of rose bushes that defended
themselves fiercely and put Charlie out of commission for
days. On a bike, his father said, Charlie would have ended
in the river. He put special emphasis on the word "ended"
and decreed that Charlie's Radio Flyer wagon would be his
only wheeled vehicle until further notice.

For the next half-year, Charlie and Aaron had accepted
this outcome as a fair decision, but Aaron was now aware of
the hair-thin line between fairness and cruelty. Some boys
would have shared the Fischer family bike pact with Charlie.
Not Aaron, who knew that worry shared is not halved, but
doubled. Some other boy might have purposely botched an
exam for friendship's sake. Not Aaron, whose allegiance to

his parents was a friendship beyond measure. His decision was to do his best, and leave fate to absorb whatever blame might result.

The last day of school was a half-day, with time allotted for cleaning out lockers. Since they shared a home room and had adjoining lockers, Charlie glanced across during the hubbub of a dozen shouted conversations. He finished shoveling debris into his satchel while Aaron was still carefully loading his own. "I got four Bs," he bragged, then noticed his pal's expression. "Uh-oh. Don't tell me," he added, meaning *tellmetellme*.

"Let's talk at the pipe," Aaron replied, stone-faced. Later, after very few words from Aaron as they trotted single-file down the creekside trail, they sat down beneath a familiar fig tree, a few yards from the storm drain. Charlie elevated his nose and inhaled strongly. "I smell coal oil," he said.

This comment was surpassed instantly by stunning news. "I'm getting a bike," Aaron blurted.

Charlie's eyes grew round. Then he had second thoughts and frowned. "Because of bad grades?"

"'Course not, you Nimrod. Because I made the honor roll," said Aaron, as if admitting a felony. Understanding flooded Charlie as his pal explained and finished with, "And my dad already made me promise positively, absolutely no riding double."

Several times Charlie framed a reply, then left it unsaid. "When we go places I could run alongside," he said finally.

Aaron's expression was pained. "Aw, guy, I'd purely hate that."

"Well then, I could pedal and you could run along . . ."

But Aaron's pain only increased. "I'd hate that a durn sight worse, Charlie," he interrupted. "Where are your skates?"

"Um, parts of 'em are under my bed, I think."

"That's what I mean. If pieces of my bike wound up under your bed my dad would make me live in the basement."

"You guys don't have a basement," said Charlie.

"He'd make me dig one," Aaron rejoined. "Look, I'm sorry about this but it's done, and we've gotta make the best of it. My folks expect me to use the bike to run errands and stuff and not lend it out or bust it, and I'll go somewhere once or twice a month to make it look like I'm having fun with it. And come on, guy, wouldn't you want me to enjoy it once in a while?"

Since the blunt truth was unspeakable, Charlie shrugged. "Once a month, huh?"

"Or twice. Times when we're not doing stuff together. You wouldn't even hardly notice, I bet. Hey, what do you care about those times?"

Put like this, it was hard for Charlie to mount an attack against a two-wheeled rival he hadn't known about an hour earlier. He sensed unseen trouble hiding in the crevices of his mind but it was plain to see that Aaron was as unhappy as Charlie himself. Charlie stood up with a sigh. In some states far away, boys sharing such a problem might have shared a handshake, or even a hug, to reduce it, but this was Texas. Charlie's comradely punch to Aaron's upper arm was so gentle, even Roy Kinney would have called it sissified.

Aaron stood and returned the gesture. "It'll be okay, Charlie. We're still pals," he said, then wrinkled his nose. "Yeah, somebody opened some coal oil somewhere," he added. And for the moment, the bike was forgotten.

Like all creatures, humans pay more attention to things they learn from their sharpest senses. The subtle movement of air currents told the boys only that kerosene, labeled "coal oil" in those days and used as everything from cleaning fluid to quack medicine by farm wives, was present nearby. It would have told Lint, whose sense of smell had a college degree, that the fluid had been thrown away as trash by a man so lazy he could not be bothered to bundle his junk. Pinero had neglected to tell his partner to take the trash where it would not advertise furtive operations in a vacant house. A kerosene-drenched towel went into the storm drain after Cade Bridger mopped up most of a quart of the fluid he spilled near the printing press.

In a way, Pinero said, the spill was a good thing. One of the properties of kerosene is its ability to mask other odors. "Counterfeiting has its own set of stinks, amigo. Two kinds of alcohol, penetrating oil, several kinds of ink—sometimes mixed with the smells that casting metal and electric motors make, but not for this job. A cop walking past an open window could've spoiled everything for us. That cleaning fluid you spilled disguised it all."

"All that stuff gives me headaches, Pinero. I don't even have a fan to blow fresh air through here." Bridger had a lot of complaints arising from the basic fact that he began with no knowledge of printing and found himself working as Pinero's janitor. By now, janitorial work was his principal duty, and made him more servant than partner.

"Don't need electricity for a letterpress powered by a treadle, and you can be glad I found this one. Foot power's enough when you're crankin' out a brand new bill every couple of seconds. Click-clack, twenty bucks. Click-clack, twenty more, and four bits of each one to us." While his rhythm imitated the muted mechanical clatter of the cast-iron press, his arm mocked the slow revolving of its flywheel. "Click-clack, stomp the treadle, click-clack, watch your fingers." He winked. "When I get it adjusted, this ol' antique will turn out stuff I could pass right here in town."

Pinero was stretching the truth here; the plates with reversed images that he had received from Mexico, originally manufactured in Germany, had made better copies when new. He knew better than to risk the entire enterprise by showing inferior funny money to an Austin storekeeper.

Bridger had seen the press work, after a fashion. Standing almost as tall as a man, the old device had the iron tongue of its foot treadle sticking out at floor level, where the printer's foot must pump it. A wooden feeding tray hung out at elbow height with its supply of very special paper. Every piece of that paper needed to be trimmed within a gnat's eyelash of perfection, too. But the heart and soul of the press was only half-visible, a reversed image of a twenty-dollar bill held rigidly in place by a metal frame. With the press in operation, the reversed image would be kissed by a mechanically inked roller before transferring that inky kiss to the paper, where the image would no longer be reversed. Every time the paper got kissed, it printed one side of a fake twenty-dollar bill.

Bridger knew the bill had to be printed on both sides. He knew that a tiny ink smear could ruin a bill at any point in the process. And he knew that Pinero intended to trade stacks of their false money to a man in El Paso for fifty real cents per fake bill. Beyond this, Cade Bridger knew so little about counterfeiting that his partner worried about his ignorance.

"No, we won't try it out in Austin," Pinero had sighed while Bridger held up their first trial bill and shared his thoughts aloud. "For sure, not this sorry piece of goods." The printer took the bill back from Bridger. "That's just my first try; gotta make adjustments. Even if you passed it at the liquor store, the first time a bank clerk saw it he'd send it to the Department of Whatever."

"The which?"

"I forget. Department of Justice, Treasury, State—federal cops of some kind. I can't keep track of all the badges, there's so many here in the States. And every one of 'em can put you behind bars in a gummint hoosegow for a long, long time. That's why we'll take four bits on the bill for what we do and let somebody else take the risk of passing the stuff in Mexico."

"We got Mex'cans here in town," said Bridger, thinking about all that cheap tequila.

"You're not listening, Cade. In this country, the day after you passed it, that bill would be in the hands of *federales*, gummint cops. People with badges would be checking out who buys our kinds of ink, our special paper, everything we need. Let's do this my way. In Mexico it takes longer for the cops to get moving."

"Then seems to me we could go across the border and pass a few pocketfuls our own self to the stupid greasers," Bridger said with a snicker.

Pinero stiffened, then made himself relax. "I'm of Spanish extraction myself, *compadre*, in case you forgot. Try not to think 'stupid,' and think 'not so familiar with American money.' But if you got caught passing it south of the border to some poor Mexican, you'd never see an American jail. Or a cop. Or another sunrise. In a country where you can't trust your cops, the cemetery fills faster than the jail."

Bridger digested this news in silence, and set aside his plans to embezzle a few bills for himself. Understanding a tiny fragment of the international counterfeiting business, he imagined that he understood it all. Pinero had told him nothing about where those plates had come from, or that Nazi Germany had created and released many of them hoping to flood America with enough fake money to start a financial panic. Pinero knew a larger fragment of this plot; knew, and did not care.

Within a few days Charlie found the flaw in his pal's promise that the bike would not bring important changes.

The flaw was this: instead of Aaron being out of touch once in a while, that "once" became most times in every while. If Charlie sought a playmate, Aaron might be off with his bike on a shopping errand for his mother. When Aaron wanted to see the Austin High Maroons play a baseball game, he could pedal a mile to the ballpark while Charlie had to walk—both ways. And the time Aaron went to Austin's sprawling Barton Springs resort to see a swimming competition, he rode there with another bike-owning boy. Charlie could not have walked several miles to the resort and, in any case, he was forbidden to cross the river.

Willa Hardin could not miss the signs of her son's misery because he made them clear. Charlie told his mom that a boy who had graduated to the sixth grade should not be punished by remaining bikeless when "all the other guys" were wheeled.

"I hadn't noticed, Charlie," she said. "Does Roy have one?"

"He's just a kid," Charlie said.

"That Rhett boy; does he have one?"

"I dunno," Charlie said, willing to stretch a fact because Jackie might have stolen one, or a dozen of them, during the past week.

"And Aaron Fischer?"

Charlie's anguish in his "He's got a new one" was almost a cry for help, and told his mother all she needed to know. She hugged him and skooshed up his hair as in earlier times, and kissed the top of his head and told him she would talk to his dad.

And she must have said something in Charlie's behalf because that very night, after Charlie and his dad had laughed at the Fibber McGee radio program for its full half-hour, Coleman Hardin patted his own thigh and invited Charlie to take a seat there. It surprised him to note that Charlie would soon be too big to be sitting on his father's knee. "I get the idea you miss your buddies this summer," Hardin said. "Want to tell me about it?"

Charlie nodded, adopting his most serious mood. Having stored up such a pile of complaints, he needed a while to explain them all.

"Your mother and I can't afford a Schwinn right now," was his dad's first wall of defense.

Charlie hurdled it with ease. "Western Auto has bikes for fourteen ninety-five."

"That's still a lot, son."

Charlie took his time now, pursing his lips as if thinking about some brand-new, very large idea. Then: "What if I earned the money myself?"

Hardin had no idea just how fast his son could have laid his hands on fifteen dollars, but he could feel Charlie vibrating as if waiting for the nibble that would catch the biggest catfish in Texas. "You're still too young, son. Even if your Grandmom Hardin gave you one I couldn't let you ride it yet."

"Sure you could," Charlie said with some heat. "You just won't."

Hardin sensed that this was no longer the Charlie who, a year before, would have wheedled and whined. But this was still the one who had reduced brand-new roller skates to an assortment of twisted pieces while testing the theory that he couldn't break his neck. "All right then, son, I won't. We love you too much to help you find new ways to hurt yourself. Maybe in a year, you'll settle down like—like other boys."

"Like Aaron," said Charlie, who almost hated his pal at that moment.

"Fischer's boy is quiet and thoughtful. He looks before he leaps. You don't look even after you leap, and you leap like a grasshopper. I don't know what we'll do with you, but I know every time the phone rings, your mother wonders if it's the hospital calling about you."

This was an angle Charlie had never considered. "Aww, Mom," he said softly, as if she could hear him.

Coleman Hardin saw that he had touched a soft spot. "So you think about that next year, when you go to a different school on a bike we'll probably get you. But meanwhile, do you remember the Carpenters? Jim and Amy Carpenter, at church?"

Bewildered by this sudden change of subject, Charlie blinked and then got it. "Gene Carpenter's folks? Yessir. They have bicycles or something?"

"It's their boy Eugene I was thinking about. He's about your age, maybe a year older. You used to like him, didn't you?"

Charlie looked before he leaped, this time, rather than commit himself. "Wellll, kinda. He's in junior high. I guess he's okay." With no other connection, Charlie wondered if his dad was about to say that Gene Carpenter's mom had gotten a phone call from the hospital. That would not have surprised Charlie because, sensing a kindred spirit, Eugene Carpenter had whispered a few of his experiences now and then to Charlie to enliven Sunday school lectures. To the best of Charlie's understanding, the only reason his father hadn't met Gene Carpenter in handcuffs was that Gene seldom chose companions to share his adventures.

But Charlie's dad was aiming in another direction today. "Eugene seems like a smart, friendly boy, and last month Jim was saying they don't know many boys his age out near the golf course where they live. I think he was hinting to see if we'd like to get you and Eugene together overnight. Your mother and I could make it happen."

Charlie did not need to mull this over for long. If Aaron could pal around with another bike owner, maybe Charlie could have another pal too. Gene was in fact several good things: smart, polite, and friendly as a playful pup. Young Carpenter also had the kind of curiosity that made him unforgettable to the few who knew his secret nature.

What might happen if a boy, adopting the voice of a young woman, called in a false fire alarm? Gene had the details. How loud was the church bell, assuming a boy could reach the bell rope undetected? Gene knew. How far could a stolen golf ball travel across a wealthy neighborhood when walloped as hard as possible by a boy with a baseball bat? Gene could have answered. And yet his parents knew nothing of these adventures. If they suspected anything, they chose to deny those suspicions. Perhaps they imagined that matching their crafty Eugene with the son of a juvenile officer might infect their own boy with civic virtue. In any case, Jim Carpenter made his friendly overture and waited for Hardin to reply.

Coleman Hardin could not have made a more dangerous decision if he had locked his son in a fireworks shed with a lit blowtorch, but he was not acquainted with what Charlie knew of Gene's unique views on innocent pastimes.

That is how it happened that Willa Hardin drove Charlie to the Carpenters' fine home one Friday afternoon, and it's why Charlie wasn't surprised when he learned that Gene had some uncommon fun in mind.

CHAPTER 12:
✈ THE FUN OF IT ✈

"Eugene! You remember Charles," Mrs. Carpenter called from her sweeping driveway as Charlie and his mother exited the Hardin Plymouth. Both mothers shed fond gazes on their sons. "Willa, come in for coffee, won't you?"

The introduction was totally unnecessary for the boys. Gene had already tossed a tennis ball across the manicured lawn in Charlie's direction, and followed this by making a comical, ferocious face. Within seconds a game of tennis-ball tag exploded toward all corners of the Carpenters' half-acre, an expanse that advertised family wealth as clearly as if they had installed man-sized dollar signs on the lawn.

Mothers seemed not to notice how many ways a game like tennis-ball tag helped boys to size each other up. Gene had been politely familiar with Charlie for years, but as a suitable companion beyond the strict limits of Sunday-school society, Charlie was still untested. In a game like this, speed, accuracy, and strength counted on the throw; deception and courage were important for the thrown-at. New tennis balls had rubber's flexibility and would sting only

121

a little. Gene Carpenter preferred last year's balls, which might as well have been flint, because he placed high value on courage and had a comic book hero's contempt for pain. Though Gene was a year older and three inches taller than Charlie, they finally negotiated a King's X on even terms. "Boy, you're tricky," the older boy panted with honest admiration, as he sprawled on the back lawn.

"You too," Charlie replied, and sat down. "Sorry about your cheek." Though he rubbed an abrasion on his upper arm, Charlie was content. He had seen his best throw catch Gene above the jaw hard enough to snap his head sideways.

"Aaah," said Gene, dismissing the wound with a grin. He spat on his fingers and rubbed a tiny blood spot from his face. Wink. "I'll tell Mother I fell in the Algerita."

If Charlie had wondered how well Gene absorbed punishment, he wondered no longer because he knew the scratches on that cheek must sting like the very dickens. It might be interesting, he thought, to watch Gene Carpenter compete against Jackie Rhett for about ten minutes.

Studying the line of shrubs behind the Carpenter home Charlie said, "They planted Algeritas like those outside the walls of my school. Almost as bad as rosebushes." In his experience with roses Charlie was an expert by now. The Algerita shrub's vice was also its main virtue: self-protection. Well known in the region, Algerita was a year-round evergreen, its leaflets stiff as metal and more spiky than holly. In spring it decorated itself with small bright yellow blossoms. Now in early summer the blossoms had become tart pink berries that were popular with songbirds.

"Let's eat some Algerita berries," Gene said suddenly.

"You go ahead, they're too sour for me." *And I'm not gonna prove how much I love sticking my hand in barbwire. Enough's enough*, Charlie added, but only to himself.

Gene had gathered only a handful of berries when they heard Willa Hardin's special three-note whistle that Charlie had been taught to respect. Charlie shouted a reply and raced around to the Plymouth with Gene at his heels.

In moments he had responded to his mother's parting kiss with a hug and as she drove away the two boys ran alongside the car as if they intended to bark at it. Gene, who knew the value of social niceties, copied Charlie in waving until the car was out of sight. Next, he waved to his own mother. Then, "Got something to show you," he muttered, and wolfed down his berries.

Here on the edge of town only a suburban street separated homes from an expanse of meadow. The grass continued for a great distance and overlooked a shallow ravine that was much too well maintained to be natural. A creek meandered the length of the ravine, glistening here and there through greenery in the late sun, artificial as a postcard. The other side of the ravine was just as attractive, with small groupings of pecan and oak carefully positioned.

Gene sat on the grass in such a way that he could enjoy both the view and his home without turning his head. "Golf course out there," he explained to his visitor. He waved toward home and Charlie realized they were still in view of Mrs. Carpenter, who waved back. She seemed about to approach them, then went back inside as if uncertain. "Let's wait a couple of minutes," Gene urged, and fell to observing the parklike view. Then he said, the way a teacher might say, "Timing is important, Charlie."

Presently Gene stretched his arm out toward the south, stood up, and ambled downhill toward the creek in the direction he had pointed. Charlie trotted along too, until he noticed Gene had stopped. "What's wrong?"

"Nothing, but we're going that way," Gene replied, jerking a thumb in the opposite direction.

"No we weren't," Charlie said, confused.

"Boy, you don't know much," Gene said, but playfully. "She can't see us from the house now," he went on. Sure enough, their heads were now below the street level, and Gene began to stride toward the north.

Charlie followed. "We're not supposed to go this way?"

"Doesn't matter whichever way," Gene confided, "so long as folks don't know, Charlie. Never let them know which way you go."

This advice was delivered with the kind of earnestness that suggested it must be important, and Charlie replied with a serious, "Uh-huh." On a parallel track, Charlie's mind began to toy with the suspicion that if a boy wanted people never to know his intentions, maybe those intentions tended to be unpopular. On the main line of Charlie's thoughts, however, lay a growing curiosity about Gene Carpenter and his rumored habits.

Gene set a brisk pace toward a gravel street some distance away, all the while talking to Charlie in a pleasant way. It was all about golf balls, and how infernally expensive they had become, and how golfers loved to buy them at half-price, and how a boy with any gumption at all could collect a dozen perfectly good golf balls in an afternoon, if he hid in bushes near the creek. And how Gene had only recently thought up a new wrinkle in the Wandering Golf Ball business, a wrinkle so new he had waited for Charlie's visit before trying it. And . . .

But Charlie's mind was working on ways to make sense of his friend's ways. The Carpenters lived more comfortably than the Hardins, yet Gene had radical ideas about the ownership of golf balls. Though he showed all the politeness a mother could ask, he had a genius for seeming to do one thing while intending a different thing. And however much he might behave all goodygood in front of his parents, Eugene Carpenter apparently made up for it when out of their sight. As the boys drew near the cross street, Charlie judged that, for Gene, out of sight meant out of control. And Gene could get out of sight quicker than a ground squirrel.

Someday it might occur to Charlie that he and Aaron—many boys, in fact—practiced the same strategy to some degree. But now, as Gene led the way stepping carefully down to the edge of the creek, Charlie noticed that the water issued as a small waterfall from a metal conduit not quite big enough to crawl through, and that the one-lane street ten feet above it was, in fact, the top surface of a primitive dam. The structure might have been in place a half-century or more, and it stretched completely across the ravine, which, here at the edge of the golf course, was no more than twenty yards wide.

Gene squatted and peered up the metal conduit, pointing. "See, there's this thing across the other end."

Charlie looked, jumped to a conclusion and shook his head. "No. Uh-unh. Over and out, lieutenant. I am *not* goin' up that thing," he said firmly.

"Course not, I wanted you to see the floodgate," Gene replied, laughing. "I figured out how it works. It lowers a big iron plate when you turn a wheel, I think."

Charlie squinted up the conduit some more. "Why do they do that?"

"They don't. If they did, it oughta shut the creek off."

"So what if they did?"

"No more water. No more creek. No more shallow pools where a jillion golf balls have been waiting for somebody to collect 'em."

An inner vision of countless golf balls infected Charlie's imagination. After a moment he said, "Yeah, but as soon as the creek stopped somebody would just turn it on again."

"If they noticed, they might. But nobody plays golf in the dark. They mostly quit about now, around sundown, and start again next day." Gene was in high spirits as he outlined his "new wrinkle," and in a moment he had clambered up the stones and cement of the old dam, drawing Charlie after him by animal magnetism. For the first time, Charlie noticed the poles of high cyclone fencing set in cement between the street and the creek. The creek extended out of sight through the middle of a grassy valley.

Gene walked quickly to a clump of wild grass just off the street and sat down. Charlie stood and faced the parklike valley, leaning on the fence.

"Get away from there, guy, you really *don't* know much! You can see it all from here," Gene said, urgency diluting his good humor. Then, "Anybody watching could prob'ly see you there on the fence," he added without heat as Charlie took a seat beside him.

"Who could?"

"The Terrys. Old man Terry used to own everything around here," said Gene. "That's his mansion over yonder."

Only now did Charlie begin to appreciate the full extent of the place on the other side of the cyclone fence. It seemed to stretch forever, and it impressed him as the owner had intended it to impress adults. He studied the huge home off in the distance half-hidden by trees, saw a scatter of lawn furniture and a barbecue grill with its own stone chimney in the valley, and whistled to himself. "I guess rich guys have their own parks," he marveled.

"You bet they do," said Gene. "And they don't much wanta share it, neither. Maybe they're afraid somebody will turn that big wheel there, and shut off the creek."

Charlie's gaze followed a pointing finger and settled on a big weathered iron wheel held by an axle that extended from the back face of the dam. To seize that wheel a boy must be on the other side of the fence. All his uncertainty about this mission disappeared in a flash. "Yeah, and I've tried to climb a cyclone fence. Those sharp tops tear you up pretty good," he said, hoping Gene could interpret a "no" without hearing it aloud.

"I know," his companion grinned, and displayed old scars on one arm. "Lucky for us, there's a gate."

"I don't see it," said Charlie.

"Sure you do. For them it's a tree. For us it's a gate." With that, Gene pointed along the street to a medium-sized hackberry tree just across the fence. It stood twenty yards away, its trunk within arm's length of the fence. The lowest branches began perhaps ten feet up, some overhanging the street.

This was familiar stuff to Charlie, and it was his turn to grin. "I've done that. You gonna go into the tree?"

"Can't reach the branches. If you were bigger than me you could grab the fence and boost me." Gene accompanied this with a sorrowful headshake.

For an endless moment, neither boy spoke. Then Charlie said, "But I bet you could grab that ol' fence and boost me in a jiffy, right?"

Something in Charlie's tone caused the older boy to look away, and a pink flush crept across his face. "You think I'm afraid, don'tcha?"

"Nope. Prob'ly not," Charlie shrugged. "The only durn thing I expect scares you is gettin' caught. But I think you wanted me here because you figgered you couldn't do this by yourself."

Gene sighed the sigh of a lost boy. As the normal color returned to his face he said, "I'm sorry. I kinda had the idea you and me might be alike, and this is a little scary, so it'd be fun. I don't blame you if you don't want to, Chuck." And as the last rays of direct sunlight floodlit the scene, Gene stuck out his hand to be shaken.

Charlie stood up and dusted off the seat of his pants. "Who said I won't? And it's not 'Chuck,' it's Charlie. This is up to Charlie Hardin. Come on," and he used the handshake to pull Gene Carpenter to his feet.

It was unsettling to Charlie, hearing a steady fit of giggles and feeling excited trembles from his partner, who took a double-handed grip on the fence and let Charlie use him as a climbing pole. The mission was in doubt only when Charlie stood with both feet on the taller boy's shoulders and leaned his thighs against the top of the fence. By the time Gene began to sag, Charlie was clinging to hackberry branches and making slow progress.

His weight was enough to bend the foliage down, and after two failed attempts, Gene had snagged a lowered branch himself. "Go on, didn't you think I'd be behind you?"

"Guy, I swear I don't know what to think." Charlie reached the tree trunk and shinnied down without obstruction. Gene following until they picked their way across to the big rusted wheel pocked by flecks of red paint from many years ago.

Gene knelt to inspect the device. "Oh, D-Word it," he muttered, "it's wired up." The wire delayed them only until Gene unwound it. Then he gripped the wheel and turned it; no, tried to turn it. The wheel budged but would not yield, and no amount of his grunting and straining made any difference.

Charlie kept up his glances toward the distant home until Gene begged for help. When Charlie added his efforts the wheel's hub suddenly squealed like a live thing, then gave way gradually, and every little screech made both boys grimace. Some distance below them, scrapes and crunches said that something was being accomplished, and now Gene could turn the wheel alone. Charlie climbed down the face of the dam near the water to inspect their progress. "There's a big old iron tray that slides between grooves. It cuts down through some twigs into the water," he said.

The wheel would turn no further. "Listen, Charlie. Hush and listen."

Without all the screeching and grunting and commentary, the place fell silent as a mausoleum. "The waterfall down there?"

"Can't hear it," said Charlie.

The reply was a whisper powerful as a steam leak. "Right, it's quit! We're done. Climb back here and I'll boost you up the tree."

Hackberry bark was so sturdy, Charlie could have climbed without help but with both of Gene's hands supporting his rump Charlie quickly climbed the tree. Gene's only way up was by gripping the trunk between his arms and legs to inch his way aloft. Meanwhile Charlie fought his way across the foliage, a practice he had mastered before, then hung by his hands and dropped onto the edge of the street. Soon, accompanied by those fitful giggles of his, Gene landed beside him.

"Now we'll see how it works," said the older boy, and raced away across the street down into the cover of creekside brush with Charlie at his heels. At the water's edge he scooped sand into one hand and used it like soap, scrubbing both hands vigorously in the shallows. It was easy to see that the creek's level was already dwindling. "You better get that stuff off your hands."

Charlie hadn't noticed his palms, which were stained as if he had been stacking old bricks, thanks to his struggle against the ancient wheel. "It'll come off," he said.

"Yeah? What if they ask what it is?" Moments later Gene forgot his own question as he spied something a few paces downstream. "Hot diggety, there's one!" And he hopscotched across shallows to collect the first ball.

Charlie wondered who "they" might be. As those soft cries of new discoveries grew fainter, he squatted and began to scrub his hands thoughtfully. It was starting to look as if, for Gene, "they" meant anybody on the planet; and it seemed that this happy young outlaw ran wild not so much for treasure as just for the heck of it.

By draining away, the creek was becoming little more than a series of pools, some perhaps a foot deep, but much of it only wet sand and limestone. Charlie found his friend hunkered down near what clearly had been a broad pool, now mere inches deep. Gene was pointing. A half-dozen small dimpled spheres crowded together at a crevice in the stone bottom, like a clutch of hen eggs in a watery nest.

"Wow, you were right," said Charlie.

"Just made sense," Gene said, and emptied several balls from his hand to Charlie's so he could retrieve his latest find. "Boy, am I dumb. I shoulda thought to hide some old sacks near the dam."

As he stood up, Charlie saw that his friend's pockets were full of rounded lumps. He recalled a similar problem with coins from a lily pond but kept silent about it as he pocketed the new treasure. "I wouldn't say dumb, guy," he said.

"We haven't come a city block and we're almost full-up," said Gene, to illustrate his own dumbness. "We'll have to hide this bunch here and do it as many times as we have to and come back for 'em all later."

"Yep. So don't say dumb," Charlie insisted. "You're not dumb. What you are is scary."

"Aw, hey," said Gene, looking as though Charlie had just slapped him.

"It's okay, Gene. You're not mean, or clumsy or anything. Shoot, you're not clumsy *enough*. I just don't know what you're up to until we're in the middle of it, you know?"

"Well shoot, neither do I. That's the fun of it," Gene explained, with a combination frown-and-grin that said, "Everybody knows that."

"There's another one," Charlie said to change the subject, and hurried downstream after a small dimpled orb he caught peeking above the water's surface. Darkness overtook them before they could survey the full length of the course, but by then they had hidden six piles of golf balls and headed for home.

In late dusk, Gene's parents seemed pleased that their son had gone "no place much" and "just played" with young

Charles Hardin, and they treated Charlie like visiting royalty at dinnertime. A big tiger-striped cat that Charlie hadn't noticed before snaked around at Mrs. Carpenter's feet in the kitchen but evaporated in a twinkling when Gene sought a pair of RC Colas from the refrigerator.

A portion of Charlie envied the way his friend was allowed small decisions without asking permission, while an equal portion of his mind argued that Gene might need a few more permissions now and then. Mr. Carpenter, a handsome older man of few words, erected an expensive camping tent in the backyard at Gene's suggestion so the boys could toy with a flashlight and sleep like adventurers. Around midnight Charlie's energy began to drain away, and after that, his sleep was deep as a coma. Evidently Gene was a sleepwalker because, sometime during the night, he imported two grocery bags of golf balls to the tent.

With morning's first sparrow chirp the boys were up again, burying grocery bags in last year's leaves behind the garage. That garage was full of little mysteries for Charlie, including a handsome bicycle locked with a chain. Gene was vague about the bike and Charlie decided to keep his guesses to himself. The croquet set looked almost new but all the heads had been removed from the mallets. The badminton racquets looked as if someone had pounded them with a hammer. "Not as good as a baseball bat," Gene confided, and Charlie supposed they had been used to whale the tar out of a few golf balls.

By the time he was burping from a late breakfast that included bacon, eggs and butter, Charlie had seen how a boy might live, given the comforts of money and parents who denied him only one thing: supervision. Charlie took wartime rationing for granted the way all his other friends did, but he found that the Carpenters lived as though rationing did not exist. From this he learned a Great

American Truth: the wealthy do not understand rationing, nor need to.

At midmorning the boys were looking through Gene's enviable collection of Big Little Books, volumes smaller than paperbacks but with hard covers and pictures on alternating pages, when a telephone rang somewhere in the house. Presently Mrs. Carpenter came to Gene's room with the news that Charles's mother would pick him up within the hour. "And Eugene, your father is having more trouble taking the tent down than he expected. I know he could use your help," she added.

Charlie followed his friend outside to find that Mr. Carpenter, though plainly surprised and pleased to find Gene offering aid, would not let a guest take part. Charlie basked in sunlight on flagstones, watching father and son puzzle at their work halfway across the yard, until the family's striped cat ambled up to him and applied for a skull-massage, which Charlie was happy to give. By stages so subtle that Charlie did not notice them, the cat insinuated itself into his lap where finally it lay on his knees in a Sphinx position, eyes shut, accepting his fingernails between its ears in catly drowsiness.

Both boy and cat became sun-stunned, so near sleep that when at last the tent was stored, Gene stepped onto the flagstones before the cat came alert. A sizzle like grease on a hot skillet erupted from Charlie's lap and the cat dematerialized in a stripy flash. "Ow, ow, durn you," Charlie scolded after the departed animal. "Thanks a lot, Tiger," he added, rubbing furiously at tiny wounds those claws had made through his trouser legs.

"Peeve, you mean," said Gene, not at all surprised at the way the family feline had greeted him. "Her name's 'Peeve.'"

"New cat, huh," said Charlie.

"Mother's had her since I was, I dunno, five maybe."

Some unspoken understanding passed between the boys. Then Charlie asked, "Why'd she name her pet 'Peeve'?"

Gene grinned that impudent grin of his. "You just said. Her pet peeve, get it?"

Abruptly Charlie did get it, and slapped himself on the forehead with the heel of his hand. "Keen."

"Hey, we don't have much time before your mother comes," Gene said abruptly. "Don't you wanta see the creek?"

Charlie fired off a grin of his own. "If there was one."

"I bet it's still there behind the dam. And if we're good guys we better turn it back on while we can."

Scampering away down to the throat of the golf course, they hurried toward the ancient dam, staying hidden in greenery. The boys reached the graveled street together and saw through cyclone fencing at the same time. One of Gene's special giggles burbled up at what they saw, but Charlie was silent with awe.

That merry little brook of the day before was nowhere to be seen—or rather, it was everywhere, but not as a brook anymore. Charlie marveled how a lazy little stream pouring twenty gallons a second through a ravine could produce a real swim-across-it, float-rafts-on-it, drown-in-it pond after being sealed off for twelve hours or so. In an instant the scene told Charlie more about multiplication tables than his teachers ever had. Wooden lawn chairs lazed across the lake surface.

"Must be six feet deep in the middle," Gene marveled, and moved over to grip fencing nearest the hackberry branches. "C'mon, guy, time to open it back up!"

Charlie rushed to obey and was standing on Gene's shoulders leaning toward the tree before he realized that somewhere far off across those fenced acres, men's voices were calling back and forth. "Hurry, Charlie," Gene insisted. "I don't see anybody yet."

The hackberry seemed to have developed claws that tore

at his clothes as Charlie reached the trunk and slid down inside the property. He slipped and would have fallen headfirst into the pond near his feet if not for the rusted wheel, and as he gripped it with both hands he could hear one of those distant voices, now much closer. No telling what it said. It didn't matter what it said.

It didn't matter what Gene was saying either, because Gene was still safely outside the fence, now lying flat in the coarse tuft grass, a cheering section of one but not a loud one. "Turn it, turn it," he chanted.

And Charlie turned it. And again, and again, and with every twist a sudden trickle became a deeper splash which begat a low-pitched rumble that created a thunderous rush so loud Charlie almost failed to hear the shout of a man in overalls ten yards away. The man was only a few paces from a capture, clinging to the fence as he approached with the obvious intention of grabbing the boy, when Charlie abandoned the wheel. Charlie leaped for the tree but knew he made an easy target, inchworming feverishly up that rough bark from a height any standing man could reach.

But not a man who suddenly lost his footing to turn sidelong and plunge backward with a despairing yell, full-length, into the lake.

As the man began to swim back toward him, Charlie shinnied as he had never shinnied before; like the boy who invented shinny. It seemed he could hear Gene Carpenter urging him on but faintly amid the Niagara roar below. Charlie's feet were running as he hit the gravel shoulder and the only reason he did not run directly uphill toward the Carpenter home was that Gene grabbed him by the belt and guided him toward the ravine. "Parking lot over the hill," was the terse explanation. "Big hedge behind it."

Charlie needed all his breath for running, but he understood when he imagined men climbing that cyclone fence and giving chase. He understood a little more when he realized that Gene's rhythmic panting carried a familiar giggle in it. And when they leaped the creek that was now visibly rising more every second, he suspected that Gene Carpenter had planned every stage of this craziness. A single glance behind him told Charlie that a solid wall of water was now hurtling from the conduit pipe like the coming of a Biblical flood as the boys sped uphill.

The hill was not high, and as soon as the boys topped it the ravine was out of sight. Charlie figured all of Gene's giggling had stolen his breath, since Charlie reached the parking area ten paces ahead. He slowed to a walk hoping to become less interesting to a man who eyed him while hauling golf implements from a car. Gene fell in step blowing like a whale, steering their progress toward a high well-trimmed hedge that flanked the gravel drive.

Minutes later the boys reached the shoulder of a suburban street and headed for Gene's neighborhood. "We'll pass by our place the next alley down and then come back from the west," said the planner, and paused to gawk at a group of men dressed as colorfully as circus clowns who stood on the golf course near a foolish little flag on a pole.

"What're they doing?"

The men were gesturing, laughing, all facing the ravine, their voices too distant to carry well. "We can see better a ways farther," Gene replied, and trotted down the street's gentle slope. A half-block away the golf course's gentle curves yielded a better view into the ravine, and now Charlie saw a knot of tiny figures there near another flag. They were yelling and waving too, but did not seem to be enjoying it much. Gene glanced Charlie's way and snickered. "Didn't think of this part," he confided.

Then Charlie saw that the unhappy golfers and their caddies all stood near the creek on a room-sized grassy patch completely surrounded by water. And the water seemed to be creeping higher on the patch. "Boyoboy, did we raise a ruckus. We gotta do this again next year," Gene remarked, and set off down the street again venting those giggles that, by now, made Charlie feel uneasy.

By the time they neared the Carpenter place, Charlie could hear the forlorn blurt of a Plymouth's horn, familiar little double toots that reminded Charlie of home as powerfully as the unmistakable sound of Lint's bark. He broke into a trot, calling as he went, with Gene at his heels.

Finally in sight of his mother, Charlie saw her wave back and slowed to a walk. His companion fell in stride, saying, "You have fun like this at home, Charlie? Could we camp out at your place next time?"

A stab of uneasiness pierced Charlie's vitals. "They pretty much make us stay inside," Charlie lied. "I'll have to ask my dad."

"You can take some of my golf balls home. I can go get you a few."

"That's okay, you keep 'em for me. Just till I come next time," Charlie added quickly, wondering whether a golf ball would still be of any use to him in a hundred years.

Gene perked up at Charlie's reply. "We have all summer, guy," he said, punching Charlie's shoulder lightly with a fist. They were smiling together as they reached their mothers, and something in Mrs. Carpenter's face said the arrivals of Eugene Carpenter were not always this tame.

As the Plymouth turned toward home, Gene ran alongside until he was called back, and then waved until he was left behind. After a single dutiful wave, Charlie settled low in his seat and released a sigh. He appeared to ignore the sodden man in torn overalls who limped along the edge of the golf course, scanning the ravine with sober intensity.

Smiling, Willa Hardin patted her son's knee. "Did you have fun with your new friend, Charlie?"

"Yessum," he said, not exactly a falsehood. Then, feeling the need to say more—much, much more—and not knowing where to start, he thrust it all away. "They have a cat," he added, and after a pause: "It doesn't like him."

"Cats can be strange," she said.

It was on the tip of his tongue to say, "Boys too," but for Charlie it was enough to grunt a simple agreement. He knew all he needed to know about his new friend. He wouldn't visit again; he would run off and join a circus, even a flea circus, sooner than invite Eugene Carpenter to the Hardin home; and he knew that the brightest, sunniest outside of a person can hide an inside as dark and twisty as a ball of black yarn. "I can't hardly wait to see Lint and Aaron," he said.

CHAPTER 13:
✈ BETTER THAN SNOOZING ✈

The rattling, buzzing chorus of locusts debating in nearby trees announced that the long sultry afternoons of summer had come. Adults sometimes called the thumb-sized insect a cicada, but boys knew it only as a "seventeen-year locust," and invented scores of myths to explain why a bug would lie clasping a twig for minutes while its motor idled, then rouse its clatter to fever pitch for fifteen seconds or so before settling again to the kind of raspy drone that could drive a person to distraction.

Sitting under their fig tree near the creek, Charlie inspected Lint's ears for ticks and described the strangeness of Gene Carpenter. Meanwhile, Aaron carefully untangled a fishing line that had small hooks tied every few feet along the "trotline" they used to threaten the sun perch of Shoal Creek. Aaron found something to disbelieve in Charlie's tale with almost every sentence. "You mean he lugged both sacks home by himself in the middle of the night?"

"I guess," said Charlie. "He never said, but they sure didn't make it back by theirself. *SHUT UP!*" His shout was directed into the trees, and though Lint flinched, Aaron ignored it. For moments after a demand like this the nearest locusts ceased their clamor, but a bug's memory was brief. Charlie went on. "The guy was trying to teach me how to be him, but he didn't wake me up for the weirdest part. I think maybe he likes to do his night stuff alone."

"What I think is maybe you better let him. Anyway, why would he wanta make somebody be like him?"

Charlie pondered the question. "'Cause nobody else is, I guess," he said at last. "Around grown-ups he's polite enough to charm your granny, almost sissified, but he's like the last of the dinosaurs, and I bet he's just plain lonesome. You pal around with Gene Carpenter once, and alligators couldn't drag you to his house again."

"Huh; no wonder," said Aaron, who had overturned his can of fishing worms and hastened to set it upright again. "You better stay away from him, Charlie; he's nutty as a fruitcake."

"Their cat thinks so," Charlie said, which concluded the topic. It was common knowledge among boys of that time that cats were superior judges of character.

Because whole weeks went by without neighborhood news worth sharing, Charlie was secretly a little disappointed to find that while he was gone the other boys had not needed him to entertain them. Jackie Rhett had been his replacement, but Jackie's misfortune was really the core of it.

Playing in the nearby park in early evening when most boys were settled into radio programs and comic books, Jackie had interrupted a romancing couple—one of several—who lay in deep shadows. Furious at being chased away, Jackie had reflected on the unfairness of young men in uniform with unTexas accents who, every night in most seasons, took charge of every secluded nook in Austin to court local girls.

Still fuming, Jackie had stuffed the bowels of a ruined tire casing with newspaper and trundled it along the sidewalk all the way from home. While Charlie was having supper across town with the Carpenters, Jackie had sprinkled the paper with lighter fluid and set it afire before sending it down into the park, a circle of flame bounding across the slopes. But while Jackie paused to count the couples he had flushed like quail in the twilight, he had been caught in mid-jeer, according to him, by a giant in military uniform who wielded a doubled belt. Jackie had gone home a sadder, wiser boy.

"Wish I coulda seen it," Charlie sighed, relishing the picture in his mind.

"You know Jackie, his giant coulda been a midget," Aaron said, "but he's got sure 'nough stripes on his hide to show for it. *PIPE DOWN!*" Again the cicadas paused. Lint sent an aggrieved look though Charlie remained unfazed.

"No midgets in the army," said Charlie, without the least idea whether he was right. "Jackie's tire burn anything down?"

"Nope, it fetched up against those stone benches at the water fountain. I helped him roll it home this morning, just a little melted and stunk up. Says he has other plans for it. I bet I know who he wants to have right in the middle of those plans, one way or another." And Aaron rolled his eyes.

"Roy?"

"I meant us, but Roy's pretty much Number One in the dumb department, so yeah, him 'specially."

Lint issued a tiny growl and shook an ear loose from Charlie's scrutiny, letting his master know there were limits to a dog's patience. "I'm not gonna worry about Jackie's plans," Charlie said, with a get-on-with-you pat against the terrier's rump. "We've let that momsie boss us around too long."

Aaron knew better than to correct a boy who resisted correction, so he didn't bother to challenge Charlie's attempts at sounding Jewish. It was a kind of compliment, in fact. Besides, "momsie" had a nice belittling tone of its own, so Charlie was welcome to it.

"Let's go string our trotline before these bugs drive me batty," Aaron suggested.

The boys felt confident that now in the endless afternoons of June in 1944 they were both too adult to be taken in by Jackie's schemes and need not be concerned about him. This attitude made it practically certain that they would soon be involved with Jackie again. Not because Jackie was such a deceptive genius; Jackie was not that subtle. And not because Jackie had leadership qualities, though with his energy and self-confidence, he did have some of those qualities. Charlie and Aaron could not avoid that involvement because in a humid Austin summer, time lay heavy as manhole covers on their idleness, and being around Jackie was better than snoozing while six-inch fish stole bait.

Having assured themselves they would avoid what they daily proved they could not avoid, they turned to applying tender inch-long morsels of worm to hooks; morsels the perch always nibbled away without penalty.

Pinero found himself wishing he had linked himself to a man with only one leg, or cooties, or almost any disability other than the one Bridger had, which was a drunkard's inability to stick to a plan for more than ten minutes.

Was special ink expensive? Then Bridger was sure to set it down where he would kick it over. Did the sturdy old printing press need careful treatment? Bridger could be depended on to fetch up against it while falling-down drunk, knocking the engraved images askew.

As for his toilet needs, Cade Bridger was seldom in that basement very long before—drunk or sober—he needed to empty the kidneys he abused with liquor that would have made better paint remover. "Look, 'migo, you have to learn to drain your lizard before you get here," Pinero told him that sweltering afternoon and pulled an empty milk bottle from the cloth sack he had brought. "Do it in this when you have to, but put it where you won't knock it over, and then take it out when we leave, okay?" He jerked, stiffened, then relaxed. "You hear that? Sounded like a woman screamed 'shut up' a ways off, out on the street," he said.

Bridger gave a headshake and took the bottle without replying, and wished he had thought of the milk bottle idea himself. On this occasion he had resolved to stay sober so that he could absorb everything Pinero needed him to learn. He had the best possible reason for this: the hope that he could run off a few hundred of those twenty-dollar bills for himself some night, without Dom Pinero's knowledge. Prices of Bridger's favorite narcotic had taken a slight but sudden jump with the long-awaited invasion by Allied troops into France on the sixth of June. With the current price of tequila at sixty cents a bottle from Austin's hard-working Mexican laborers, if he spent only one of those bills a month he could stay as cross-eyed drunk as a congressman for the rest of his life. Moments later Pinero glanced up again. "Crazy gringa's still yelling," he said, realizing Bridger hadn't heard it.

"Wha'd she say?"

"Sounded like 'wipe town,'" said Pinero and, seeing the puzzlement in Bridger's face, added, "Not important. Now pay attention how I tighten this clamp."

On this occasion the lesson went well, Pinero insisting on using ordinary paper for tests and using a small high-powered magnifier to study the counterfeits they produced. When Bridger asked about the poor quality of metallic glitter that small portions of new bills were supposed to have, his partner was almost pleased.

"That's why we'll take all the bills and tumble them in a tub of dirt," Pinero said. "Look at any old genuine bill.

You see after it's used and wrinkled the shiny stuff mostly goes away. By then nobody thinks anything about it."

Bridger thought it was silly to filthify new money until Pinero convinced him that in ordinary use most paper money was thrust into so many grimy hands, tainted pockets, mildewed mattresses, mouldy crevices, dusty drawers and other palaces of bacteria, it was little short of miraculous that people dared to keep the nasty stuff around. Bridger declared he was satisfied to live with it anyway. He gathered the copies they had made for Pinero to take away as trash of the most dangerous sort, trash to be burnt in Pinero's fireplace and its ashes stirred for good measure.

But while his partner took these things to his car, Bridger found a pair of rejected bills fallen next to the rag bin. They had been printed only on one side but slightly off-center, and some trace of caution told Bridger not to leave this evidence out in the open. While emptying his milk bottle of its yellowish fluid through the escape hole he had bashed into the storm drain, he crumpled the useless bills up and discarded them in the storm drain's rubble. He saw no point in letting Pinero know his first attempt to clean up the place had been sloppy. There would be plenty of time to remove the stuff another time.

Or maybe not . . .

"Pilot? You aren't not neither." It was the day after the latest trotline failure. And Charlie pronounced this ritual triple denial with scorn.

"Am so too," said Roy, folding his arms to stiffen the firmness of his stand. "Jackie said."

"Nobody pilots a tire," said Charlie. "You guide it or drive it or push it or shove it if you're big enough, which you're not, so even if some people did, you couldn't."

"Betcha a million bucks," Roy insisted. Then, seeing that this had no reality in their world: "A dollar, then."

For a moment Charlie considered this, if only to call Roy's bluff. But if Roy ever had a dollar, by now it would be in Jackie's pocket, so Charlie ignored the offer. "Well, Mr. Tire Pilot, where's Jackie gonna be while you get it going? Seems like he'd want to do the piloting himself."

"I ast that too. Says it needs somebody big to stop it and take it back home with him. He'll be down the hill across the street where he can catch it."

Charlie pondered this. Jackie had drawn little Roy into his plans only that morning, while Charlie and Aaron were downtown at the hobby shop. Waiting for plans to mature was not one of Jackie's strong points. If Roy could be believed, it was Jackie's intention to let Roy guide the old tire casing as it gathered speed down the street beside the castle wall. This adventure would start at the top of Castle Hill (adults called it Eighth Street), and continue for a steep block downhill through the Nueces Street intersection, where Jackie would bring it to a stop as it began to climb a gentle rise.

This was all in theory, a theory none of them had ever tested. Though he could not have explained in so many words, Charlie understood that an experiment this complicated has more variables than a boy has excuses. And every thing that can vary in such a setting can do it in umpteen ways. Picking a complication at random, Charlie imagined an innocent bicyclist passing that intersection. If the cyclist believed traffic would obey a city stop sign, which was a pillow-sized iron pimple bolted to the macadam with the raised letters S T O P painted in red, that cyclist just might sail through the intersection to be collected by twenty pounds of rubber going in another direction at high speed. It was not to Charlie's credit that his vision made him smile, but then, Charlie didn't own a bicycle.

Roy hurried off to whatever fate held in store and Charlie ambled away until he was sure he could not be seen by Roy. Then Charlie ran the necessary few blocks as fast as he could toward the Fischer place. "Jackie's tire—down Castle Hill," he was panting, two minutes later.

Between Charlie's gasping and Aaron's translating, the boys were both hurrying back toward the Eighth-and-Nueces intersection before Aaron got it straight: Charlie hadn't been chased down the hill by a flaming tire. Moreover, as for what was about to happen, perhaps no one on Earth had a decent guess. Anyone who wonders what boys were created for might be directed to situations like this.

At the intersection they found Jackie peering up the hill, cursing, hands on hips as he watched a small figure at the hilltop wrestle a slightly smaller object that seemed determined to escape. He turned to see the newcomers settle at curbside and grumbled, "If that dumb B-Word rolls it in the gutter once more I'll let one of you guys do it."

Aaron: "Awww. You'd do that just for me?"

Charlie: "Your lucky day, Aaron." The sarcasm was elaborate.

Jackie could tell he would find no willing helper here. Always sensitive to teasing, he turned and glowered. "Or I could just pound your head up your A-Word if you get smart, Hardin."

"Sure, after you chase me up that tree." And Charlie took a few steps toward the same oak, fifty yards away, where Jackie had taken his lumps so recently.

Jackie calculated the distance to the oak and sprang forward with, "If you think I can't . . ."

But Aaron interrupted with, "Here it comes, guys," and the contest was instantly canceled. Judging by the slow wobbles and wavering atop the hill, no one could tell at first whether little Roy Kinney or the tire was controlling its descent, and Jackie stood transfixed, swaying from side to side as if hoping to steer them by example. A Packard sedan appeared on Nueces and cruised slowly past Jackie, the driver staring mystified at him without glancing higher to find the reason for the plump youth who seemed to be dancing a slow hula.

Charlie decided that no collision was likely with the car but, just in case, turned his face away hoping to remain anonymous. Aaron, carefully estimating the terrain in general, trotted backwards along the curb away from the intersection. If Jackie failed to corral the tire—now gathering speed at a frightening pace while Roy sprawled headfirst behind it—the job of stopping it might fall to Aaron.

With no other cars in sight, Charlie sprinted across Nueces and up the street's incline to Aaron while keeping his eye fixed on the tire, which now emitted a raspy humming whirr as it neared Nueces Street, and its noise must have been a song even Jackie could not ignore. It sang, "Here I come, all gooey burnt sticky twenty pounds of me, heading straight for you at forty miles an hour, and *you better be ready*, boy."

Jackie thought of the two impudent upstarts somewhere behind him, and his dimwit apprentice limping down the hill toward him, and chose courage over good sense. The tire hurtled down the exact center of the street, its hum now a musical note, and Jackie must have seen a split second beforehand that it would hit that S T O P sign squarely because he braced himself and prepared for the tire to rebound into him. He was prepared for it to sting a bit, but after all, it was only rubber.

What he didn't prepare for was the tire's Olympian leap from the iron pillow that was the stop sign, soaring over Jackie's shoulder to continue past the intersection as Aaron had suspected it might. Jackie floundered and spun on his heel, and saw the tire rush only a little more slowly toward the two witnesses as he shouted, "Grab it!"

The boys traded glances and shook their heads as one. "Rassle Porky Pig's unicycle? Nope," Aaron called, including the insult because Jackie was too busy to make him pay for it. Jackie hurled himself forward in pursuit of his property. As it passed Charlie in the street the tire had slowed further, moving roughly as fast as a boy might run, cresting the small rise and moving down the even gentler incline with nothing to stop it before West Avenue and, beyond that, the Shoal Creek bottomlands.

Meanwhile Roy trotted up favoring one leg, hoping he could draw enough attention to justify the spasm of boohoos he was saving. The others ignored him, too familiar with Roy's habits as a sympathy sponge. It seemed for a moment that Jackie might catch the tire but now it was gaining speed again. "C'monnn, Jackie," cried Aaron like a cheerleader.

"C'mon, tire," Charlie retorted, at which Aaron laughed so hard he snorted, then sat down on the curb holding his stomach. It was becoming more likely that no one would catch the tire until it found an obstacle, and Charlie joined Aaron in enjoying the situation. It may have been this lack of earnest support that made Jackie send a furious glance over his shoulder.

Roy inspected a rip in his pants. "He mad at me?"

"At everybody in the world," said Charlie, and Aaron could only nod.

"Boy, that durn tire musta been doing a million jillion lillion miles an hour," said Roy.

"That's crazy. I have an aunt named Lillian," said Charlie.

"She must be really, really big," said Roy, which set Aaron off again.

"She's little and kind of skinny," said Charlie.

"Then why do they call her Lillian?"

"Shut up, Roy," Aaron gasped. "I can't stand it."

The three boys sat on the curb and watched while Aaron caught his breath and Jackie grew smaller in the distance. As the tire entered the driveway of a stately home on West Avenue, Charlie squinted and shaded his eyes. "He better leave that thing where it fetches up," he said.

"Not him. He's no quitter," Aaron said, wiping his eyes.

A moment later they heard a faint, resounding *thump* as Jackie was trotting down that driveway, followed quickly by a symphony of breaking glass, as if all the old milk bottles in Austin had jumped off a cliff together.

Roy looked at Charlie, who looked at Aaron, who said, "We're two blocks away. Who's gonna blame any of us?"

"Whoever saw Roy start the tire, is who," said Charlie, and in an instant little Roy had left them, racing for home in the storm of tears he had thought he'd forgotten.

The two boys argued whether to walk in Jackie's direction until, minutes later, they saw him trotting back toward them. The tire was conspicuously missing. Though he wasn't moving fast, Jackie gave every sign of wishing he could, his chest and belly heaving with every step.

As Jackie drew near, Aaron stood and approached him but Jackie's exhausted headshake made questions pointless. "Castle—Bushes," were all Jackie could muster. Following the sore-footed Jackie across the street, they sank down half-hidden by grass between a spreading pomegranate bush and the castle's stone wall. Normally reddish, Jackie's complexion had become pale around his mouth but gradually he recovered enough to speak. "Tire's lost," he admitted.

"You mean like you can't find it," Charlie prompted.

"I know where. Under preserves," Jackie said. "Stuck under busted jars and shelves." As he fought for more breath, the silence built.

Aaron guessed, "That old garage was fulla preserves?"

A nod. "Back wall, on shelves. Oboy. Smelled like peaches. Some woman yellin' in the house but I got away."

Charlie and Aaron traded glances before Aaron said, "You wiped off what Roy chalked on the tire, then."

"He didn't write nothin," said Jackie.

"Said he did," Aaron insisted, "just before he started it

down." A pause while Jackie digested this idea. "Scared you'd kill him if it got away."

Jackie lay back on the grass and shut his eyes. "Maybe I'll kill him anyway. What'd he write?"

"He did you a favor," Charlie supplied, and looked at Aaron again. "Least he thought he did."

With all the energy he could muster, eyes still tightly closed: "*What'd he write,*" Jackie demanded.

"It said, 'Propety Jackie Ret.'" Aaron spelled it out. "Nobody knows who that is. You know Roy can't spell."

Something like a tiny strangled sob escaped from Jackie. "Nah," Charlie chipped in. "But just in case, what'll you say if they come for you?"

It was remarkable, under the circumstances, how quickly Jackie roused himself to hurry off for home snuffling. The others managed to keep their conspiracy silent until Jackie had turned a corner a block away. Then Charlie said, "What will he do when Roy tells him there wasn't any chalk?"

"Nothin'," Aaron shrugged. "Roy says the first thing that comes into his head."

"I reckon Jackie will have a choice. Believe a ten-year-old who still writes letters to Santa, or you and me."

"So Roy will prob'ly get the slats beat out of him anyhow. Doesn't hardly seem fair," said Aaron.

"It's what he gets for bein' Jackie's pal. You know how dumb he is," Charlie replied.

"Jackie, or Roy?"

"You choose," said Charlie. "I bet they spend the rest of today under beds somewhere." The boys grinned at each other, pleased with their deception.

And in the duration of a heartbeat, they forgot the whole business. Aaron said, "You know what? I really liked that orange box kite we saw at Woolworth's. Forgot to bring money."

"I know where you can get some. Kite line too, if you're

not scared to go after it," said Charlie. To sweeten the challenge while Aaron considered, he added, "And I'd buy an RC Cola for a guy with a new box kite."

The next second, they were trotting toward Shoal Creek with no idea of the danger they would soon face.

CHAPTER 14:
✈ PLAY MONEY ✈

While only halfway to the creek, Charlie noticed a rising lack of enthusiasm in his pal that soon became a list of reasons for not entering that storm drain. To one objection he replied, "Naw, we don't need my dog with us. Anyhow, what do you care, he's a worse scaredy-cat than you are."

When only a block from their goal, Aaron wondered out loud whether he could drive himself any farther through mortal exhaustion. "Jump on my back, I'll carry you the rest of the way," scoffed Charlie, who knew a flimsy excuse when he heard one.

Finally, when Charlie hopped up to the mouth of the concrete pipe, Aaron balked like a pony. "I didn't bring my flashlight," he said, refusing to accept a helping hand.

"Course you didn't. It's here, though. I left it up inside, remember?"

Aaron decided that Charlie's grin was a trifle too smart-alecky. "And how smart was that," he sneered, "when we'll have to feel our way up there in the dark just to reach it?"

"And so you get yourself a case of the sissy vapors, afraid

we might get lost in a plain straight pipe," Charlie retorted, refusing to back down an inch.

"I just don't feel like it today," said Aaron. "Hey, why don't we go to the castle and invade Normandy? We haven't done that yet. Yeah, that'd be keen, we'll wade ashore on Omaha Beach with tommy guns and you can be the fierce ol' sergeant and—"

"—And you can be the hero corporal who druther invade a million Nazis than go get your own money that's ten feet away."

Converting a hundred yards into ten feet as Charlie did for purposes of ridicule gave Aaron his turn to scoff, and he did it in tones loud enough to echo in the pipe. Had Bridger or Pinero been in the basement at this moment, several futures might have been less perilous. But the echoes faded while Charlie took a heroic pose, pointing into darkness.

"Okay, it's up to Charlie Hardin to go get you some light. When I turn the flashlight on up there, that's when you follow me. Right?" He took a step, then turned. "Right?" No reply.

Charlie knew his friend well. He had a vague understanding that some of Aaron's expressions, and his cautious ways, were flowers from seeds planted by a culture older than Rome. When a boy is soaked in the mysteries of a thing, that thing's power becomes magical. And some magical things can be awful, far worse than anything real—in the mind of the boy.

Charlie's magics were not as deeply rooted. He felt sure that once Aaron dared to stand in that pipe, to feel his wealth in his fingers, another fearsome fanged booger would evaporate from his imagination. So Charlie held his commanding pose and said very slowly, "Aaron Fischer, I've been up that thing and back. There's lots of money in there that already belongs to you. In fact, I just might put mine somewhere else but I won't move yours. In a minute there's gonna be a flashlight shining on it and if you won't come up and get it, I reckon somebody else would be happy to, if I told him it was there."

"Somebody like who?" Aaron did not like where this conversation was headed.

He liked it less when Charlie said, "Oh, anybody." The boys stared at each other. Aaron hesitated, reflecting that they knew one boy who was not a fearful sort when facing anything less than a police badge.

Sensing that the stakes needed to be raised, Charlie said, "Even some little kid. The dumbest kid you ever saw. A kid so dumb he'd tell everybody and show the treasure around and let some bigger kid cheat him out of it."

Aaron let a brief movie run through his mind. He knew exactly which dumb little kid and which bigger kid Charlie had in mind. The prospect of watching this happen, or hearing about it, or even thinking about it afterward, was a thorn stabbing into his sense of right and wrong. And it would be embarrassing in a way that Aaron rarely experienced. And Charlie, blunt and direct as a billy goat, was a kid who could make it all happen. "I hate your guts, Charlie Hardin. Help me up there," he said.

Charlie was pleased to lead, imagining that all was well again, familiar with the gloomy aspect of the pipe ahead and the way it seemed well lit when he glanced behind. He could feel the hand grasping the back of his belt and kept up a commentary intended to be useful. "You wanta straddle the grit, and keep a hand on the side of the pipe to steady you," he said, and, "Look back now and then and see what we passed," and "Up ahead there's a littler pipe that comes in on the left side, maybe big enough for your ol' booger cat." This earned him a set of knuckles jabbed hard against his backbone. "Well, don't blame me, it's your stupid cat," he joked. "And anyhow, it's where our stuff is." He found, also, that it was easier to be cheerful in such a place if he kept up a constant stream of chatter.

Presently they came to the smaller pipe where, as he expected, Charlie found the money, marbles, and flashlight. Aaron wasted no time in flicking his flashbeam on and off, directing it here and there while Charlie implored him to keep it on the treasure. "You wanta get some of this stuff or not?" Charlie asked crossly.

Aaron said nothing, but he counted out a small trove of coins, paused, then took a few coin rolls. "It's funny how we can't see ahead but we can see our way back real easy from here to the creek, even without the light," Charlie said. And because he was getting no replies, he went on, "Want me to show you those ol' bottles that broke and we dropped them down here?" Aaron turned away without a word and set off up the pipe ahead of him using the flashlight.

With Charlie now in the rear they advanced farther into the storm drain. Charlie was encouraged by the way his pal moved forward, and imagining that his role in Aaron's progress was a cause for self-congratulation, asked, "Now, aren't you glad you're not scared anymore?" Again Aaron ignored him, but stopped and squatted when they reached the glistening shards of bottles they had disposed of months before. Aaron studied the faint daylight reflected down from the street grating.

Then an errant flick of the flashbeam revealed something in the pipe farther ahead, and Aaron advanced near enough to recognize debris in a large rupture in one side of the pipe.

Charlie stepped forward as Aaron looked again at the jumble of stuff in the pipe. "I'm sure glad I made you come up here," Charlie prodded, hoping for a reply, only to be disappointed. By now Charlie was growing impatient for conversation and made a comment he thought might provoke a response, the way a boy might set off a Baby Giant firecracker in an antbed. "I reckon you're real lucky you have a buddy good as me to look out for you, guy. If it wasn't for me—"

"If it wasn't for you I'd be out in the sun flying a kite," Aaron burst out, and his flick of a switch put them into near-perfect blackness. "I wouldn't be in a hole in the ground that stinks like dead stuff! I'd be just fine outside by myself, or across town on my bike with some other guy who's not so pea-brained dangerous his dad won't let him loose on wheels without a babysitter!"

The fact that Charlie was in darkness getting shouted at into his face so near he could feel the spray of spit on his cheeks made this explosion more flabbergasting. Then the flabbergaster flicked the light switch on to see the flabbergastee's reaction. Charlie stood slack-jawed, in need of time to fully realize how far his good intentions had gone astray. Could this loud, furious accuser be even distant kin to the quiet, calm Aaron he knew so well? Had Charlie in fact just possibly said or done some eensy teensy little thing to light Aaron's fuse? Charlie hung his head and thought about this. And then he focused on the debris at his feet and his thoughts expanded.

Aaron half-expected his pal to shout back. The other half of his expectation was that, after hearing a few things about himself that Aaron had kept in a shadowed corner of his soul, Charlie would turn all remorseful and beg his pardon for being such a blossoming bumptious inflated strutting common Christian jackass.

But Charlie did neither of these things. Instead, he kept his gaze down, moving his lips slightly as he sometimes did when his thoughts were most creative. Or when, as Aaron had seen many times, his friend was trying not to laugh but close to doing it anyway. Well, he'd better not be about to laugh now. If he was, he'd get a bloody nose for it. He'd wind up here by himself in the dark with—"Charlie Hardin, you better not laugh. I'll pound you one in your piehole if you snicker at me," Aaron said, near angry tears.

"You're not even looking," Charlie replied, and bent

down. "Here's a dollar, right here next to us and you don't see it. Neither did I. How long you think it's been here, guy?" And with that, he pulled a small green piece of paper from a scatter of dirt-flecked trash.

"That's not ours," Aaron whispered. "It looks new, even if it's crinkly." Charlie gasped as he stretched the wrinkles from what appeared to be a twenty-dollar bill, then found another similar scrap of paper. Both bills went into Charlie's pocket immediately. "Forty bucks, Charlie?" The change in Aaron's voice was sudden. "Aw, I get it. Play money." His sigh had an echo. "This is why you brung me, to see junk you put here before. Caught you, didn't I?" His anger faded on deciding that he had outfoxed his trickster.

"Shine the light over to the side again," Charlie said, in tones that suggested he wasn't listening. "No, over here," he insisted, and put a hand over Aaron's. "Yeah. I thought I saw something funny through the hole."

The flashbeam shone partly on concrete but also beyond it, through the man-sized hole that someone had bashed in the pipe. Both boys now knelt and peered through loose earth into what seemed to be an ordinary basement with an ordinary door through which they saw part of an ordinary staircase in the distance. "Golll-leee, this must be somebody's bank," said Aaron, awed by the idea.

"It was ours first," Charlie said firmly. "People can't just go put stuff in a guy's hideyhole without asking. It's no fair."

"I dunno. You ever been in a real bank, like those buildings downtown where it says 'Bank' across the front?" To this Charlie could only grunt. "Well I have, with my dad a long time ago, and we weren't the only ones there. And you were supposed to go up to people behind cages like they were in a zoo."

"Like the circus wild man from Borneo?" said Charlie. "That's weird."

"No, there was a big hole with a shelf in front of the cage so I think the bank guys coulda crawled out if they wanted to. They talked to you when you went up to a cage. My dad doesn't talk Borneose so I guess they talk like us. I don't remember, I wasn't tall enough to see in the cage. Besides, other folks were doing stuff at other cages. I think they give their money to the cage guys."

"I still don't think it's fair," said Charlie.

"My dad agrees," Aaron replied. "Banks aren't fair. They lost a lot of his money back when I was a baby. But he still goes there, I think. I don't understand why. It's kinda confusing."

While engaged in this talk of high finance, they continued to peer into the basement as Aaron let the flashbeam wander. They could see shelves with boxes, rags, and jugs of fluids as well as a large metal gadget standing tall on legs that threw fitful shadows against a wall. Finally Charlie said, "What if this is the cellar of a bank where they make the money? I mean, it's gotta be made someplace. They keep money in banks; I figure they probably make it there. Why don't we go in there and see?" And with this, Charlie took a careful forward step.

But with that, the flashbeam was no more. "Nope. This is some big bohunkus trick of yours with play money, and you're gonna get us both in trouble, only I'm not gonna let you."

"Durn if you're not. Gimme the flashlight."

"No. That's how I know you're not gonna." Aaron had moved back now, only a dim shape amid deeper blackness. "It'll be black as the inside of a cow in there. If that's a bank, with you stumbling around knocking stuff over, they're gonna hear you. There's two kinds of guys down in the bottom of a bank: bankers and robbers. If you're not one of the bankers . . ."

To keep from having to hear the rest of this prediction,

Charlie burst out, "You're not the boss of me. I'm gonna get me a flashlight,"

"Not right now you're not," said Aaron.

"Well I just bet I will too," Charlie said, and lurched sideways to grab the nearest portion of Aaron. But all portions jumped away instantly, so that Charlie slipped in the pipe debris. His quarry was as quick as Charlie himself, and though still bent over, Aaron managed a staggering trot toward the distant dazzle of the outdoors. He ran safely ahead of Charlie whose threats only made Aaron run faster.

In only a moment Charlie could tell that his attempt to snatch the flashlight was hopeless, and he was reminded of his marbles and coins in the simplest way: he banged his ankle against the lip of the smaller pipe they lay on and then fell on his stomach.

The Charlie who hobbled out of the drainpipe a minute later moved a lot slower than the Charlie who had tried to grab the flashlight, and once he was out of the musty cool dark he had to admit to himself that an adventure into the basement of somebody else's bank was perhaps not the most brilliant idea of his career. He sat down under the fig tree to inspect his offended ankle and felt a bit better when he saw the trickle of crimson there. Anything that stung so much, he felt, had better bleed a little. Too bad Aaron had sped off like a rabbit; there was always a measure of manliness in blood.

"Bunged yourself up, huh?" said a familiar voice. "I wondered why it took you so long."

Now Charlie saw his pal peering from behind the trunk of a towering pecan tree fifty feet away. "I had to get my stuff, didn't I," he called, and held up the marble bag with one hand. With the other he used a fingertip to smear blood around on his foot in an arrangement he thought might add a dramatic touch.

Aaron moved away from concealment with the wariness of a boy who wasn't quite sure the chase was over. "Cut yourself in those busted bottles?"

"Nah. Just a scratch," said Charlie, telling the truth as if it were a huge understatement. Yet something in Aaron's tone suggested that he wasn't as impressed as a wounded hero might wish. To prove he was still capable of adventure Charlie pulled some of the stuff from a pocket, studied the contents, and said, "Trade you my roll of nickels for that ol' flashlight."

Aaron turned his back to check on his goods. A moment later: "Shoot, Charlie, it cost me more'n that."

A pang of irritation shot through Charlie, seeing that Aaron would take his dare as far as this. "Okay, twenty bucks. Right here," he said, holding up a bill.

Aaron moved forward, drawn as if magnetized by money. "You're not going in there, guy."

"You see if I don't," was the retort. Charlie hadn't intended to actually follow up on his foolish impulse, but Aaron's resistance had lit a fire under that impulse.

Aaron moved still nearer, holding the flashlight. As Charlie stood up, Aaron said, "Just drop the money down in the gravel there and I'll toss you the light." Instead, Charlie limped down to the storm drain's dry watercourse and placed the bill on the gravel. Aaron motioned him back, then tossed the flashlight across and knelt down to grasp the bill while watching his old friend for any false move.

Charlie caught the flashlight and watched Aaron. "Think you're so durn smart," he said, starting to convince himself that yes, D-Word it, he *would* go back in there and show that cowardly Aaron what's what and who's who.

But Aaron had backed away again to a safe distance. "I'm smart enough for the honor roll. And a bike. Not like some guys I know," he said.

"But not smart enough to know plain ol' play money

when you see it," Charlie said, with a teasing singsong cadence. And waited for Aaron's fury.

Which seemed almost to develop, until overtaken by laughter that would be hard for Aaron to fake. Aaron held the bill with both hands, turning it over again and again, and then waved Charlie off. "Go ahead, I dare you," he said, still laughing. "I'll wait. Double dare. Triple," he added as Charlie limped to the drainpipe.

Charlie glowered at this. A guy's best pal, even one you're mad at, wasn't supposed to issue a challenge that potent. Goaded to this extreme, he set off hobbling into the pipe. Ten seconds later he emerged again, keeping his face as free of aggravation as he could. He thumbed the flashlight switch back and forth several times without result, confirming what he had just discovered in the pipe. "What'd you do, Aaron?"

Aaron held up a single dry-cell battery between thumb and forefinger. "Took this out. It needs two. Trade you this one for the rest of your coins," he said, in a singsong that imitated Charlie's much too well. In an attempt to simmer down, Charlie took several deep breaths, standing wordless, hurling mighty frowns in his pal's direction, then dropped the flashlight on the ground and began to study the contents of his pockets.

"Awww, Charlie." Aaron's tone shifted into some near neighbor of begging. "I don't want your money. Don't do this, guy. I wouldn't trade you this lousy ol' battery now for everything in the world."

Charlie's question was equally passionate. "Why not?"

"'Cause I don't want you to get in trouble, so I did what I had to do."

"You pulled a dirty trick on me, is what you did."

"We pulled dirty tricks on each other at the same time, and no matter how bad you want this battery, bunged up like you are right now you can't catch me and you know it, and there's something we need to think about that might be a lot more important than which one of us gets his way. Everybody knows you're the crown prince of stubborn, okay? You win. You're the stubbornest cuss I know."

Gradually, Charlie's face went through subtle changes of shape and of color too, as his inner juices ceased bubbling to the point where he could say, "Wellll, at least we got that settled," as if satisfied that he'd won a major point in their contest. Then he took his place below the fig tree again, smoothing out the paper from his pocket. "It's about what to do with this play money, right?"

CHAPTER 15:
✈ FINDERS KEEPERS ✈

The greatest arguments fester around the grubbiest details. Charlie's first impression of those bills was that they were real, and worth what the numbers said, so he held fast to that position. But Aaron, instantly favoring the idea that Charlie had placed the bills there, maintained that they must be worthless play money, part of some infernal plot of Charlie's.

The discussion was soon marked by claims so loud they vibrated in the storm drain. "Even if it's like Monopoly money, somebody else put it there," Charlie said at last. "And it looks real. Half-real, anyhow." He turned the better of the two bills over to study its blank side, then made a hopeful guess. "Maybe it's worth half of what it says. Ten bucks, prob'ly."

By this time they sat side by side, loud arguments being preferable to wrestling around in the shrubbery. "How about this one, then?" Aaron said, squinting at the other bill. Most of it looked genuine but perhaps a fourth of it was badly smeared.

"One end's just crud. I wouldn't give you more'n five or six bucks for that sorry excuse for money," said Charlie.

"You wouldn't give me a penny for it," Aaron countered, "'cause you know it's not real."

"Wait a minute." When Charlie shifted down to a studious tone it suggested a new line of reasoning. "My mom found some money in my dad's pants once in the washing. And when she dried it out it was still good. Play money would, I dunno, fade or rub out or get all gooshy or something. Wouldn't it?"

"How would I know, you're the play-money expert. Why not try wetting it in the creek?" Aaron began to doubt his plot theory the moment Charlie nodded and limped down to the ankle-deep stream that was Shoal Creek. Aaron followed, reflecting that Charlie's willingness to test the bills might mean he was not scheming but truly curious.

After squatting to dunk the bill, Charlie rubbed it and eyed it closely. Next he repeated the experiment, rubbed some more, then glanced up to his pal with a vexed expression. "It doesn't run or fade, but it kinda peels a little. Real money's more like cloth, I think."

"I thought so. Play money," said Aaron. "Where'd you get it, anyhow?"

"For the last time," Charlie began, standing up, his face stormy.

Aaron waved his hands before him, discarding the last of his theory. "Okay, I take it back; they weren't yours. So they've gotta be from whoever owns that bank you were gonna rob."

"I never!"

"Well, you woulda gone down in there if I hadn't stopped you," Aaron amended, stepping away to prepare an escape.

But Charlie stubbornly continued to use logic. He limped back to their cozy bower under the fig. "Going down there, yeah. That's a durn sight different." Aaron's tiny snort conveyed more argument, so Charlie demanded, "Is taking a look the same as robbing? Is your bike the same as a Greyhound bus? Nuh-uh. If I robbed an actual bank my dad would skin me."

"You mean, after you got outta the jail he put you in," Aaron reminded him, settling his rump, forearms resting on knees.

They stared gloomily at the wrinkled mysteries on display at their feet, so deep in thought that the buzz of locusts went unnoticed. Finally Charlie said, "Banks are supposed to look like banks, right? But if you stand in the street outside and look across the front yard from the curb, you don't see a bank. It's just that ol' gray haunted house nobody lives in with the sign in the yard. Who would have a secret bank?"

"We would, that's who," said Aaron. "Maybe some banker downtown makes all their money here."

Charlie considered this. "He sure makes some trashy stuff," he said, then brightened. "I bet that's it. When he bakes up a bad batch, the guy just throws it away. Like this."

"They don't bake it," said Aaron, and saw the urge to argue rise in his pal again. "Awright, maybe they do. And if a person found their trash and spent it, like a special sale, why would they care?"

"Yeah. They're rich," Charlie said. "It's not like it was costing them anything." A pause, as their eyes met. "You thinking what I'm thinking?"

"Yep, if you're thinking we didn't go into their basement so we didn't do anything wrong. If it's not on their property, you said yourself, finders keepers."

The boys were nodding in unison now. Charlie smoothed out the two bills, folded and pocketed them. "Only thing is, we need to find out if this is worth something. My dad would prob'ly know. Or yours."

"Oh, suuuure." The reply was rich with sarcasm. "And then you get to explain where we got it, and you and me get to hang out with each other once a year. C'mon, guy, the only way we get to play at the creek is because everybody thinks we're someplace else. If my mom had any idea you bullied me into that sewer pipe, dad would have to coax her down off the roof. And I don't fib and neither do you, exactly." Aaron's "exactly" admitted the way they tiptoed around falsehoods, making sure they never made a foray along the creek without going elsewhere as well so that, if asked, they could always name another location.

"Well, we could just go downtown and ask a bank," Charlie said.

This new point had to be thrashed to splinters in the usual way, until Aaron hit on a variation both simple and direct. "Okay, why not ask the bank people in the haunted house? I don't give a rip what the sign in the front says, we know somebody's there."

To Charlie this idea had charm because it could be tested in moments. Its drawback was that somebody else had thought of it, but Charlie was prepared to be generous. "We have to make 'em promise not to tell our folks," he said.

So it was agreed, and in another five minutes they had followed one of several footpaths worn up to the street by generations of boys.

Whoever first labeled the old stucco-clad house as haunted had done the owner a favor. Boys playing "tag" or "kick the can" tended to stay beyond its grounds while claiming a total lack of fear. On this late afternoon in a dazzle of sunlight, the place did not seem forbidding for the two boys. Together they marched up to the front porch past an untended yard where weeds fought for survival. A few of last year's faded newspapers lay unclaimed near the door. Charlie sought a doorbell in vain, then knocked.

"Banks aren't locked in daytime," Aaron said, tried the doorknob, then shrugged.

"That's all you know," said Charlie, and knocked harder with the same result.

Next they peered through the one front window that lacked a fully drawn shade, seeing only a few old magazines and footprints in the dust of a floor without furniture or carpet. "Heck of a bank this is," Charlie grumped.

"Kinda late. Maybe they went home," Aaron said, turning his head westward for a quick judgment of the sun's position, their usual timepiece. "Hey, I gotta go home too, pretty soon. Mom wanted me to go to the store before dinner." And he started placing his goods on the porch, reserving a few cents for a pocket. Charlie followed suit. Their problem of the moment, too well-understood to need conversation, was bulging pockets; both boys were convinced that their mothers had the eyes of hawks. To avoid questions they squatted on the porch and unfolded a yellowed copy of the daily *Austin American Statesman,* wrapping bundles that Charlie would be obliged to smuggle home somehow. In the process, they agreed to return in midmorning when they expected that bankers would all be hard at work printing money.

Charlie found more cause to grumble while walking the last blocks home alone carrying an assortment of stuff he would not have wanted to explain. He had half-decided to hide it all in someone's shrubbery before he arrived home, when he remembered that he had made that mistake once before with a pair of yellow organic hand grenades. He might never learn when Roy Kinney had found those terrifying eggs, but the Kinney boy had a troubling habit when he played alone: he would sit concealed by whatever was handy and watch the world do whatever worlds do. For all Charlie knew, instead of hiding indoors after the Runaway Tire Experiment the smaller boy might be somewhere nearby, hunkered down like a toad, watching him at that very moment.

Presently a squirrel scooted across the street, and as he reflected on the banking practices of these furry little rogues, Charlie's frown softened. His face became tranquil, then began to show signs of downright pleasure. It would suit him just fine if Roy was spying because the more Roy longed to swipe this stuff, the more he would be frustrated by a place he was too small to reach.

Charlie squeezed between the bars of the castle courtyard and made a final inspection of descending branches from the huge live oak to assure himself that Roy was not tall enough to imitate him. Then, with a parcel stuffed into his shirt, he made his way high into the tree and chose a crotch near its center. Needing two trips, he made his deposits in the tree and minutes later as he strolled within sight of home, he whistled for Lint.

Charlie often wondered where the terrier roamed when left to his own dog-gone affairs. Often as not the dog would be away on some solitary business, but beyond doubt, if Lint knew Charlie's whereabouts he would try to be there too. Lint was an outdoor dog, not because he or Charlie wanted it so, but because Willa Hardin's rules applied inside the house. If she'd had her way the Hardins might have had an indoor dog instead, one of those pocket-sized trembling, snapping, yapping mites unfit for real live weather, with long yellow fur sticking out as if its nose is stuck in a light socket.

Lint had been accepted because Coleman Hardin, raised with farm dogs, could not abide a pooch that cringes from kittens and looks like a muff on legs. In comparison to such a joke of a dog, Coleman felt, Lint was a regular fellow eligible for an occasional headscratch. To Charlie's dad, Lint might have been welcome inside the house if not on Charlie's bed. Yet Mrs. Hardin had a horror of fleas, and she had noticed that Lint could usually scratch up one or two when he needed them for company. While he was only a pup Lint had found the need to add Willa Hardin's *"shoo!"* to his vocabulary.

So in fairness to all, Charlie and his dad put an outside doghouse together from scrap lumber and old shingles, adding a decrepit remnant of carpet for its floor. When the weather turned wet or frigid Lint might be found inside, nose poking out, eyes bright with hopes of entertainment.

Long after midnight, Charlie's eyes snapped open. If a dream prompted him, it was one he could not recall, but whatever the cause, he was instantly alert, responding to alarms that clanged in his head. Every detail of the situation might as well have had searchlights trained on it. He had been so amused, so proud of himself for being as smart as a two-pound acorn thief, making sure that even if sneaky little Roy were watching him establish his hiding place, Roy could not climb up to burgle it.

Not by himself, no. *But Jackie could.* And Roy was often so lacking in wit and so desperate for companionship, he would attach himself to bad company. While Charlie lazed at home, and later slept the sleep of innocence, what was to prevent Roy from teaming up with Jackie in the crime of the century? Judging from his everyday habits, Jackie had scribbled "finders keepers" across the inside of his skull.

It did not occur to Charlie that Roy thought he had reason, at least temporarily, to avoid moving within arm's reach of his criminal mastermind. Or that neither of these larval criminals had any idea whether Charlie's hiding place held anything worth taking. Or that even if Jackie took up such an expedition he would be a raving lunatic to do it after dark, and if he had done it in daylight, nothing could be done about it now.

What did occur to Charlie was the nagging fear that, if Gene Carpenter could extract a bazillion golf balls from a creekside alone in the dead of night, some other boy might climb the great-granddaddy of all oaks in darkness for more valuable stuff. Would Jackie do such a thing? He might. Would Aaron? Too careful. Would Charlie? He might have saved himself the effort of asking because two things made the answer obvious. Any legal risk Jackie Rhett might take, Charlie felt required to take. And if that tree-crotch held goods that were Aaron's property—*for which Charlie was responsible*—no doubt remained. So . . .

It was up to Charlie Hardin.

As soon as summery weather allowed, Charlie always shoved his bed so near his bedroom window that, with the window fully raised, he could push his pillow onto the windowsill and sleep with his head touching the wire screen. The screen was kept from swinging out only by a hook-and-eye arrangement, and the flowerbed below it could be reached without jumping. Charlie had never thought it useful to unhook the screen. Until now. To tiptoe outside through the kitchen meant certain arrest because between his bed and the kitchen door lay at least three floorboards guaranteed to creak a symphony of parent-alerts.

Short pants and a T-shirt lay at the foot of his bed. With the first "snick" of the screen hook a faint growl sounded somewhere near, but the sentry investigated in silence and as Charlie slid out past the sill headfirst, his cheeks were bathed in canine kisses. Neighborhood porch lights were rarely lit in the wee hours. The glow of the nearest streetlight was distant, with trees providing shadowy cover for a small person in a hurry.

The night was so still Charlie could hear the padding of his own bare feet and the nails of Lint's paws as they scuffed a curb en route to the castle. Something rustled in a flowerbed and Lint made a rough comment but stayed at his master's feet. Something else hurried across the street in a noiseless glide, a temptation Lint resisted with a repressed whine. The tune Charlie hummed was intended to bolster his dog's spirit but it worked just as well for the hummer. The car that sped down Nueces avenue did not catch boy or dog in its headlights because the stealthy pair had passed between iron bars into the castle courtyard seconds earlier.

The night sky of a small city has a glow of its own, created by commercial lighting. But in Austin, a unique kind of false moonlight added to the luster. Decades before, celebrating the coming of the Twentieth Century, city fathers had decided on modern street lights—and yes, by jingo, Texas-sized lights while they were at it. As the capital city of a state gifted with more money than good sense, Austin could have spidery steel "moonlight towers" if it wanted them.

It did want them, dozens of them spaced across the city, each with six lamps hanging a hundred and sixty feet in the sky. By now, Austin children who visited other cities often felt uneasy in places that lacked a swarm of moons above their horizon all night, every night.

Before this Charlie had always thought of his city's perpetual moonlight in a friendly way, but as a slinker through the night he now saw it was a treacherous guide, casting shadows that made ordinary objects seem undependable. The first time he missed a handhold in the tree, Charlie nearly fell. The second time was worse; this time he slid sideways while straddling a limb as thick as his waist, and regained his balance with enough struggle-and-grunt that Lint, on sentry duty twenty feet below, sent whines of concern his way.

And that was where Charlie stopped.

Not by intention. It was not part of his master plan to twist and turn and scrabble and strain and fight and cuss and squint and discover that a thumb-sized oak stub had somehow snuck through one of the empty belt loops in the back of his pants to hook him firmly on his perch, but by the time he tired himself out he had discovered that the most masterful plan can go wrong. To Lint's encouraging whine he could only reply with hoarse whispers and resume his struggle. If he could see the wooden culprit clearly, he might slide around enough to slip away. If he could tear that sturdy belt loop loose, he might at least climb back down. If he could unbutton his pants and climb out of them, he might be on the way to success in his birthday suit—but none of these things was possible. In a city known for producing dusk all night, Charlie had trapped himself in a tree that furnished deep shadow. His only hope, short of shouting for help, was sunlight, and in late June the dawn would come early enough that a boy snared by his own muddleheadedness might speed home before anyone missed him.

So for several years—or roughly three hours as adults would measure—Charlie straddled his branch and first, to avoid dying of boredom, composed explanations that might come in handy if he had to yell for help. Then a taxi raced down Nueces at breakneck speed, its identity light flickering, and Charlie invented tales to explain its hurry. Later he was slumped almost asleep, held upright by a hundred leafy twigs, when distant sirens began to warble on another street, to strengthen with roars of laboring engines, and finally to fade away to provide him with more fables.

At some point, he realized that this twilight imprisonment had its own romance. The paper boy on a bicycle with a single powerful headlight never stopped, but he had a big leaguer's arm and the smack of morning papers against porches along the street suggested he had done this many times. A milkman's chugging old vehicle must have stopped a dozen times while in view and took that many minutes to do it, but when he was gone, Charlie sort of missed him. The most peculiar passage, though, was one Charlie had heard about, though never seen. A shadowy figure of his own height led a goat by a cord, both almost trotting, in the direction of West Avenue where Mexican families lived along the opposite side of the creek where Charlie and his pals played.

Charlie knew there was little grass in the Latino neighborhood, and no parks there. Plenty of forage for a goat in the little parks near the center of town, though. Some Tex-Mex teenager was grazing the family milk-ewe through the city's small hours. Shortly afterward, he heard the first sleepy chirps from neighborhood sparrows. Dawn crept into his leafy prison as Lint remained on guard.

Renewing his struggle to escape that stub branch, Charlie gained only a crick in his neck until, at last, he was able to see that the stub wasn't projecting in the direction he had imagined. When his belt loop popped loose he almost fell, so exhausted and gritty-eyed by now that every step was painful while he retrieved the treasures he had come for. With Lint trotting beside him Charlie scurried home composing excuses, slumping in relief when he discovered that the Hardin household still echoed a duet of snores.

He hid his valuables in the garage. A quick hug for his companion, a slow climb past the windowsill, weary exertions to latch the screen and slip from his clothes, and Charlie lay once again on a cool cotton sheet over a friendly mattress. He was asleep in seconds and didn't stir for hours.

CHAPTER 16:
✈ A WAY TO PASS THE BUCKS ✈

It was Charlie's habit in summertime to be up and buzzing before the cicadas, so his mother worried when she had to rouse him at midmorning. "I swear, sleepyhead, you'd think this was a school day," she said fondly, and laid her palm across his forehead to check him for fever.

Charlie managed a grunt but not much else, eyes still closed as he relished the cool of his mother's fingers. His ankle hurt a little and his neck was stiff as rawhide, but even half-asleep he knew better than to complain about either. During the school year he would have made a life or death issue of his stiff neck, and Willa Hardin would have just as surely evicted him from bed, with a splash of cold water down his back if the situation required. Summer ailments were another matter. She valued a school-year pain at one-tenth its value to Charlie, and a summer pain at ten times its Charlie-value. So he yawned and blinked with no sign of discomfort as those soothing fingers touseled his hair.

When the fingers withdrew, they held something that made Charlie's blood freeze like a popsicle. It was an oak twig, a pair of tiny leaves spread winglike from it. "Charlie,

Charlie, Charlie," his mother said softly, sitting down on his bed, "what are we going to do about you?"

Three Charlies in a row made it serious. Because it would hurt his neck to shrug, he murmured, "I dunno," and waited to be slathered in guilt for sneaking out and accidentally spending the night in a tree. His dad tended to aim thunder and lightning in his direction but spiced the mix with sarcasm. His mother's punishments submerged him in a syrup of loving disappointment that was worse.

"We try to keep track of your needs, we really do," she said, idly untwisting ends of the sheet that had coiled around his feet. "Your father is a good provider. You don't lack for clean sturdy clothes. Coleman insisted that you have a room of your own, and I try to see that your meals match the appetite of a growing boy."

She turned a sorrowing gaze on him and Charlie gazed back, in full agreement with all she said, more ashamed of his failings with every passing moment. He waited to hear her reveal her deduction that he had been adventuring while she slept. "We take an interest in your schooling; we don't ignore the kinds of playmates you choose. You even have an allowance."

Now he saw the moisture in her eyes and forgave her for the skull-rattling blunder she had made so recently by setting him loose in the care of a seemingly presentable outlaw genius like Eugene Carpenter. This was not the moment to bring up such things, and he could only nod. At that instant his feet appeared from his bedding and seeing them in the full Technicolor of dirt, grass stains, street tar, tree sap and shreds of bark between his toes, she gasped in dismay, still holding the oak twig in her free hand. "But this is how I let you go to bed, like a wild Indian waif without a parent in this world," she finished, leaning down to take him in her embrace. "Forgive me, Charlie." And she began to sniffle.

Charlie needed a few seconds while understanding flooded into his noggin. He had been prepared for this catalogue of parenting virtues to be followed by a list of the ways that he had failed them. Instead, his mother had ended with—could it be?—a confession of *her* imaginary sin!

Charlie patted her shoulder. "Aw, Mom," he said, pulling an offending foot back under the sheet.

But she was not to be denied. "Donald Charles Hardin, don't you hide my flaws under that sheet for another second," she said, abruptly recovering now that she had hit on a remedy. "You're going to take that hot bath I should have made you take last night. Be sure to get the shrubs out of your hair when you wash it. Meanwhile your lazy mother will change your bedding and fix you a decent breakfast."

She pulled away the covers, noticing the scratches on his hide, accepting them as reproaches to her mothering. Charlie scrambled from his bed before she could count all his new blemishes, hurrying to the bathroom with what might have been suspicious speed in a boy who wasn't overly fond of hot baths.

His long soak in hot water did wonders for his neck. Afterward, while mouth-watering fragrances floated out from the kitchen, he found a fresh pair of knee-length khaki pants and a hated short-sleeved shirt of the ironed-for-Sunday variety laid out on his bed, and something told him that on this one day he would be wise to wear whatever his mom had chosen for him.

Sure enough, a single place-setting waited for him in the breakfast nook and the ruins of three oranges in the sink promised freshly squeezed juice, a treat he had last enjoyed at his birthday breakfast. Two fried eggs and a stack of miniature pancakes shared his plate with fingers of pork sausage—his favorites, and a rarity. He used too much butter and far too much molasses and knew his mom watched him do it without protest, and he considered asking for a quarter to spend on a toy but relented out of a sense of fair play. It was likely, after all, that he had recently accumulated more wealth than her purse held.

He cleared the table himself to prove his gratitude, sealed it with a kiss on her cheek, and took its twin in return. By this time Charlie felt like the rascal he was, brimful of breakfast and topped off with guilt. He hurried off with the disclosure that he "might see Aaron at the playground," to leave the impression that the schoolground was his goal. In his mind this wasn't perjury; Charlie was sure to see Aaron, and almost every other boy he knew, at the school playground—sometime during the next few months, anyway.

His first thought was to seek Aaron at home but found out, en route, that Jackie had already made peace with Roy. The two knelt down the street by a curb in full view of the giant oak that had held Charlie prisoner, and they were entertaining red ants with a magnifying glass. Charlie declined the older boy's offer to take the glass and "touch one up" because Jackie declared it was worth a nickel to see one of the hated half-inch stinging demons shrivel to a cinder in the glass's bright pinpoint of sunlight. When that bid failed, Jackie floated the idea that Charlie might at least pay a penny to watch someone else punish the ants. Yet he saw something in Charlie's eye—or heard it in his refusal— that he often met in older boys. It was a mix of patience and scorn, and it sent Jackie back to the big sandy circle the ants had cleared of all vegetation. A circle of utterly bare dirt as wide as a truck tire, with a pencil-sized hole in its center, was the signature of an active red-ant bed.

As Charlie turned to go Roy said, just to be sociable, "Aaron came by on his bike, 'way earlier. Headed to town."

Jackie looked up from his instrument of torture. "Big important business, I bet," he said, his tone denying it.

Roy had not grown old enough to know sarcasm

when it surrounded him. "Yeah, maybe. In a big hurry," he put in.

Of all the things Charlie could do without this morning, a confusing and disagreeable conversation with Jackie ranked high on the list. Nor did Charlie think anything could be gained by revealing any of his recent discoveries so, "Reckon I'll just go paste stamps," he sighed, and turned toward home. This was intended to ward off attempts by either boy to tag along, and it worked. All the boys had experienced Charlie's stamp collection and all shared a single opinion. Even Aaron had proclaimed this venture "the world's boringest way to poison yourself" after helping lick dozens of tiny cellophane tapes that affixed stamps into a booklet. Roughly once a week, at times when he wanted to be by himself, Charlie vowed to go paste stamps. In truth, he hadn't seen that collection in months and wasn't sure where he had put it.

Charlie intended to call to see if Aaron had returned home, since his own mother was in such a tolerant mood. The Hardin telephone was normally reserved for adults because in 1944 the telephone company had not yet added signals that let a user know, while he is talking, that someone else is trying to call. Charlie's call proved unnecessary because, as he greeted Lint and angled toward the family driveway, both heard a squeal they knew as the voice of Aaron's bike brake approaching from downtown. Bikeless, Charlie watched with a twinge of hope. Aaron had already developed a devil-may-care mastery when dismounting his steed on loose surfaces, and when he eventually bashed himself to shreds Charlie didn't want to miss a second of it.

Avoiding a spray of gravel, Charlie greeted his pal with, "Your mom send you downtown?"

"Nah. Had a great idea," Aaron replied, "and went and checked. A kid can just walk right into a bank alone! There's even a little bitty cage off to itself with a guy with bars over his counter where they have bills I never saw before behind a glass case. Lots of different colors and names like peso and sol and stuff. I ask if they print all that different money downstairs and he laughs and says there's banks all over the world. So the money we have isn't the only kind there is. You ever hear of a bank of Scotland?"

"Nope. Don't care neither," Charlie replied. "I can't even speak Scotlandish. They print that in the basement too?"

"I don't know, a guy stopped me when I started downstairs to see where they print their money."

The boys moved into the garage to discuss it with their treasures close at hand. It was on the tip of Charlie's tongue to describe his misadventure during the night, but decided the story wouldn't shower him with respect. Instead, he took a listener's role.

Aaron hadn't been allowed downstairs at the bank because, he said, "This guy told me I needed a safe deposit box. I said no I didn't and he said that's all they had down there. Well, I know that's a lie, we saw a bank print shop yesterday."

"What's a safe deposit box?"

"Beats me. Anyhow, then he says do I have an account and I says on account of what and he looks at me squinch-eyed and says do I know what an account is and I'm not a big fan of being laughed at, or lied to, so I walk out intending to slam the door."

"What'd he do then?"

"Nuthin'. You can't slam a revolving door, Charlie."

After mentally chewing all this over, Charlie said, "I think maybe you wasted your time."

"Durn if I did. I found out there's all kinds of money besides what we buy stuff with. For all we know, the bills we found are what they spend in Oklahoma. Maybe I'll go to another bank and ask; I won't go back to that one, for sure."

"I don't blame you. Well, there's one bank that'll know

about our bills: the one in the haunted house. If they print 'em, they've gotta know. We'll just go bang on the door 'til somebody lets us in." And with Lint capering beside them, they took a roundabout route that avoided Certain Other People frying ants down the street.

Cade Bridger's mother hadn't raised him to be an undependable sot, so her brother must have done it; that is, Bridger's uncle, who manufactured bathtub gin in the 1920s and paid his nephew to help. Once young Cade took to sneaking samples of their product, he developed a strong liking for the way alcohol teased him, made him see double, numbed the pain when it made him fall, and distanced him from his uncle's curses. Because he hadn't been blessed in the brains department, his family soon discovered his weakness for booze and managed to find him honest work where other members of the Bridger clan could keep tabs on him. And it had worked tolerably well until he met Pinero.

Bridger hadn't heard boys rapping on the front door of the gray bungalow the previous afternoon because it had been a workday, and he had been part of a city work crew filling in a ditch at the time. Today was also a workday, but not for Bridger, whose hangover had been fierce enough to drive him, about midmorning, onto nice cool dirt in a shadowy corner. He had been caught in midsnore by his boss's boss. A smarter man might have taken his tongue-lashing gracefully, but a hangover tends to steer a man's language into other shadowy corners. At ten-thirty that morning Bridger replied that the big boss was a four-eyed B-Word who could S-Word in his hat, and at ten thirty-one he was an ex-city employee.

Now, as noon approached, he sat on a basement step under the bungalow, thinking and waiting for Pinero. And as he waited he took little sips from the stuff he had hidden down there weeks earlier for emergencies: a Nehi soda bottle full of Wawdeeos he had traded for a tamale. (Its one virtue was cheapness but after his first taste of it, Bridger asked Pinero what it was. Pinero took one sip, made a horrible face, and said, "Waughhh, Dios!" as he spat.) So Wawdeeos it was.

Bridger had cause to ponder as he sipped, having saved from his city paychecks the same way a grasshopper saves for winter. He was deciding to tell Pinero how he had bravely quit his job to be more available as a printer, when young voices filtered down the basement stairwell, growing louder as footsteps sounded above. Something about safe deposit . . .

Bridger stuffed the neck of his Nehi bottle with a rag and wondered if he could make it up the stairs and out the back way without being recognized. Meanwhile, he froze. He was still only half-foozled, able to realize that those voices were boyish. Perhaps he could force his way between them, or bluff them into retreat. But so far, freezing in place seemed to work. He continued to listen.

Voices were clearer now, and the sudden rapping at the door reminded Bridger that the door was locked. He eased a few steps up the stairs and heard one boy say, "You think they might just take the money away from us?"

But Boy Two said, "How come? It's not theirs, money in a sewer pipe is finder's keepers," and with sudden understanding of that reply, a wee surge of weewee warmed Bridger's shorts.

More rapping at the door. "Oh shoot, nobody's here. Maybe they only print the money once a week or something," said Boy One. In fact, Pinero had hinted that they might run a few hundred bills this very evening, but if Bridger reported this discovery to him there might be no printing at all. Now the same boy added, "Or maybe once a month, 'cause it looks like nobody's home today either."

"I got an idea," said Boy Two. "What if we just go to the Ice House and see if we can spend one of these things on root beer and stuff?"

Boy One scoffed, "Twenty bucks for root beer?" Hearing this exact number, Bridger knew the bill they spent would be one bearing his own fingerprints and let an almost silent groan escape him. Even with his brain sopping up more alcohol as his belly passed it on, he was still barely sober enough to know the bills he had discarded would never pass any adult inspection.

The boys didn't hear his groan, but other ears were more highly tuned, and a single sharp bark squeezed out an extra teaspoonful of liquid downstairs.

"Lint! Hush. Well then, root beers and Baby Ruths and some firecrackers if they kept some from New Year's, and prob'ly a lot of change too. Coming here didn't work out worth a durn, how else are we gonna find out if—"

"Here, you take half the money," said Boy One with more foot-scuffings, and Bridger heard imaginary police whistles trill in his mind when the boys walked off the porch. He tiptoed up the last few steps and risked one glance through the front window, as a dark-haired boy of twelve or so took wrinkled paper from a sturdier boy of the same height while a terrier trotted beside them. Only the dog looked back to see one bleary eye peeking from inside, then quickly picked up its pace to accompany the boys.

Bridger said aloud to himself, "You ain't gonna let those fool kids go tradin' funny money around. You purely cain't." But neither could he chase them down and catch them and steal the bills back and beat some sense into them because they'd plainly said their goal was the Ice House, the little all-hours market only two blocks distant. And it was noon, not the best time to be whopping the tar out of kids no matter how much they deserved it, but something had to be done fast. Bridger stumbled up to the floor level and hurtled toward the back door without the slightest idea what that something might be.

"If they do let us buy stuff with this," said Aaron, "it pretty much answers our question." Their pace on the sidewalk was moderate but Lint began to lag.

"Yeah, but the bills don't look the same, and you couldn't carry twenty bucks' worth, not even fireworks," Charlie replied. After a pause he added, "I got it: I'll try to buy somethin' with one bill and you buy somethin' else with the other one. Then we'll both have a lot of change, or we'll know which bill they don't take."

Now each boy eyed his bill. "Come on, Lint," Charlie said. The dog had stopped, looking back, and now Charlie saw a figure in work clothes a block behind them, crossing the street at a stumbling run, arms flailing for balance like a man on a tightrope. "Huh. That's funny," said Charlie, watching as the man abruptly straightened to dart off behind a hedge.

"What's funny?" said Aaron, only now looking back.

"Nothing." But Lint had a different opinion, growling until the boys sweet-talked him toward the Ice House with little kissing noises.

CHAPTER 17:
✈ THE HAUNTED BANK ✈

The Ice House had grown as the town grew. Before Charlie's time it had been a tiny office that clung to a windowless insulated shed crammed with nothing but blocks of ice; big blocks, little blocks, fill-your-car's-trunk-sized blocks. The place reeked pleasantly with the smoky perfume of cork insulation. Buyers who could not yet afford a newfangled electric refrigerator during the 1920s hauled blocks of ice home to their oldfangled iceboxes, metal-lined wooden chests where perishables were cooled.

Then, as war approached and income rose in the late 1930s, more refrigerator owners bought less ice. The storekeeper, an old Danish immigrant, began to sell a wider range of goods as well. The tiny office grew like a farm shack, bit by bit, and managed to compete against regular grocery stores by staying open until late, stocking small amounts of everything from hardware to fireworks and aspirin.

Charlie's earliest half-forgotten experiences included fumbling open the latch of the cork-lined Hardin icebox at age three to steal a gob of butter whenever he could toddle to the kitchen unwatched and plunge his fat little fist into the stuff for licking. By now the family icebox was long gone. He could not have explained why he loved shopping—and inhaling—in the Ice House, with its corky musk that would linger as long as the building stood.

The old Dane storekeeper was not mutt-friendly, and Charlie knew it. Repeating "Sit!" the necessary three times that said he really, *really* meant it, Charlie pressed Lint's rump down on the Ice House's concrete porch for good measure and followed Aaron to the soft-drink cooler that squatted on the porch just outside the office. No one else was inside but the proprietor. Lint stayed in place, but stared back down the street muttering canine curses to himself. Aaron pulled a Hires root beer from the ice-filled cooler and entered the shop, then began to scan the shelf of candy bars with a barely audible hello to the owner. Charlie, keeping his pretense of not-shopping-with-the-other-kid, stepped inside the shop holding a bottle of Delaware Punch before he heard shoes scuffing on cement and heard Lint's rising growl.

A glance through small panes of the single window told Charlie that the runner in overalls now stood wavering on the cement porch, glaring down wild-eyed as he aimed kicks at something Charlie had never seen and scarcely imagined. It was an enraged Lint protecting the doorway, ears flattened, eyes slitted nearly shut, neck ruff standing on end as he dodged kicks; he bared his teeth at a stranger in ferocity that could not be misunderstood, and the message was plain: *"This far but no farther, for I am not this man's best friend."*

With something between a snarl and a bark Lint dodged another kick while backing away a few inches. Charlie had no idea who the kicker was. He darted back to the doorway, horrified, with a cry of, "No, Lint! Hey, wait, he's my dog," making a dangerous mistake by dropping to his knees to hug the furious terrier. Many another dog in a mood sweeter than Lint's might have bitten anyone, even his own lord and master, who fell over him at such a moment.

Lint was not one of those dogs. Since leaving the gray bungalow, he had done everything but grab a piece of chalk in his teeth and draw little doggy diagrams to tell the boys they had alerted someone who was up to no good. His nose had told him when this man, while inside that house, had identified himself, without intending to, the way dogs do on purpose against a fireplug, and that same signature was on these overalls. A faint groan from inside the bungalow had given Lint's ears a detail that human ears could not decode, and this man's wheezing had made that groan, and Lint had heard the same wheeze following the boys from afar, all the way to this spot. Though Charlie might know many things that were beyond his dog, in this matter Lint was the expert. He flinched as Charlie grabbed him, but he did not bite.

Aaron, surrendering his bottle of root beer to be opened while holding a candy bar, was about to ask the owner if he still carried those tiny one-cent packs of Yan Kee Boy firecrackers under the counter. In Aaron's other hand was his travesty of a twenty-dollar bill, and the old Dane's first glance at it told him that this would be absolutely, positively No Sale.

When Charlie hurtled outside shouting, the commotion unnerved Aaron so much he dropped his candy bar and spun on his heel, bursting outside with the bill forgotten but still in his hand.

The Dane had ruled his tiny kingdom for longer than Charlie's years and knew perfectly well who these two kids were. Not by name, but by their familiarity. They sold him discarded bottles for honest pocket money; they argued and joked together while they shared candies; and they had never tried to shoplift so much as a blob of Fleer's bubble gum. Now, to see one of them offer an obviously bogus bill of high value astonished him beyond words. He assumed the dog belonged with the boys, and ordinarily any dog in combat with a customer would be met with his broom. But

through the window he recognized the man in overalls—
one who apparently cut his hair with a lawnmower and
combed it with a leaf-rake—as the one who occasionally
bought a bag of Bull Durham tobacco for cigarettes and
whose breath could stun bees in flight. In the Dane's mature
opinion, the dog was the better customer. With a wordless
shout, he rushed to the doorway.

Cade Bridger did not like dogs, because dogs did not like
Cade Bridger. After running a few blocks in half-drunken
panic without knowing what he intended to do when he
arrived, Bridger did not like anyone of any species, least of
all the terrier squinting at him as he reached the porch.
When the dog growled, Bridger aimed a mighty kick to clear
his way to the open door forgetting that a drunken sot needs
both feet firmly beneath him. He would never quite
understand how he managed the next few seconds.

One of the boys appeared on the porch hovering on all-
fours over the dog, shouting something, and abruptly a bad
joke of a twenty-dollar bill fluttered from the boy's hand to
the cement, and then it was in Bridger's hand as he squatted
to snatch it in the doorway. Lurching to his feet, he
confronted the second boy, who faced him so near Bridger
could have embraced him, but the kid threw up a hand to
ward him off—and that hand held the other counterfeit bill!

In an eyeblink of time, blotto as he was, Bridger snatched
that second accusing bill with a shout of, "Gimmethatthing!"
and reeled away with a bill in each hand, missing the step
from the porch to sprawl headlong on the sidewalk while
the terrier began to bark furiously. Bridger couldn't be
certain his recovery of those bills had been noticed by the
portly old fellow who appeared bellowing in the doorway,
but he was certain he had no further business at the little
store today; for that matter, maybe not ever again. With this
scrap of good sense rattling around in his skull by itself,

Bridger lurched to his feet again intending to get out of sight as soon as humanly, drunkenly possible.

But alcohol works pretty much the same awful magic tricks on all men, including Bridger. Just five minutes before this he had been guzzling his favorite poison, and it takes a few minutes for alcohol to worm its way from a man's stomach to his brain, which meant that with every moment Bridger was soused worse than he was the moment before. An amateur of alcohol, with this much of it in him, might have blundered into a hedge or pitched over to break his head on the sidewalk. But this was a man with years of experience in his condition, practically a specialist at it. Somehow Bridger managed to stagger upright.

The soonest way out of sight was to get behind the Ice House, and he made it in five bumbling steps, but he could hear a lot of loud commentary, including the dog who seemed to have a lot to say and not much of it approving. A few paces behind the little building lay a brush-covered slope leading to the creek with its trees and meadows, and tribes of boys had worn a path so clear not even a dolt like Bridger could miss it, though he was seeing double by now.

But he could flounder into bushes several times on his way along the path, the last time losing one work shoe in the ankle-deep mud of Shoal Creek, so that he was obliged to stick the counterfeit bills in his mouth because he couldn't find his pockets. Besides, he needed both hands to scramble toward that big, dark, broken storm sewer that he knew would lead him back to the familiar welcome of his Wawdeeos.

The old storekeeper was no fool, and knew better than to charge off in pursuit of an arm-waving drunk when armed with only a broom. His two young customers seemed only shaken up, and their spirits improved when he gave them free soft drinks. The dog took more time to settle down. If his master had released him there might have been a chase ranging along the creek.

"Dat man," said the Dane, leaning on his broom, fixing the boys with a firm gaze as they sat nursing sodas, their feet off the porch as Charlie patted and soothed his terrier. "You boys know him?" He couldn't bear to ask point-blank if one of them might be kin to the thief.

The slender boy shrugged, then shook his head. The boy holding the dog muttered, "Nossir." Then with a glance that included his friend he added, "You know, I bet he followed us all the way from the bank. Maybe that's why Lint kept growling."

"Dat money, den," the Dane probed. "Not from any bank, neh. Yours, or his?"

As if they had practiced a duet, the boys looked at each other, blinked in a pantomime of considering something new, then said together, "I dunno." The dogless one went on, "We found it, and we wanted to see what it's worth."

"Maybe it was his after all," said the doggy one. "Durn sure swiped it like he thought it was."

"And you try to see vat it vas vort' in my store, hah?" The boys shared a longer glance, and finally the dog-boy nodded. "I tell you vat it's vort'; *long time in prison*," the old man thundered. The boys' heads lowered between their shoulder blades; they looked toward their feet, but found no help there.

After a long silence, the Dane went on more quietly: "I see him before. But today dat fellow act like a crazy man, boys."

"Yessir, and his breath stunk like rubbin' alcohol," said the dogless one. "Made my eyes water."

The Dane thought about that briefly. "Neh, drinker's alcohol, you bet. But he knew vat he came for, and he took it. Yep, I tink he vas yust after your fake money." Another pause before, "Vere you find dat stuff?"

The dog-boy took a long time choosing his words: "Real close to a haunted bank."

The Dane knew that American kids used a lot of strange slang, but this soared miles above strange. "Haunted bank," he said, trying the idea on for size.

"Yeah, real close," said the other. "We don't actually know if the bank's haunted. For rent, though. Says so on the sign."

The Dane moved back to the stool next to his cash register, drawing the boys through the doorway by personal osmosis. He was half-convinced that this whole incident had been some vast, childish practical joke of the kind that fun-loving Americans played on one another. Perhaps he should settle back on his stool and dismiss all this foolishness and stoke his long-stemmed pipe and enjoy the rest of his day. And yet . . .

Yet the man had been falling-down drunk, in no mood for joking, and intent on his getaway the instant he had the counterfeit bills in his grasp. The Dane tried to imagine such a spectacular clown following two boys and a dog all the way from a downtown bank, but his imagination refused the assignment. And all the banks were downtown, and whoever heard of a bank with a "for rent" sign? "Boys, vat bank vas dis?"

Two shrugs. After a second thought, Dogless said, "Ol' empty house, couple of blocks away. We call it that 'cause it's where they print the money."

The Dane sighed. "De haunted bank, hah? Only not haunted, and not a bank. Still, dey print money. You know de house number, boys?" Twin shrugs again. "I bet he see you find dat money. People vit money like dat go to prison."

"We went and knocked because we wanted to ask about it," said Dogboy. "We even went twice. Then we came here because nobody was ever there."

"You stay away from dere," the Dane said sternly, maybe too sternly.

Dogboy: "What d'you think he'd do?"

Without a word, but with a maniac's wide-eyed glare, the old man drew his forefinger across his throat. Slowly. The boys stared at each other. The next instant brought a two-boy-and-a-dog stampede, leaving the Dane alone with his thoughts.

He served a few customers during the following hour, then filled his pipe with Prince Albert and hid his face in a wreath of smoke for a bit of contemplation. Every question he asked himself about the morning's excitement led to an answer involving innocent—well, relatively innocent—kids and a guilty counterfeiter. A guilty and drunk counterfeiter. A guilty and drunk and possibly very dangerous counterfeiter, who upon sobering up would realize that a certain European-born storekeeper might figure out who and where and what was going on here. The lives of those boys might be in the same danger. With these facts in hand, any bright citizen would know enough to contact the police. And the old Dane was as smart as they come.

But he was not a citizen. He had learned English in Canada before seeking warmer winters, back in a time when Texas officials did not ask a bushel of embarrassing questions of honest working men. Like many immigrants, he had made himself useful, even prosperous. For many years he seldom thought much about his citizenship, or rather his lack of it. This war had brought many disturbing changes, though, and a man without proper legal papers was wise to avoid the notice of lawmen. To make matters worse, when that drunken fool ran off, he took the evidence with him. The old Dane could do nothing more than plead his case, in broken English.

He must contact the police.

He must not contact the police.

* * *

They had covered a quarter-mile of creekside trail far past the storm drain, with Aaron in the lead, before Charlie called, "Why are you running?"

"Because you are," Aaron called back.

"But you're ahead, guy. Only one chasing you is me."

Aaron risked a glance behind them, then slowed. "Durn."

Charlie fetched up beside him. "You want 'em to chase us?"

"Nah. But look, now I've jiggled all the spunk out of my root beer." Aaron peered into the bottle he had held all the way. His face was glum. "Here, you can have the rest."

"Worth two cents empty," Charlie joked, and swigged the remaining ounce or so.

"Uh-huh, and worth your throat cut to go back there if the crazy guy is watching."

Here the path wound through a tangle of briars and bunchgrass, the meadow stretching toward a line of decrepit fences intended to keep boys and other wild animals out of the untended backyards of the well-to-do. Winded from their long sprint, Charlie led the way to a shrubby hummock where they could sit in hiding without actually admitting it. "I'm kind of glad that crazy guy took our money," he said after a moment.

"I guess," said Aaron. Lint, who had just begun to warm up during their run, stood around waiting for it to resume, but Aaron spoke again. "Maybe it sure-enough was his."

Silence, and one of their thoughtful eye-to-eye gazes. At last, "Then we know where he lives," said Charlie. "He just wouldn't come to the door."

"Good! I purely hope he never comes to *our* doors," was the reply. Aaron followed this by crossing himself, the complicated hand-gesture that Charlie vaguely recalled seeing a Catholic boy make.

"Why'd you do that?" Charlie asked.

"For good luck, I think," Aaron said, having asked that very question after observing the same boy. "My dad saw me do it once and laughed like the dickens. When I explained he said oh well, it couldn't hurt so long as I don't do it in Temple."

So Charlie did it too, getting it all wrong, but perhaps the Almighty was off catching a nap in some other corner of the universe because no heavenly lightning bolt punished either boy.

After dissecting their Ice House experience at length, they concluded that a man who would furnish free sodas while lecturing them for their crimes was a man whose word was probably good. If he had decided not to herd them into the ice cooler for trying to hand him worthless bills, maybe they could apologize by bringing his bottle back—but maybe not today. And now that they knew the storm drain was actually a kind of informal back door to the gray bungalow, Charlie had no interest in further investigation.

It was Aaron who brought up the need to tell parents, and how much to tell, and how to go about it. But it was Charlie who furnished answers neither boy could stand to consider. "One of us'll get sent away," Charlie mourned. "At least to another school. Or to juvie hall, if the Ice House guy tells on us, where they turn us into murderers and I don't know what-all."

During this recital Aaron's head began to rock back and forth, and Charlie was soon doing it until finally, forcing back tears, Aaron put up a hand, palm out, to stop him. With an effort, he sat up straight and stiffened his neck. "Then there's only one hope, Charlie."

Charlie thought he had never seen his friend take on such a heroic look, and whatever idea Aaron had found, Charlie felt it couldn't be worse than his own catalog of cruel fates. This time, it was fine that the decisions would be up to someone else. He became the obedient sergeant; he even saluted. "Cap'n Aaron, sir," he said, "what do we do?"

Aaron set his jaw. "We're not gonna tell 'em," he said.

CHAPTER 18:
✈ TRAPPED ✈

After the boys agreed that the morning's events would remain secret, their shared worries drove each of them toward solitude. For much of the afternoon Charlie sat near the family victory garden, basking in the sun like a lizard with Lint to help him do it. The dog soaked up more than his share of pats from a master thoroughly proud of the way his twenty-pound terrier had stood firm against a grown man.

Reading through a mixed stack of *Planet* and *Captain America* comic books, Charlie reveled for a while in freedom from responsibility. Aaron had shouldered that heavy load, and Charlie knew well that Aaron would be feeling the weight of his decision. For the moment, Charlie's own guilt was no more bothersome than a speck of gravel in his shoe.

But gradually, that speck began to grow to the size of a marble, then a brick. When his mother sent Charlie off in midafternoon to buy groceries at the Checker Front store, he actually rejoiced to have the chore as a distraction. Lint, having judged that the gathering clouds might bring cold winds, wagged a farewell and crawled into his den.

As he walked, Charlie reflected on how much more agreeable the world would be if a guy could just revise little pieces of reality here and there. He imagined other ways the storm drain discoveries might have happened, and was taking a shortcut down the grocer's alley when Jackie Rhett called to him. Jackie was itching to show off his just-discovered skill in smoking a discarded cigarillo he had found in Checker Front's garbage. The absolute prohibition against Charlie smoking, or even the pretense of it, was made more galling by the grand gestures Jackie made in his efforts to blow smoke rings at the sky. It was Jackie's self-admiration as a young man of important skills that prodded Charlie to spin out his wishful version of the morning, in which Charlie was important too. After all, it wasn't as if Charlie were telling what had *really* happened.

And the part he told about the fearsome storm drain leading to the bowels of a bank fitted all too neatly into Jackie's beliefs. For some weeks past, he had felt increasingly sure that Charlie and Aaron had somehow become capitalists.

In late afternoon when Pinero moved down the basement stairs, he knew even before he heard his partner's snores that something was amiss. For one thing, the place stank of that whoopee juice Bridger drank, though Pinero had warned him against it a dozen times. Also, when Bridger weaved up from his squat on an overturned bucket it was plain to see as well as to smell that he had wet his overalls, and a pair of those botched counterfeit bills lay in plain sight, flattened and torn on the press.

"You were supposed to burn every piece of that bad paper," said Pinero, wadding the bills together in contempt and tossing the wad at Bridger. "All of it. You think if you wrinkle it up enough you could pass it?" He wore an unpleasant grin, intending his question as sarcasm.

To Bridger, whose brain churned with doubt about youthful invaders in the storm drain, this sounded as if someone had told Pinero about the scene at the Ice House. "It wasn't me," Bridger slurred. Anxious to point blame away from himself, he went on, "Those crooked kidsh." But when he saw what passed across Pinero's face, he wished he had held his tongue.

Pinero sat down on the stair and looked at his partner for a long moment, the way a wolf might look at some kind of rabbit he had never thought much about before. Then—but casually—he said, "What wasn't you, Cade? What crooked kids?"

"Why, the ones that broke in from the storm drain," Bridger stammered, realizing that his partner had not found out about the Ice House foolishness after all. But Pinero seemed very interested now: had the boys seen the press? Hard to tell, Bridger told him, but in any case he had driven the young thieves away before they could take anything.

And when had all this happened? Bridger did not own a wristwatch and was not clear on the question, but he figured it had been about half a bottle ago. Further questions, with replies rooted half in fact and the other half in more of Bridger's fantasies, left Pinero convinced that all his hard work would amount to nothing. But if the weather signs could be trusted, he might have a stormy night to work in, undisturbed.

By now, from studying the look in Pinero's eye, Bridger wanted his artfully decorated details to be true so much he half believed them. He mentioned a big dog, and a challenge near the creek where he had wrestled the bills from two youths the size of adults. This had the added feature of explaining how one foot was encased in mud he had forgotten to clean off. Because Pinero's calm seemed so dangerously brittle it might shatter with further explanations, Bridger thought it better not to mention anything about the Ice House. Furnished with this balderdash, Pinero understood the day's true events about as well as a snake understands a footrace.

"Well, with their break-in to explain, they're not likely to be yelling to the cops," Pinero said at last. "If they had, you'd be behind bars already. All the same, they could be back up that pipe any time now, and they've seen our operation." He fell silent for a moment, his mood dark.

Bridger simply stood with arms at his sides, awaiting whatever fate held for him, weaving slightly as he blinked. If he had any remaining doubt about his partner's mood it evaporated after he said, "So what do we do?"

Pinero's hand lashed out in an open-handed slap. It caught Bridger full across the cheek and sent him reeling against the nearest wall. Pinero took a step as if to follow this with heavier blows, then mastered his fury, his breaths long and hard as he watched Bridger stumble away. "What *I* do is try to do one little print run, to get something out of this mess. What *you* do is plug that pipe enough so we could still get out, but if your thieves tried to come back we'd hear them. Can you understand that much? And don't pile things up where they could be seen from creekside. Plenty of concrete chunks around here." This was true; when breaching the side of the pipe weeks before, Bridger had simply shoved broken hunks of concrete into corners of the basement.

As Bridger hoisted pieces of concrete to the level of the pipe, he could hear occasional scurryings up there somewhere. He decided the sounds might have been a rat, or the trickling of rainwater punctuated by occasional mutters of distant thunder that echoed along the pipe from curb gratings. Pinero had never struck him before this but seemed ready to do it again. Bridger thought of escape, to stumble down the pipe and disappear into the twilight never to return, but the odor of ink and Pinero's feverish haste to—

finally!—create useable counterfeits overpowered the drunkard's sensible fears. Panting, grunting, Bridger began to stack fragments of broken pipe in a way that would let water continue to trickle down toward the creek while preventing boys from climbing past without making an obvious clatter.

Meanwhile, Pinero set his mind firmly on leaving this very night, now that their hideout had been discovered. He began arranging adequate light and cleaning his equipment so that he might print a stack of twenties before abandoning this entire operation. At worst, he might have to abandon the heavy, foot-operated old press. He had stolen one press and he could steal another. Far more important were the engraved Nazi plates, no heavier than metal bricks, the only things he could not replace.

The summer rain took its time. Charlie arrived home before the first big spattering drops could do more than moisten his grocery bag. His mother chased him out of the kitchen with only an apple because, she said, it would be dinnertime in an hour. Soon he was lost again in the adventures of Captain America, but now in his own nook under the workbench in the garage with Lint curled like a parenthesis beside him. From time to time, brief freshets of rain drummed against the metal roof corrugations.

As evening approached and Coleman Hardin set his parking brake in the driveway, he smiled at the sight of his son, who stood waving a welcome in sprinkling rain even though he stayed fully dry, which suggested that Charlie had been elsewhere seconds earlier. It was almost, he thought, as if the boy had some kind of radar. In fact, this is exactly what Charlie did have—in his dog. A hundred cars a day might move downhill toward the Hardin residence without drawing the least show of interest from Lint. Brakes squealed, or whined, or did a half-dozen other animal imitations down that hill, but the Hardin sedan's faint screech was a whispery song that Lint distinguished from any other. That song was too faint for any human ears but whatever the dog might be doing, when those floppy ears came to attention Charlie knew which Plymouth, of all the vehicles on earth, was about to enter their driveway.

The weather often chose which dinner Willa Hardin would prepare. Today the signs of her choice had hung in the air like delicious dust: chicken and dumplings, a Hardin favorite on evenings like this, when storm clouds hung in blankets over the city.

Charlie and his dad were ravaging their dessert of oatmeal cookies when the telephone rang. Coleman Hardin sighed and stood up because, while his wife answered the hallway phone—their only phone—as all good wives were expected to, calls were almost always for men. But Willa Hardin announced with a hint of "la-de-daa" in her tone that the call was for Charlie.

People of Charlie's age were encouraged in those days, and for no very good reason, to leave telephones to adults, as though electrons were very expensive things not to be spent by children. A faint pang of alarm sounded between Charlie's ears to share space with the guilt he had nearly forgotten, but he moved into the hall with a show of nonchalance.

Charlie's inner alarm rang louder when he heard Aaron's warning. "Listen, guy, I've been thinking about Roy," said Aaron.

"Then I reckon you don't have a whole lot on your mind," Charlie retorted.

"I wouldn't, if you didn't live across the street from him," Aaron said, in no mood for banter.

"Is that all the reason you called?"

Aaron pressed on. "I guess you remember how Roy likes to tattle. It bothers me to think what a pesty little cuss he is.

If you had anything you really, *really* didn't want other folks to know, Roy's the last person a smart guy would tell about it. Just wanted you to be careful."

"Why sure, anybody would know that much," said Charlie. "Even if Roy wouldn't have the gumption to go check up on whatever I told him, which I won't, Sue Ann might," he joked.

Aaron, without amusement and just to prove his point, said, "Or Jackie." After a moment he added, "Charlie? You there?"

"Uh-huh. Listen, I gotta go. You know how my mom is."

"Yeah, mine too." But now Aaron was talking to a dial tone.

Ordinarily, Jackie would have hidden the stub of his cigarillo and hurried home as the storm approached, knowing how his gram feared lightning. Furthermore, she had a carved-in-granite rule that whatever villainy he was up to in the afternoon, he must be home by five o'clock without fail. Gram was a real boogerbear about that.

But it was still only the dregs of afternoon, and Jackie felt sure he could beat Gram's deadline. Besides, the prospect of a fast run to the creek and a foray up that old storm drain, a dare he had never considered until a lesser boy claimed it on this very day, was a risk Jackie could not resist. It should take only a few minutes to learn, one way or the other, how much of Charlie Hardin's tale might be true.

Jackie was rain-soaked enough to feel a chill wind before he climbed up into the mouth the drain pipe and hunkered down to catch his breath. The gooseflesh on his arms and scalp owed less to the weather than to the stench and the deep forbidding blackness ahead, but hadn't Charlie Hardin done it? At least he'd *said* he had. Charlie had made no mention of candles or flashlights, but the pack of paper matches in Jackie's pocket was nearly complete. And later he could always claim he hadn't had any matches, just to gold-plate his boast. Jackie lit a match and scuttled forward shielding his source of light from a faint musty air current.

Very soon he bunged his toe a nasty wallop against a D-Word smaller pipe, fetched it a mighty curse, and had to fumble for another match in a darkness that was not quite so deep when he turned around to face the creek. After two more matches he noticed that the blackness was less profound as he moved forward, and this made him bold enough to continue despite a soft rasping that got louder with every step. He recognized what it was, finally, because Gram made noises like that when sleeping off her wine sozzlings. Funny that Charlie hadn't mentioned snoring but in Jackie's experience, when a person snored like that you had to wake her with a Chinese gong.

When Jackie reached the pipe's broken sidewall, he saw that a kerosene lamp several feet below the break provided soft light that streamed from an ordinary basement, and that the raspy snores came from a man in muddy overalls who squatted on an inverted bucket wearing only one shoe, arms crossed over his knees, head on his forearms. Until this moment Jackie would have bet heavily on a whopper of a lie by Master Charles Hardin. And then he saw what looked like money lying atop some kind of big metal thingamajig, and in that millisecond Jackie's curiosity became greed. Was there more money in those boxes? Was money stored at the top of those stairs in the shadows? If somebody filled his pockets with it, would the sleeper ever miss it? And if he did, would Jackie give a hoot?

With a man sleeping so near that Jackie could have hawked a loogie on his shoe, this was no time to take another step without thinking it over. The several minutes Jackie spent studying stairs, supplies, even the stinks of the place, seemed like hours but his first cautious step across the pipe caused a tiny landslide that produced whispery sound effects on the basement floor. A snort escaped the sleeper and Jackie froze for a thirty-second eternity. Then gradually the snoring resumed, and Jackie slow-crept past the break in the pipe to observe the scene from a slightly higher perspective.

Jackie's spirits were not helped by sounds from further up the pipe, where a tiny but growing waterfall trickled from somewhere near to become part of the brook between his feet. He heard a familiar medley of noises and recognized the squish of water between pavement and automobile tires. Creeping up the gentle slope of the pipe, Jackie soon discovered a complicated molding of concrete that fed water down into the storm drain from an iron grating. Moreover, he could feel a rough disk the size of a barrel top set into the uppermost part of the molded concrete, and knew it must be a manhole cover. He pushed against it; pushed again, harder. It did not give him even a shadow of a hint that it might budge. He put the crown of his head against it and shoved until it made him grunt, and only then did it move ever so slightly. He would have needed a second Jackie to do more.

He knew roughly where he was now, though he could not quite see the occasional cars that passed. In early dusk made more gloomy by the approaching cloudburst that had threatened all afternoon, he could see flashes of lightning that terrified his gram so much. It was time for him to be home with her, or even without her. He turned and waddled down the pipe, rainwater running between his shoes, intending to continue to the creek.

That is, he did until he heard that stairwell creak under footsteps a few yards away and heard someone with a Latino accent growl, "You were supposed to burn every piece of that bad paper."

Jackie heard every word that followed, leaning toward the pipe crevice barely enough so that he could watch the men through one eye. Jackie heard that someone—Charlie, no doubt—had broken into the place, and not alone. He learned many other things too, including a strong likelihood that the sleeper in overalls had a gift for embroidering his exaggerations. Either that, or Charlie and Aaron had turned ferocious and Lint had grown big enough for a man to ride. After the Latino's vicious slap, Jackie also learned that the water level was rising steadily in the pipe and that if he had the brains of a dandelion he would make a dash for the creek this very second. Or the next, or the one after that, as soon as his courage returned.

But courage was still in short supply when the drunkard began to raise hunks of concrete to the drain pipe crevice, and the big Latino turned to his task at the strange machine before him. And if the man in overalls had only turned to stare up the pipe he would have seen, twenty feet away, an overweight schoolboy with eyes like saucers, his shoes awash in a stream. Above Jackie's level the thunderstorm flashed and boomed and threatened to expel anything hiding in the drain system. A few yards below Jackie's level, fumbling to build a pointless dam in a growing torrent, a poor fool struggled to obey the orders of a bigger fool. And mere yards away, petrified with fear and more waterlogged by the second, crouched Jackie Rhett.

Trapped.

CHAPTER 19:
✈ PROBABLY A RUNAWAY ✈

Given his druthers, Charlie would have listened to favorite radio programs in his room all evening, but the approaching storm had contrary ideas. Radio waves of that time could be turned to hash by nature's big static discharges. When mighty lightnings flickered across Texas in 1944, constant outbursts of static snarling out of a radio speaker made every program sound like a fight between two cats yowling in a gunnysack. Charlie shrugged and turned to the pages of *Boy's Life*.

But later, because he read quietly, Charlie heard his dad answer the telephone. The conversation was brief and businesslike. Then husband and wife spoke hurriedly in low tones. Though Charlie did not usually overhear details of a juvenile officer's work, he knew his mother was sometimes told.

The discussion became clearer as it moved to the kitchen. "Boy's grandmother called the station," said Coleman Hardin between hurried rustlings of his raincoat. "Redmon gave me the address, it's not far. She insisted the boy never stays out this late without telling her. It's an even bet we'll find him at the Greyhound terminal."

Charlie missed his mom's next words but not his dad's reply. "Because I know his family situation, if you can call it that, and he's probably a runaway. That old lady's no lady."

Moments later the back door banged and the Plymouth thrummed off into the dusk leaving Charlie to wonder at the mysteries of his father's work. But the mystery and the wondering fled when he left his room and saw the hall light fall on the telephone note pad. Imprints of familiar handwriting had left shadows on the blank page, and Charlie knew that surname, and his mind leaped to connect the day's events. In an instant he knew that his father lacked some important facts.

When he announced that he was going "out back," Charlie knew his mother expected that he would be continuing some project in the garage, which was nowhere near as "out back" as he really intended to go. To support her impression he turned the workbench light on before he left at a run without a jacket, forbidding Lint to follow.

He *tootle-de-oot*ed from the eaves outside Aaron's bedroom until he was dizzy, but at length his pal raised the window a few inches. As the patter of rain increased they did not need to speak in whispers. The last piece of Charlie's bulletin was, "And you know he'd never hide from his gram; shoot, Aaron, she's the one that hides him. You know why he swipes things. He's like he is 'cause he's like *she* is."

"And you had to go blab everything to him, like a dummy," said Aaron, disgusted.

"Not everything. In fact, I left a lot out."

"I know you, guy, and it's just like you to stick a barrel of made-up stuff in, like a dummy."

"Will you quit saying that?" Charlie begged.

"I will when you quit doing it," was the reply. "Does your mom know you're here?"

"I'm supposed to be in our garage. And I bet I know where Jackie is, and it's in a nice dry basement next to a sewer pipe. But I'm not going in there again." Charlie shivered, though the stormy breeze was not chill. During the past few seconds a distant clamor had drawn nearer from up the street, loud enough now to compete with a heavy sprinkle of rain. Charlie put up a hand for silence. "Hey. You hear that?"

Both boys listened with gazes locked while the siren of a speeding police car told them, as clearly as if in words, what it was doing. It slowed through that block and stopped not far beyond, as the whine of its siren subsided to a gurgle.

The distance from Aaron's home to the Ice House was exactly one and a half blocks. "Uh-oh," said the boys in unison.

Jackie's gram had wondered out loud why a juvenile officer was lallygagging around on her porch when he should be combing the city, and she said so, in colorful language. Coleman Hardin thanked her and drove to his office at the police station, then sent a pair of plainclothes officers to check the rail and bus stations.

Moments later he learned that his friend, police lieutenant "Cotton" Redmon, had taken a call only minutes before from a Mr. Yansen concerning boys and a drunken counterfeiter. Police radios fared little better than commercial programs in such troublesome weather, but the police dispatcher had Yansen's address. Hardin could see at a glance that all this sudden muddle of police business was not far from his own neighborhood. Was it possible that young Jackie Rhett was involved? He could settle it one way or the other if he followed Cotton Redmon.

The old Dane had finally mustered his courage enough to call the authorities, but found himself tongue-tied when a uniformed police lieutenant showed up with siren wailing. The combination of his Danish accent, the growing fireworks of the storm, and the old fellow's case of nervous hesitation when facing a uniform, stole most of his English and tested the officer's patience to the limit. When Coleman Hardin arrived a few minutes later in a business suit under his raincoat, Mr. Yansen recognized him as a customer and then the facts practically tumbled out. In truth, the facts poured forth in such a heap they needed sorting out like soiled laundry.

Before disappearing from home Jackie had paused long enough to promise Mrs. Rhett a considerable sum of "new money." Now, Hardin asked whether it was, perhaps, counterfeit money? Yansen could not vouch for any names, but he recognized the description of Jackie. Neh, he said, not dat thieving scamp. But he declared that the bills he had glimpsed were false beyond any possible doubt; practically parodies of money.

The two boys, said Yansen, were often together, sometimes with a small dog of forgettable features. At this, Redmon glanced at his companion. "Coleman, doesn't your boy have a dog?"

"A joke of a dog," Hardin replied, smiling. "Not a snarl in him. The one that stood fast against a reeling drunkard sounds more like a bull terrier. I expect Lint is at home hiding from all this thunder about now."

Yansen had been sitting thoughtfully, drawing now and then on his pipe, but now he perked up. "Lint? Yah, de only name I heard."

As the men exchanged blinks, lightning struck so near that its blast of thunder began with the air-ripping flutter of an artillery shell.

Redmon spoke first: "The house can't be far off, but we'll need more men for a search."

Hardin sighed. "That radio in your car might as well be a tin can and a string, Cotton. Mr. Yansen, can we use your phone?"

☆ ☆ ☆

Aaron needed ten seconds to solve the immediate problem, sliding out his window and leading Charlie to the Fischer garage. He located his old Cub Scout tent, a rectangle of canvas that would barely cover two boys, and helped Charlie drag it up to branches of the backyard hackberry tree. In the long ago of second grade, high up that tree, they had fashioned their crow's nest. Its one virtue was that a boy perched higher than any neighborhood roof could see halfway to Mars—or at any rate, well beyond the Ice House. The little store was near enough that patrons might be identified from that rickety perch. But short lengths of two-by-fours nailed to branches by children had not served them for more than a season, and no one had monkeyed up that flint-barked tree for years.

Aaron struggled up inside the canvas next to Charlie and took a death-grip on a branch the thickness of his thumb. He would have refused to plant his rump on this flexible swaying contraption now except for one fact: the hackberry was on Fischer property, sort of. Aaron could honestly face his parents and claim he had not left home at night in such weather. Also, he could not deny that this demented notion had been his own idea.

As a Plymouth sedan pulled up beside the distant police car, Aaron stiffened. "Charlie, is that your dad?"

"Shut up," Charlie advised. "I'm thinking."

"Better late than never," said Aaron.

"You're hogging the tent," said Charlie.

"You want me to get wet?"

"Poor you, and tell me who thunk this up. Listen, they're gonna find us drowned up here anyway," was the reply. "So if you're so durn smart, what are we supposed to do up here?"

"Watch, I guess."

"You mean watch which one of us gets blown down from here first?" The storm's answer was a thunderclap.

Aaron's was almost as loud. "Maybe! I believe I remember somebody all out of ideas, two minutes ago, sneaking up outside my window and hoo-hooing for help."

"Yeah, so you brung me out here up a tree in a cloudburst. Closer to the lightning. Thanks a bunch, guy," Charlie shouted back.

"You're free to leave any time, Charlie Hardin."

"Not 'til you let go of my belt," Charlie said.

Doing his best to sit erect high in a wet swaying tree, Aaron saw in lightning flashes that the most secure thing for him to hang onto was Charlie. He found another branch to grasp but Charlie remained firmly planted. After a moment Aaron said, "I have to go."

Charlie, scornful: "What; you have homework or something?"

Aaron: "No, I mean I have to—you know—*go*." A lightning flash lit the heavens near enough that the boys heard its artillery shell imitation.

A numbing thunderclap, and a pause from Charlie. Then, "Well, if that didn't do it, I reckon you can hold it awhile."

"Nope, but I can reach my buttons right here. But if you ever tell anybody, guy—"

Thunder rumbled a reply. Charlie snickered. "You're gonna let 'er rip up here? Okay, so will I; shoot, nobody can see us anyhow." And the boys tended to their trouser buttons, and other needs, with sighs of relief as they made their contributions to the rain.

Charlie was buttoning up when he saw headlights go on near the Ice House, and spotted his dad hurrying back into the Plymouth. The two cars swung parallel, motionless, long enough for a brief exchange before the police car parked at the corner with a red spotlight shining upward. The Plymouth moved away into the neighborhood scarcely faster than a walking pace, its big spotlight spearing into front yards as it went.

The city had not installed a police radio in the Hardin Plymouth, and it had never occurred to Charlie why his father had made such a point of having the handle of that clear-lensed spotlight set into the Plymouth's door. Now, for the first time, he realized that though Coleman Hardin did not own a handgun, the handcuffs in his coat pocket suggested that his job sometimes became actual real-life police work. Charlie imagined his dad searching front yards for the missing boy; knew that a spotlight from the street was not a tool likely to be of much use; and came to the conclusion a wiser Charlie would have reached long before this.

The downpour was stronger now, which made everything slicker and gave fair warning that one clumsy move could bring a person hurtling down out of that tree a whole lot faster than he had shinnied up it. But in a flash of clarity to match the lightning, he saw that he needed to be involved in some useful way, not hiding out in a crow's nest built long ago by seven-year-olds.

Once again, it was up to Charlie Hardin. "I'm no sissy," he shouted back at the thunder, and eased off the shared perch, and lost his balance. And fell.

And was snagged by the fork of a branch just below, painfully enough to make him gasp, but with both arms flailing he found a useful grip that led him to the tree trunk and then downward at a reckless pace.

Aaron's descent was only a little slower and on his way down he called,

"Where are we going?"

"You don't have to. He needs me," Charlie called back.

Aaron: "Which he?"

Charlie thought of his dad, peering into rainy darkness, and of Jackie Rhett, probably shouting dirty words at a crazy man in an outlaw's den. "Both *hes*," he called. "You better go back inside." And then he was pelting away through the downpour.

Only minutes passed before the Plymouth's spotlight reflected from a rental sign, and Hardin made a cautious decision as he parked two houses away in a driveway masked by a hedge. If that darkened bungalow was really the lair of counterfeiters, a man whose badge was his only weapon would be foolish to inspect the house alone when armed officers were already on the way. He had left Charlie in his room not long before, and he had no reason to suspect his son had stirred from there. The police dispatcher might force a radio message through the storm giving this location to Redmon and others, but that message would have to begin with an ordinary telephone call. Unarmed, Hardin knew he would be cautioned to remain at that telephone and await further instructions. A knock at the nearest residence and a show of his badge would be his best move toward a telephone, and he made that move without hesitation.

No sensible dog would brave a rainy winter night when he had his own snug one-room apartment, but this was warm summer rain, worrisome only to fleas. Lint waited until no one could claim he was dogging Charlie's footsteps, though he intended to do that very thing. Then he let boredom propel him away from home for a stroll while he cussed the booms of distant thunder. He knew his boy well, and sensed that any time Charlie set off at a run in such conditions as these, something very interesting must be afoot. The tangy odor of Charlie's shoes was fresh in Lint's nose but fading fast in the wash of raindrops. No matter; if Lint lost that familiar beloved scent, well, this was a route he knew by heart. At its other end lay Charlie's second-best friend, Lint himself claiming the top position. And there was no hurry; it was not as if Lint had pressing business elsewhere.

Several blocks further as he trotted along a sidewalk, he was drawn to a familiar bulky shape half-hidden by a hedge and gave it a good sniffing-over. Between those irksome outbursts from the sky he could hear Charlie's dad in that house talking with someone, but that someone was not Charlie so Lint filed it all under "boring" and resumed his stroll for a half-block. By this time the storm center had crept directly above the neighborhood. In spite of the rain's warmth, increasing crashes of thunder had begun to set Lint's teeth on edge. He was considering a return to his bed as he crossed the street and hopped a gutter stream that was fast becoming a creek now, and heard the rush of water as it dropped through an iron grating. The rushing water, and— something more.

Lint remembered that grating. He had watched Charlie shove broken bottles into it one Saturday morning, after Lint and Charlie's wagon collided. He was not so much intrigued by the grating as with the hole under it, which he decided must be the mouth of a den hiding the biggest woodchuck in all creation. At the moment, if Lint was any judge, that critter down there would be doing the backstroke. At any rate, it was doing *some*thing, because the sounds issuing from the hole were sounds of something in trouble. Maybe something human.

Abruptly, standing atop the curb with thunder's insults still ringing in his ears, Lint forgot the storm's hissyfit. He flopped down on the sewer's big circular iron manhole cover, stuck his nose out over the grating to read any bulletins coming from below, and gave a gruff little half-bark to whoever might be within earshot.

CHAPTER 20:
✈ THE HERO BUSINESS ✈

The person nearest to Lint was Jackie Rhett, petrified and whining almost noiselessly with fear, only a few feet away. Jackie hid motionless in the big pipe as rising water surged around his ankles, but he was separated from the terrier by solid concrete. In Jackie's view, no help could have come from anything less than his own personal Bengal tiger. The longer Jackie hid in that flooded concrete tube, the more abuse Bridger took from the Latino outlaw. And the more of it that Jackie heard, the more he became convinced that this was a man who would wring a boy's neck while whistling "La Cucaracha."

When he started up that storm drain, Jackie had held his usual opinion that he understood his world and the kinds of people in it. But a few minutes spent listening to Pinero had taught the boy about a type of man rarely found behind a truant officer's desk. Jackie's fear grew so great he was not aware of the silent tears that poured down his cheeks. The splash of water, Lint's excited comments, and the clatter made by a second man stupidly trying to build a barrier in a growing torrent were loud enough to mask Jackie's

scuffings and whimpers. Without knowing he did it, Jackie
Rhett gradually crowded himself further into the molded
concrete that guided water down from the street. Water fell
mere inches from his body, and he pressed the top of his
head against the underside of the manhole cover. Now, every
bolt of lightning brought him a one-second view of the
world above. For some moments Jackie's view was full of
anxious terrier, and then it suddenly changed.

The storm's tantrum raged so high that when the
patrolman had summoned Coleman Hardin out to his
police car, their conversation was chiefly by pantomime.
They sped off in the squad car needing only fitful lightnings
to show the way and skidded around a corner, then quickly
turned down an alleyway. Pinero's panel van was one of two
vehicles that already stood dark and motionless in the
backyard behind the gray bungalow.

In the other squad car sat Cotton Redmon. The three
men conferred inside Redmon's car before the patrolman
shook Redmon's hand, secured the top button of his
raincoat, and transferred crucial hardware to a pocket he
could reach instantly. That hardware included his wallet with
its bronzed badge and a Police Special revolver. One corner
of the bungalow's front porch was supported by a pillar the
width of a man, and under Redmon's orders his man would
stand immobile against that pillar. Anyone in the house who
thought the front door was a means to escape would
discover his mistake in a hurry.

The uniformed officer was very young, and impulsive,
and he pounded through shrubs to the bungalow's front
porch without bothering to step lightly. And then, without
the least awareness that he had made a commotion like a
wild-horse stampede, the officer tried to make himself a wee
bit smaller and leaned against the pillar as he stared toward
the door. Somewhere near in all this chaos a small dog was

barking a call to arms, but it was not the kind of thing to interest a young officer who was intent on more important things, or imagined that he was.

In a time when many lawmen cared little about thoughtful behavior in their work, Cotton Redmon was the kind of police lieutenant who struck a balance between common decency and his passion for duty. He did not forget for a moment that Coleman Hardin's work was almost entirely with juveniles, nor that Hardin sometimes dealt with dangerous youths and yet always went unarmed. This is why, when preparing to invade a house that might contain armed counterfeiters and a troubled boy, he gave Hardin the role least likely to involve gunplay. Redmon chose a riot gun for Hardin because it was a shotgun, meant to be used only at short range and relatively harmless at any distance beyond half a city block. But up close and very personal, a shotgun's muzzle looks like the business end of a cannon and sounds like one, too. If a juvenile officer needed a deadly weapon, the choice of a riot gun would be hard to beat. Leaving Hardin inside the squad car with his scary blunderbuss, Redmon knocked hard on the bungalow's porch-screen door with his heavy flashlight, keeping his police revolver holstered. It was not strictly according to the rules for him to tear at the screen, but someone had damaged it previously and when his knock went unanswered he reached through to fumble for the lever with his free hand.

In the storm's tumult no one could have heard the roar of lions outside, much less the alarms of one small dog. And when Coleman Hardin had hurried out to the police car in darkness, no one had seen the terrier's small form almost a block away. In his quest for more information, Lint left the curb to stick his nose almost into the flood that gushed along the gutter and down through the iron grating.

It is well established that Lint's ears deserved Olympic

medals. Between peals of thunder, he detected tiny moans of human fear and then identified which human was making them. A dog that harbored grudges might have trotted off then, having recognized the moaner's voice, but Lint's moral code was extensive. It even extended to the obnoxious Jackie Rhett.

Charlie's favorite radio programs included *Gang Busters* and *Mr. District Attorney,* and no one had ever suggested to him that the superhuman wisdom of police in those dramas might be stretching the truth. So, thanks to those muddle-headed radio plays, Charlie assumed that when the good guys left the Ice House, they knew everything they needed to know. Justice would triumph; crime must pay. If Jackie was somewhere near and fooling around a haunted bank seeking loot, well, Charlie figured his dad would have it all straightened out in a moment. But meanwhile, Charlie was plunging up the street in a thunderstorm remembering he had seen the family Plymouth only minutes before, and asking himself where the H-Word was it now?

By this time, Charlie could not have gotten any wetter by swimming up Shoal Creek, and the pounding of a jillion raindrops did their part to add more clatter to the brawling of the storm. Charlie did not recognize the new chorus of barks—which had a deeper sound when echoing from a storm grating—for whose they were until he was sprinting up the sidewalk within fifty feet of Lint. Then, interrupting the barks, a high penetrating whine escaped the dog, and it speared into Charlie's very soul like a dagger. No other creature could manufacture a sound that spoke to Charlie with quite such a cargo of need, of loss, of pure yearning. Charlie dropped to his knees beside the grating to hug his dog.

"Lint! You stuck? What is it?" As he spoke, Charlie peered into the grating. Lightning flashes showed little more than terrier paws flicking against iron as if to dig through the metal. A darted glance around him was fruitless; the young policeman standing in wait and unseen fifty yards away might as well have been on another planet, hidden on a porch, staring in the opposite direction with his collar turned up.

As Charlie crowded nearer to the grating Lint backed away, relieved that he could turn this spectacular problem over to his young godlet. Some ancestor of Lint's had probably herded sheep in Greece because it had endowed the terrier with the ancient Greek view of all gods, who must be allowed to run things even if the product of their ideas is mostly mischief.

The uppermost thought in Charlie's mind was to locate his dad, mingled with a new impression that Lint had lost his doggy mind. But in the bursts of light while peering at a common sewer opening, Charlie saw two impossible things. The first was a tiny shudder of motion from the iron manhole cover. And the second was a pair of boy-sized eyes from the gloom of the sewer, staring back up at him.

For the scrawniest fraction of a moment, Aaron was comforted by the idea of retiring from this water-soaked fracas that his pal had drawn him into. But he had caught the tone in Charlie's dismissal, and its central message had been "*no sissies need apply for this job.*" Aaron hoped his father would someday understand why Charlie must not be left to finish his mission alone. Splashing almost in Charlie's tracks, Aaron began to chase after him only seconds behind.

Charlie had just commenced ruining his fingernails on that cast iron manhole cover when Aaron spotted him with both knees in the gutter, huddled over the sewer opening. Since he had already committed himself to whatever craziness his pal was into, all Aaron could think to splutter into the pounding rain was, "What are we doing?"

"Crowbar. Screwdriver. Knife," Charlie gritted, redoubling his efforts to get his fingers under that lid.

The only metal thing in Aaron's pockets that was remotely similar to the needed items was a nickel that he thrust into Charlie's empty hand. He still had no idea why Charlie attacked the lid's edge with a coin, and peered at their surroundings wondering if he should run home for a kitchen knife. Then in a long blink of lightning he saw the FOR SALE sign glistening wetly a few yards away, and in a few precious seconds he had pulled its wooden stake from the ground.

Now Aaron jammed the pointy end of his stake at the crevice between iron and concrete near Charlie's fingers, prying back and forth, the cardboard sign missing Lint by inches as it waved about. Charlie only grunted, but kept up his attack and was rewarded with a faint metallic scrape. It seemed to Aaron that his makeshift tool had inserted itself slightly deeper into that crevice, and he thrust harder.

"Ow, ow, ow," Charlie advised, and shifted his body. "Come help," he added, which carried a hint that if the stick was help, it was harm too. Something in the brevity of that message told Aaron that his own fingers were wanted in that cruel slot as well.

Those extra fingers were the difference. With a louder scrape, the heavy lid grated up and across concrete until, with both boys holding it vertical, it rolled away to fall onto the nearby sidewalk with a mighty clang. Charlie flopped onto his stomach and reached both arms down into the blackness of that hole, and Aaron, now on his knees, was astonished as the next flash revealed a pair of hands that reached up toward them, seemingly from the bowels of the earth.

Pinero tried to keep track of all the noises around him, including the slosh of water that now began to pour steadily into the basement from the broken pipe and, worse, sounds that might be footsteps above him and knocks at the screen door inside the house. Pinero thought fast. "Cade, the wind's blown that back door open," he called. "Go fix it right now!"

Bridger slid down to the floor from the broken pipe and rushed to obey without a word, leaving muddy tracks up the stairs. He was almost sober by now but beyond caring whether Pinero's orders made any sense. In Bridger's tiny mind, anything that kept him safe from more of Pinero's threats had to be a fine thing. It did not occur to him that Pinero might send him upstairs to check on the likelihood of something more troublesome than a screen door banging in the wind.

And a few words carried from the pipe and deepened by its echoes were the last straw, all that Pinero needed to cancel his entire operation. A pair of valuable Nazi engravings in heavy metal plates were the only things a printer absolutely must save to try the scheme again someday, and it was the work of moments to wrap them in pockets of their special leather purse. If cops were really at the door, Pinero figured, he could count on Bridger's stupidity to create a noisy three-ring circus upstairs. Meanwhile, a smarter outlaw like himself could sneak away through the storm drain and emerge at creekside in welcoming darkness. He might lose his car, but not his freedom; Dom Pinero had tasted the joys of Texas jails and intended to avoid refreshing his memory no matter what the cost.

With these thoughts, Pinero struggled up to the pipe and paused long enough to draw his revolver. He resolved to shoot any lawmen—or blundering kids, for that matter—who dared come up that pipe. Standing ankle-deep in water now, he released a brief grin imagining Bridger's sacrifice as the drunken fool met his fate upstairs. Seconds later he heard things too loud to suit him, and too near also, from up the pipe. Silence was no longer his friend. Still unable to see beyond a few feet into the pipe in either direction, he fired one shot up the slope of the pipe to halt any pursuit from that direction and was rewarded by a screech louder, if possible, than the revolver. Then he bent double and began to stumble blindly down the pipe toward the creek, one hand feeling along the pipe, the other holding his weapon.

As he moved along the central hallway toward the back porch Bridger saw a flashlight beam sweep across the porch floor, and realized a man was entering the house. He ducked into a vacant bedroom while the beam speared sideways into the kitchen, and flattened himself against the wall listening to footsteps approach. The bedroom was entirely bare of furniture so he had no place to hide. When a deep male voice announced, "Austin city police," every one of Bridger's bones turned to oatmeal and leaked away somewhere. He could not have taken a step to save his life, but he could stand rigid as a plank against the wall waiting to be speared by that flashbeam, so that is what he did. There is no telling how long he might have lingered there if not for the single gunshot downstairs, which brought the police lieutenant running along the hall, his flashlight leading the way. The beam did not stray into the bedroom.

The beam did not stray into the bedroom! God bless Dom Pinero, thought Bridger, for creating a diversion to save his partner in crime. Medicated back to vigor by the ruckus of a policeman bounding downstairs into the basement, Bridger found his bones magically renewed in an instant. He darted back into the hallway and aimed himself toward the screen door, careened through it, then bore its remains along with him as he stumbled down the slippery outside steps.

Lightning is unruly and makes up its own mind when to strike, so it chose not to flash until Bridger had fallen to his knees beyond the steps, still wearing parts of the rickety door frame like a cloak. Squad cars of that time did an awful job of keeping moisture from the insides of windshields, so Hardin did not see Bridger emerge from the house. He quickly wiped his palm across the inside of the glass, which made him blink, because now the screen door was no longer in view. He did not notice the dark shape that slid ghostlike into Pinero's panel van.

However, he was thunderstruck when the old vehicle's starter began to whine ten yards away, and he came boiling out of the squad car while the van's engine was still coughing to life. Bridger kept his headlights off and trusted the heavens to provide his light, but the van could only creep into motion before Hardin planted himself squarely in its path and aimed the riot gun.

Then the van moved faster, and Hardin did what he had to do. To Cade Bridger the flash and roar must have seemed like lightning and thunder combined.

Redmon heard a pistol shot fired in the basement, and an answering cry from somewhere near it, then descended the stairs two at a time. His gaze darted around him though he saw nothing move in his flashbeam, which now furnished more light than the oil lantern's faint gleam. As he stood in a spreading puddle and sent the beam probing here and there, he found a concrete storm sewer at the height of his belt, the pipe so badly damaged that a man might climb through the hole into which a torrent was now pouring. In fact, he thought he could hear someone moving away. Maybe people moving away in both directions.

Meanwhile, the only thing of note in that basement was a sturdy old printing press, and unless his trained ear had lied, in the past few seconds someone outside had fired a ferocious blast that could only be a riot gun. He raced back upstairs because for Lieutenant Cotton Redmon, the voice of a riot gun was as serious as business can get.

* * *

With a boy pulling on each of Jackie's arms, he managed to wiggle up through the manhole far enough that his chin was level with the pavement. None of the boys had breath to spare for shouting, and at this moment those flocks of shoplifted candy bars, those throngs of second helpings of mashed potatoes, those gangs of extra pounds Jackie wore to dominate other boys, all crammed him in place as a fleshy cork in a concrete bottle. Some regions of his broad circumference were free for water to drain, but his belt buckle scraped and so did his rump, so perhaps Pinero's warning shot was, after all, a helpful one.

Charlie had no idea that Pinero or his weapon existed, and he flinched at the reduced yellow flash and report of the revolver in the pipe, thinking it seemed unfair that lightning could attack from such a place, but Jackie had seen the weapon and knew instantly what caused that searing pain across his backside. Aided by the bullet that grazed his bottom and two boys pulling him by the arms, he rocketed up from imprisonment with the shriek of a lost soul and set off for home without a word of thanks.

Two boys and a dog found themselves staring mystified into that vacated manhole. Aaron was first to admit his curiosity. "What just happened?"

"We were heroes, is what. Maybe something bit him," Charlie said. "Your old ghost cat, maybe," he added out of spite.

Aaron opened his mouth to counterattack but was struck dumb by a thunderous explosion and a wink of yellow light through the trees, not at all like lightning, from somewhere behind the bungalow. As the boys glanced toward the house they were astonished to see a dark shape materialize from the porch and hurtle out of sight. Seconds later Aaron offered some revised thoughts. "People are shooting real guns around here, guy. I think Jackie got shot."

"Didn't slow him down a lot," Charlie said. "I bet Jackie will have to admit we're heroes, too."

As the rain began to pound them with less fury they gradually lowered their voices and Aaron spoke almost normally now. "You know what, Charlie, this isn't a lot of fun anymore. I'm gonna see if I can sneak back in our house. This hero business can go to the devil, I think maybe I hear my mom calling." He turned to leave but flung over his shoulder, "In fact, I wasn't even here."

"Me neither, if I can manage it," said Charlie, and scratched his dog between the ears. Then they were gone.

CHAPTER 21:
✈ PINERO'S FATE ✈

During the few minutes Charlie needed to reach home the storm lurched away, and through its final sprinkles he heard his name called again and again. As he reached the backyard he sensed a note of panic in his mother's cry of, *"Don Charles Hardin!"* Half-illuminated by the workbench light she stood gamely outside, but huddled beneath her umbrella, she somehow appeared smaller than usual.

"I'm here," he called, managing in those two short words to include overtones of, *I've been right here under your nose, where else would I be, why would anybody suspect I might be somewhere else,* trotting into her view a few steps behind Lint. When his mother saw him, the furrows at her brow relaxed and made him five years old. "I'm with Lint," he said, as if she couldn't see that for herself.

"So I noticed," she said, and drew herself erect with perhaps more self-control than necessary. "This seems to be a night for all my menfolk to go scooting off to worry me half to death." Then, as Lint made a major production of shaking himself dry, she went on more gently, "I've been calling you two for ages."

231

"I didn't know where he was," said Charlie, who knew perfectly well that an age, for his mother, could be half a minute or half a day. He busied himself with an old bath towel from under the garage workbench, first drying his head, then applying the towel to Lint.

"Of course," said his mother, and bent to pat the dog. "Poor little scalawag, I didn't think about how all that thunder felt to his ears. It's a wonder he didn't crawl under a house somewhere. Where was he?"

"Just right down the street," he said, hoping she didn't reflect that the creek was also down the street, and so was the other side of town, and so were Dallas and Mars. "I got nearly as wet as he did. See?" He made a display of his obvious condition. "I didn't know I was gonna get this wet."

"Charlie, fish in the sea don't get that wet," she scoffed. "You might let me know next time before you run off like that in the worst thunderstorm we've had in years. Now get yourself into my kitchen and out of those soggy things, and be glad your father can't see you looking like a drowned ragpicker."

Charlie produced a puddle on the kitchen linoleum by simply standing there, and put on dry clothes as his mother brought them. Meanwhile she continued to vent aloud all the worries she had collected during the short time when she understood that her only son was missing, at night, with a knockdown-and-dragout lightning extravaganza directly overhead. In her relief she allowed herself to believe that Charlie had remained at home for all but a few moments, catching the frightened terrier after a brief search, while rain soaked them both like a pair of sponges.

By the time he took the first slurp from his cup of hot chocolate, Charlie liked his mother's version of his absence so well he saw no reason to improve it. There were things to be said for another boy's rescue, but the truth would have filled a five-gallon bucket with questions Charlie didn't want to answer. Besides, he could name folks who might argue that more glory would have resulted from *not* saving Jackie Rhett's ample bacon.

And had Jackie really been in danger? The answer might never be known, and the least dependable source of missing facts would be Jackie himself. Maybe that little yellow flash and bang had been only a firecracker; maybe the big flash had been one too. And whatever Jackie might claim, he hadn't trapped himself down there on purpose. Charlie wondered what his father would make of it all, and entertained a hope that Jackie had run away.

That hope died an hour later when his mother answered the telephone. From dramatizing a Captain America comic book at his desk by supplying the *pow* and *bam* noises, Charlie began to turn the pages very, very quietly. He learned from his mother's replies that Coleman Hardin was curious as to their son's whereabouts. "He's in his room," she said, and listened for a moment. Then, "I caught him chasing after the dog in the rain like a ninny, but they're both fine. Will you be home soon?"

The answer made her gasp. "Hospital! Are you hurt?" Charlie's blood froze, but regained its warmth when she went on. "The same boy? That's just awful . . . Oh. But I thought all gunshot wounds were serious . . . And then you'll be home, hon?"

Her wait was longer this time. Then, "Oh my lordy, you might've been killed. A gang of counterfeiters with guns is hardly a problem to leave with my husband . . . You didn't!" Now she laughed aloud. "Well, I'm glad it was only a tire . . . No, he's been playing in the garage by himself this evening. I'm sure he was with the Fischer boy this afternoon, I suppose you can ask him if you're home before bedtime."

From all this, it seemed likely to Charlie that he would be answering questions about the Ice House and his encounter with the crazy man, and he quickly decided that this had been a very long day. When Willa Hardin finally replaced the telephone in its cradle, she noticed that the light was off in Charlie's room. Opening his door, she called to him softly—twice—then assumed he was asleep and breathed a little prayer of thanks for a son who slept so full of carefree innocence.

Charlie awoke to find his father's fingers tousling his hair while early morning light bathed his room. Coleman Hardin sat on the edge of Charlie's bed, still wearing his suit from the previous night. In quick succession, a hundred details freight-trained through Charlie's memory and his first impulse begged him to find some illness he could claim. But his dad looked as if he needed sleep, and the squeeze on Charlie's shoulder was gentle, and those things made a difference. "You and Aaron had a busy day yesterday, son," said his dad, and Charlie nodded.

"You know old Mr. Yansen?" To this, Charlie shook his head with evident puzzlement. His dad tried again. "Immigrant; owns the little grocery down on Sixth."

"Oh. Ice House," Charlie said, stifling a yawn. He waited for his father to continue. Finally he sensed that his father already knew a great deal, and was giving Charlie a chance to confirm it. "Yessir. I was, uh, gonna tell you." His dad lifted an eyebrow and Charlie added, "Later, though."

"Someday after I retire, you mean."

"Before that. Old guy scared us plumb to splinters about jail and stuff when all we did was find some money that looked funny. We just wanted to see what it was good for."

His dad issued the ghost of a smile. "That's what they call it sometimes; funny money. Not funny at all, though; the official word is counterfeit, and passing it is a federal crime. Mr. Yansen could have put you in serious—well, never mind, he didn't, and you boys gave him some story about finding it, and the man who attacked you to get it back was one of the gang that printed it."

"We didn't swipe it," Charlie objected. "We really did find it."

"In the house where it was printed," said his dad, sighing.

"We never!" Suddenly Charlie was supremely glad that he hadn't clambered down those few steps into the basement. "Nossir, we never once went in that ol' house. Right outside it, though. Main thing we did was knock on their door to ask if what we found was real."

Now his dad managed a chuckle. "At the haunted bank, I suppose."

It seemed as if the old grocer had perfect recall of yesterday's conversations, and Charlie felt that his dignity lacked support. "Aw, we didn't think it really had ghosts and stuff, even if we figured it might be a bank, but nobody ever came to the door, so we all went to the Ice House to ask Mr. What'shisname."

"All?"

"Me and Aaron and Lint. Dad, you never saw a dog stand up for a guy the way he did."

"Wonders never cease. And Mr. Bridger followed you."

"I dunno who he was, but he stunk and he acted crazy, and he tried to kick the slats out of my dog," Charlie said, indignant.

"We have Mr. Yansen's word on that," said his dad. "Pretty much as you say. Did you follow Bridger?"

"Huh! Follow a crazy man? Not hardly, I never saw him again. After the Ice House guy bawled us out we ran home. Then Mom sent me to Checker Front and I saw Jackie. I told him a lot of stuff about the fake money, mostly baloney like the stuff he's always telling."

His dad nodded to himself and thought for a moment before, "You told him a lot of bull," he said, with that familiar accusing eyebrow trick.

"All the time, Dad. He tells us a lotta bull, we tell him a lotta bull," Charlie said. "You know Jackie Rhett?"

"Better than you think, sonny boy. It'll suit me if you avoid young Master Rhett after this. You won't see him for a while in any case, Charlie; he got his rump nicked by a bullet last night." Charlie's open-mouthed silent "oh" was genuine, and satisfactory to his dad. "He was lucky at that. He'll recover at home, but he won't sleep on his back for a while, I'm afraid."

Charlie suspected his dad was squelching a smile when he looked away, and to direct the discussion elsewhere he said, "Did the nutty guy shoot him?"

"Bridger? No, it seems that Mr. Bridger was on his way out of the house to make my acquaintance, even though he didn't know it yet. Another man did the shooting, Charlie, we think it was a really bad egg named Pinero. We have the name from Bridger, and that poor fool is behind bars." His dad vented a yawn that equaled three of Charlie's. "We'll know if it's Pinero soon; whoever it was, he used up all his luck getting away to a creek in full flood."

Charlie considered the little yellow flashbang from the storm grating, which had evidently been a sure-enough gunshot, and recalled the much larger one. "Did somebody shoot him?"

Charlie's dad considered the question briefly, dry-washing his face with both hands, then shrugged. "That's probably what the morning paper will say, because I fired a riot gun for the first time in my life and woke up everybody in town, I'm sorry to say, but all I did was blow Bridger's front tire to kingdom come." Charlie's father looked away at nothing for a long moment, then nodded again. "It must've changed his mind about trying to run; when I killed his tire he just eased out of the car and lay down on his face in the mud."

"You say the other guy got away," Charlie prodded.

His father's denial began with a headshake. "Not very far." More slowly: "Couple of hours ago, while Shoal Creek was settling down about dawn, an officer spotted him tangled in some bushes. Not much doubt he had tried to escape down that storm sewer because he was weighted down by the kind of engravings counterfeiters use."

Charlie sat up, and needed two tries to say it: "Alive?"

The reply was soft, almost respectful. "Not after a few hours face down in water, son. I don't suppose it matters whether he drowned or cracked his head open or whatnot." Now Charlie and his dad were face to face, and each of them appeared to have aged. "Charlie, you've been in that old storm sewer." This was spoken without heat or scorn.

Charlie dropped his gaze. "Yessir." Measuring the next words as if they cost him a dollar apiece: "Lots of times."

When the only response was a sigh and a glance toward the ceiling, Charlie said, "How could you tell?"

More to himself than to Charlie: "Confounded nuisance. I mean to have bars welded across it." Then, putting a hand on his son's shoulder: "For any boy of mine it's bait, Charlie. It has to be irresistible to a daredevil, and I know my son. Muttonhead."

Then Charlie gripped his father, and it was returned, in a hug more fierce than any in his memory. Finally he said, "I'm not gonna do it again, Dad. Not ever. We were just dumb."

His dad stood up and grinned back at him. "You and who?"

"Me and Lint," said Charlie, but he was blushing.

"And you're worried that I'll start asking whether young Fischer took any part in this." Charlie's nod was silent. "Maybe you ought to worry a little, son. Get a small taste of what your parents go through about three hundred and sixty-five times a year." But he didn't ask about Aaron.

"I get it. Thanks, Dad," said Charlie, reaching for his blue jeans. "Really. You know what? I'm glad all this stuff happened. Last time you and me talked this long together was, uh, maybe not ever."

"Only a few minutes," said Hardin, glancing at his wristwatch.

"Still," Charlie said.

The father pondered that bulletin for a moment, gave his son a mock salute, and said, "I can fix that. Consider it a promise, Charlie." He cocked his head and added, "And unless I'm very much mistaken, I'm smelling good things from the kitchen. What do you say we go and see?"

AFTERWORD

The briefest backward glance at Charlie's herd convinced me that life was simpler for us all then, so we stumbled into World War II as simple folk. Coleman Hardin was an unbending juvenile officer who believed in the rights and virtues of our species, an exact replica of my father, who assured me that all bullies were cowards and that a truth will always defeat a lie. That taught me that nobody—*nobody*—is right all the time.

My mother would have seen herself in Willa Hardin, a slender, pretty, farm-raised brownette who ruled her kitchen firmly, even though she gave a newspaper composing room forty hours a week and sang our church solos. Three older brothers taught her to be a perfect lady but failed to crush her flashes of whimsy.

Lint was drawn from life, a two-tone fox terrier who learned why not to chase cars the first time he caught one. His shoulder mended but for the rest of his life, when under suspicion for some offense, he would suddenly remember to limp and snivel and avoid eye contact in a way that made you want to kick him. And then hug him.

Gene Carpenter combines two boys who bamboozled adults with an amiable veneer to conceal the demon under the skin. The sociopath hid behind his merit badges and prospered. The jolly prankster flunked his last risk at high speed, and I'll bet he was grinning.

If Roy Kinney's original had been my age he might have been our leader, but in our habitat little kids got no respect. He would spy on older boys and had a genius for copying only our most villainous habits. He would attach himself to you like a barnacle if you weren't spry. You had to outrun him.

Whoever first used the phrase "Nasty, brutish and short" had to be thinking of the kid who was almost Jackie Rhett, only smarter. After others learned that being Jackie's companion involved bushels of self-sacrifice, his options narrowed down to Roy or nobody. Tough choice, so it varied. For most of us, the almost-Jackie was the key to extravagant parties thrown by the Kinneys, the point of which was to invite every kid in the neighborhood except the one Roy was mad at. Which was nearly always Jackie. Which was why we promoted discord between them. I live in abject fear that one of them will now read this.

Although the Nazis did try to sabotage the U.S. economy with schemes to counterfeit our money, I don't know if they did it with scoundrels like Bridger and Pinero. I had to invent them because I never knew anyone like them. After all, they were the kind of guy you meet only in a sewer.

Aaron, it's not my fault you're only half-Jewish; it took two guys to steer Charlie between the ditches. Any kid with two pals this loyal, cautious, industrious and forgiving is rich beyond measure. If Charlie had much value to you it was probably as your hood ornament. Friendships of this grandeur do not fade; they're only interrupted now and then. Because, as I've noted before, integrity is thicker than blood.

As for Charlie himself, I may be the least qualified person

to give a fair account of him. My middle name, by some immense coincidence, is Charles, and Tex-Mex schoolmates nicknamed me "Chollie Huevos." I have no earthly idea what that implies. Charlie contains cupfuls of two cousins, a teaspoonful of my neighbor Jimmy, and a smidgin of a knowitall kid I loathed in class. Charlie was merry, and sturdy, and sly, and overconfident, and lazy, and deceptive, and sometimes a dimwit, and occasionally the opposite. Dad warned me that if I were ever arrested he would be obliged to penalize me more than others. This may account in part for the fact that officers never caught the youth they followed across Austin rooftops in what is known today as parkour.

Only after I turned Charlie loose did I begin to realize how deeply World War II changed nearly all Americans, saving perhaps only the few insulated rich. At the time, battles in headlines were romantic distant adventures to boys—with startling exceptions. I met a sixteen-year-old combat veteran, honorably discharged after medics discovered this wounded Marine had managed to keep his youth a secret for a year. A few eighteen-year-old vets returned to finish high school, and to play football against fourteen-year-olds. The romance of war faded early for the vets, but eventually for the Charlies too. We all accumulated bruises of one kind or another, and for me, a few broken bones and teeth. This was Texas high-school football, remember.

My dad, like many another, felt so guilty drawing a princely salary in an aircraft plant that he enlisted in the Army for a tenth of that sum, rising to the dizzy elevation of Private First Class. I won more stripes than that, but on my backside, from my mother. I could claim I didn't earn them, but the facts would keep getting in my way. At work my mother commanded a huge machine of many small parts, a Mergenthaler Linotype, that composed newstype column by column. Women became welders, assemblers, riveters, and ferry pilots, and in the process feminists. Combat vets who returned expecting to find their wives unchanged, joked that they needed a treaty in the war between the sexes.

Many things changed by just disappearing. Our big-little books, metal toys, and old tools went into scrap drives. Postwar replacements, when they came, were unrecognizable. Balsa was a war material, and the rubber-powered flying model hobby never recovered. And does anybody *not* know why I still grieve for my *Action Comics* #1, introducing Superman, that went into a scrap drive in 1943? A fine copy recently sold for over $2 million.

But it wasn't just *things* that, in changing, changed us as well. A new and more knowing (some would say "cynical") set of attitudes crowded older ones aside. I was tempted to slather Charlie's days with the special flavors of Southwest mythology, but much of it, today, would be met with glaze-eyed disbelief from my grandlarvae. A sample: before the war it was well-known to many of us that a single remedy was favored by Grandma for baldness, acne, poison ivy, sunburn and assorted bug bites. The remedy? A poultice of fresh cow patty. After the war, even little kids realized that the world is not quite what they were told it is.

Of course, a few old myths lurch ahead into this century. Not always because they make sense, but because they're still fun. I fondly recall how therapeutic it was to sneak up and burst a paper sack behind the head of a person in the throes of hiccups. If he hadn't had hiccups, well, now he would. The time that head was my fearsome Uncle Fred's, I escaped justice only by insisting I'd been almost certain he'd hiccupped.

Or maybe that was Charlie.